"But for the lady on my arm, I should not spare you."

(See page 82)

THE REGAL BOX

BY

ALEXANDRE DUMAS

AUTHOR OF

"D'Artagnan the King Maker," "The King's Gallant," "All for a Crown," "Count of Monte Cristo," etc.

TRANSLATED BY

HENRY L. WILLIAMS

Fredonia Books
Amsterdam, The Netherlands

The Regal Box

by
Alexandre Dumas

ISBN: 1-58963-285-0

Reprinted from the 1902 edition

Fredonia Books
Amsterdam, the Netherlands
http://www.fredoniabooks.com

In order to make original editions of historical works available to scholars at an economical price, this facsimile of the original edition of 1902 is reproduced from the best available copy and has been digitally enhanced to improve legibility, but the text remains unaltered to retain historical authenticity.

CONTENTS

I—The Penny Show	7
II—The Tyranny of Management	14
III—The Legend of the Well . . .	21
IV—To Save a Life	27
V—A Humble Victim	35
VI—"Who Shall Keep the Keepers?"	42
VII—The Forcing-bed of Talent . .	49
VIII—A Dish for the Gods . . .	60
IX—"The Little Man in the Camlet Cloak"	69
X—Any One Can Cry "Stand!" But Another Delivers . . .	76
XI—The Hagar of the Stage . .	86
XII—Success	92
XIII—Grist to the Mill	96
XIV—A Diplomat's Wife	103
XV—The Love for a Prince . . .	110
XVI—How the Last Act Went Off . .	113
XVII—Sky Rocket, or Lamp? . . .	117
XVIII—A Torch to the Taper . . .	131
XIX—An Eminent Scandal-Monger .	142
XX—An Appeal to the Nobler Self . .	151
XXI—Genius Out of Place . . .	161

XXII—A Fleeting Show 167

XXIII—A Tragic Picture 173

XXIV—The Rage for the Stage . . . 184

XXV—Gideon's Weak Hand . . . 190

XXVI—The Fox Attracts Customers . . 199

XXVII—A Host in Himself . . . 209

XXVIII—Equal Footing 214

XXIX—The Pantomimist . . . 219

XXX—The Full-blown Rose . . . 225

XXXI—A Convincing Bill . . . 230

XXXII—Genius or Madness? . . . 238

XXXIII—A Man in Love 248

XXXIV—"Tarry, Sweet Soul" . . . 254

XXXV—The Prince Finds a Way . . 261

THE REGAL BOX.

Of all the customs clinging to England, few are prettier and appeal more directly to the heart than "the coming of age." The interest redoubles if the person involved is a youth destined for a high station in the Senate, the circle of finance, commerce, fashion, or simply the army or navy.

In a minor way this "homing" of the fledgling is like a year of jubilee.

All obey this unwritten law, in all its branches, without acknowledging its potency. Debts are forgiven, canceled or renewed, feuds are buried, and for some days all don the mask of joviality, and rejoice with those around the Fortunatus.

This summer ray spread in all its glory over Freefolk village, Southampton, where the inhabitants and neighbors for leagues around had assembled, in their best, and with "bowpots," that is, bouquets, breastknots and favors, to hail Stephen Brinkwell, now Lord Newell in full, coming into his paternal estate as well as his manhood year.

His father had died after his return from the Peninsular wars, and his mother, who had crossed the sea to nurse him, had passed away soon after his entombment, literally, with his fathers. This sad immolation to war had led them both to urge their executors to prevent the son's leaning to belligerent aims.

Stephen was, therefore, educated in Luxembourg, at a religious college, where certainly "Cæsar" was read solely for its Latinity. Unfortunately, the good fathers had kept him ignorant of about all an English gentleman of rank and means ought to know. He came here to the manor unable to drink heartily, ride a day long, sing a merry song or give a jovial toast. Besides, except by letters, he did not know his own kin.

His brother, Jessamy, had an advantage on this head. He had been educated at home, and not at the great schools, but his tutors had isolated him, as far as possible, and hedged him around on his Continental tours, during which he had seen something of his brother.

Hence there was much curiosity about the pair, but the heir came in for the greater share of attention. The second son is put very much in the background on such occasions.

It could not be said that either won, on this presentation.

Both looked delicate. The elder was pale and sallow, with the waxen tint of prisoners, whether in jails or cloisters. His hair, being black, enhanced this unwholesome, or, at least, un-English hue inherited from a crossing of the Spanish strain, relicts of the Armada having paid ransom, but wisely kept in England, not to endure the wrath of the incensed Philip of Spain.

Jessamy was understood to be prepared to enter the Church, but as yet he had not displayed any proclivity for the miter, and even less for sword or marine-glass.

His chief aspect was of resignation. He felt like one who, reaching out his hand for a bag of money, perceives that some one has been before him, and has put his name on it as possessor.

But the programme of the week of festivity would have relaxed Jacob in his quest to oust Esau. The great house, once a hunting-box when the Norman monarchs chased the buck in the New Forest, so rang with revelry and was so redolent with scent of feasts, old wine and fresh flowers that one must have smiled.

Jessamy made himself even more agreeable than the young host, who was as embarrassed as a novice.

While all the county magnates jostled one another here, the tenants, laborers, hinds and hangers-on gathered in the village.

The war taxes had sorely straitened the toilers, and no one was vexed at the announcement that the Newell funds which had been accumulating during the minority and were swollen by some excellent investments of the late Colonel Lord Newell in Portuguese vineyards and "loot" in Spain, enabled the newcomer to avoid raising rent this quarter.

The farmers, therefore, had a light heart to help themselves to the good cheer. This generosity was reflected on the subordinates, so that all wore a jocund mien, not excepting the humblest whose rendezvous was the inn.

Not only was everything free there, but all scores had been wiped off at the new lord's expense.

Moreover, since one does not live for beer and beef alone, the mental appetite had been thought of, in accordance with Lord Newell's college breeding.

He ordered that all entertainment should be paid for by his steward.

But as, on hearing of the rejoicing at Freefolk, some of the traveling shows had not hastened, but put the place on their programmes, according to their route, some had arrived after the steward had finished his arrangements with those amusement mongers upon the ground.

Woe to the late comers, therefore, to the stands, "stoopes," booths and hovels turned into auditoriums for the rustics.

These, who had to cope with competitors insured against loss, could only make wry faces—not laughter-raising ones—and quit, unless they dared to wrestle with the odds on the other side.

Nevertheless, one arrival stood its ground. It secured the inn, that is, a floor and the outhouses. It planted its large caravan, or living-wagon, against the inn side. It turned a story into its theatre.

As for the steward, he scowled, for he had feared that this would prove a demand on his purse, and nothing does a steward so abhor as an unexpected item. He well knew that it was impossible, had a question arisen, to ignore the famous "Richardson's Penny Show!"

Richardson's was known as the Penny Showman's, from the extreme midland to Blackheath. It was known to the frequenters' fathers; children had been lullabied on songs learned in its arena; jokers repeated its jester's jests; and, if two boys got a cudgel apiece, it was to rehearse, under the hedge, the "double-robber" combat seen last fair time at Richardson's. Hampdens struck attitudes in claiming right of way, borrowed from *Coriolanus* (of Richardson's) and "mute, inglorious," Miltons saw in Richardson's heroine of "The Murder in the Roadside Inn" a spirit of their muse.

Half the money paid to see the performance was really put up for the transient glow of pride and pleasure at being allowed to go up on that platform ("parade," technically), by which one entered by a window of the tavern into the theatre hall, to touch elbow with the kings of England, Queen Bess, Old Nick, with his mouth full of fired tow, and the clown!

Children saved up for "when Dickson's comes round," and the adults cheerfully paid the penny extra for the front seats!

Mr. Biggins, the steward, feared that this potentate of festivity would be warranted, on such an occasion, to appeal to his master to have his terms granted, so that his unparalleled exhibition might also be free. But, luckily for him, at the first intimation that he had come too late for "the *honeyrarium*," "Muster" Richardson flared up with his blunt indignation at not being appreciated properly.

"This is scandalous magnesia," said the broad-shouldered and broad-spoken showman, flushing up red as his long waistcoat; "time were when the motter in the show purfession was "a country" fair field, and no favors!" Look a' here, young sir"—though Mr. Biggins had more white hairs than he, and more years by twenty—"if this here be a plot to bring me in empty benches, by the Lord Harry, it will be the biggest failure on record! Richardson's has made its way—you can repeat this to our master, *word-batim!*—into the hearts and the pockets of the English pipple! these years, more nor less! It is accepted by culpable judges, ay, and justice to boot, as the acme of the climax of draymatic conglomerations! But I see your drift, young fellow! You want to screw me down low, so that you can fob me off with shillin's when I ought to pouch pounds, if I thought for a blessed minute to be bought off!"

"But I said I had no more money for motions and pup-petry——"

"Motion! Puppetry! My show a galanty one—a penny poppyshow!" roared the lusty man, redder than ever. "Know that I give twenty turns, both day and night! Know that I was the werry fust to prove that the Bard of Havon, which he is known as Shakespoke to the iggorant multitude, is the draw. I purduce more hoften "Romeo," "Gamblet," "King Queer," and all them pus-sonages, than the two patent theayters of Lunnon and the minor ones to boot!"

"I doubt," said Biggins, imprudently, but, wincing sorely, like all bullies, at being browbeaten, "I doubt that, with all those shows wide open, you will get a boy of eight to go in to see your dolls represent all Spakeshear!"

"Shikspur!" roared the other, enraged at being cor-rected in a name which ought to be correct in his limited vocabulary, "Shakespeare, or Shavespoke. I warrant, ay, I wager that I will bring all the poppylation of the manor and the subbubs into my house, while no one, not for nothing, will go into those larned-piggeries and tumblers' booths! I tell 'ee!" cried he, as the parting shot, "I have singers in my show that your master's vocalists could larn notes of—dancers that their bonny skipjacks could not shake a leg to—and, as for femininny beauty and graces, why, let your fine ladies come and see me put 'The Dame of the Social Cream' on my boards; see Mistress Carey, late of His Majesty's Own Theaytres R'yal, show them how a real fine lady wiggles the smellin'-bottle, whisks the fan, and——"

But Mr. Biggins, around whom the crowd had flocked, and who could not get another word in, had sneaked away, downcast.

"Hang him, their chief turkey-cock!" muttered he. "They are all willains, wagrants and wagabones! If I catch them whisking linen off the hedges or laying night lines for the tench, or yet wringing a pheasant's neck, why, Master Constable shall give them the novel exit of whipping them out of the Newell seat at their own cat's tail!"

The fact is, coming of age is the *crux*-time of a steward; he has to render his accounts with an exactness not insisted upon at other periods.

Spite of Mr. Richardson's pride of having inculcated the loftier drama, after his fashion, during many years, it must be avowed that between the bundle of hay that was labeled "free" and the other labeled "one penny," the great ass—the public—of Freefolk did not starve. Without hesitation, it ran straight into the stalls of the gratis halls of mirth.

In vain did Richardson's trumpets blow, the thunder and the leather-lunged "heavy man" split those lungs, even the venture of the maiden-victim of man's false love and other perfidies, steal, with studied timidity and long-practiced coyness, like a vapor along the plank, as though a pirate were making her walk it—all was useless.

For the first time in the memory of the British dramatic muse, "the Penny Showman's" show was given the cold shoulder.

The old Romans were an acute people, after all; to give either circuses or bread avails, but, to give both, with beer into the bargain, is consummate policy.

Richardson had among his virtues a firmness—call it not bullheadedness—quite his own. He resolved to bring back the wanderers to their discarded idols. He went indoors, and, with the help of his scenic artist and his property manager, harried out of the packings all the wonderful paintings, which, decorated with different titles, try to convince an indifferent public that all the marvels on the canvas without can be realized on the other side.

Meanwhile, charged to bear in mind that their exertions must be multiplied on the next and early occasion of their being summoned to the contest, the actors were given a slight liberty.

It is regrettable to admit that, without reflections on anything but the Richardsonian larder, for he boarded some of his company, more or less, these fugitives from art descended into the inn and those hovels where sundry concoctions dear to the rural heart called "spruce," "mead," "nectar" (O ye gods!) and "sherbet" (shade of Omar the Persian!) and other "waters bewitched" regaled those who could not get near to where the exhausted tapster drew malt and barley beverages.

Nor did they neglect the stalls laden with similarly rustic edibles, dispensed on the same generous principles.

Richardson's enemy, wishful to load down his sprightly troupe, could not have worked more hindrance, if it be true that fasting stimulates genius.

CHAPTER II.

While these weaklings, succumbing to the tempter when they were to make the greatest effort of their career to induce stolid people to pay for intellectual banquets, while sordid refreshments ran free, one of their party separated himself from the suddenly joyous set. Like a philosopher, he sauntered up and down the single street, watching with sympathy, for he was very young to play the cynic, the sinking of the tempted into the dens and caves where they would become as Circe's swine.

He also had an eye to the rush made upon those other temples of the drama, rivals for many years to his employers. He was named Edmund, and was the showman's right-hand file, or, not to express it militarily, his leading man, or, rather, his do-all.

Most of the Richardsonians were double-handed; that is, they played one or two musical instruments as well as acted, sung or danced. But Edmund, while engaged ostensibly as tragedian, was compelled by his task-master, aided by the overweening conceit of the youth who has talent, to undertake practically everything on that tolerably wide and comprehensive field, the stage of the traveling Thespian.

Born in London, placed early under the care of persons attached to the stage in menial capacities, he "went on," or, more strictly, was carried on, as Cupid in a nest. As soon as he could walk, he was a boy actor. In his teens he experienced all the dangers and difficulties of a young player's life.

Tugging at his pseudo-mother's apron-strings, he accompanied her on tours of the provinces. The pictures of Hogarth and many pathetic or grotesque memoirs show that life. As for him, he was put into all lines, leaping as harlequin, grimacing as clown, tottering as pantaloon. When too large for the baby, important in all melodramas, he stalked as the ghost. Then, as his voice became hoarse and strong at puberty, he was let assume the most onerous parts, luckily abridged by the time pressing at Richardson's. He boasted of his "Richard the Third" in ten minutes and "Romeo" in twelve, with the balcony scene complete!

This master do-all of the troupe was a youth whose face was deeply interesting; here was thought which defied gloom, humor which relieved intense application, gluttony for mental work, a kind of inextinguishable lamp with two lights—eyes the most penetrative that ever existed. It would be flattery to call him "indifferent plump," for he was starved on his half a guinea per week, with his share of the candle ends, by which he studied the plays in the whole text.

That this drudgery was ill paid went for little. When one has his heart and soul in his profession, he must fly or burrow.

He awed Richardson whom a bull would not have turned from his path across a field. But he also charmed him, and the old itinerant niggard, because he had found his first hundred pounds so hard to amass, many a time doled out a trifle at a pinch, lest he should lose the lad of promise.

This character out of the common road, in an age when sons were not ashamed to wear coats cut out of the paternal mantle, so excellent was the weave, compounded with his taste and youthful yearning for butterfly garb by wearing remainders of the wardrobe, shaved to fit his slender figure, graceful as the willow, and neatly put together by the Mistress Carey mentioned. She took a pride in decking him something like a "lordling" disavowed.

Still, there was more black than colors, and scarcely did the young man, when dismounted from his theatrical pedestal, agree with the enchanted auditors' idea of what he appeared off the stage.

So he was little heeded as he continued his promenade.

But he was vain. His idea was, perhaps, true as to the theatrical nature of the ornaments worn by the *beaux*, but his means were insufficient to carry them out. His ornaments were profuse, but the gold was a mockery and the diamonds at shoe and knee and collar were paste. There were miscellaneous charms on his fob-chain, but one might doubt whether the hidden end was attached to a watch. As for the snuffbox, he only handled one on the stage in suitable parts; he was above that kind of superfluous concomitant—an evidence of nervousness unbecoming a gentleman.

At least the malacca cane he carried was fit for a fop; its head was of cornelian, and the gilt collar was untarnished. The silk tassel and loop to suspend it to the wrists were unraveled. Cuffs and ruffles were there, white and lacelike, but oft-mended, and "the ladders" taken up; a little more and they would be like the traditional spendthrift's shirt, which could be cleaned only by being pinned up to the walls and the suds thrown at it! It follows that his boots were patched and well greased to hide defects. The gloss of his high, hard, almost pointed, hat was a filmy dream; but he bore it jauntily, as though, like the master's of Newell Manor, it had just come down from Bond street, out of the royal hatter's.

All the morning the bumpkins had roved the street, munching, swilling, stumping up and down, "goggling" idiotically until they could not wink their protruding eyes. Satiety had come. They sat by the roadside in groups, silent as the bucolics are, drawing at clay pipes and looking wonderingly at the inn. For the first time in their history, the scores had been wiped off, the credit-board taken off its .peg, and nothing scored for the unusual drafts on the pump and vats. Freefolk was a newcomer in Elysium. They wished for nothing more—not even for dewy eve to come.

If not Arcadia, it'was Jack-Cade-ia, thought the actor. Indeed, all ate and drank at somebody's score.

They were too replete to chat, but a dull, deep grunt of contentment escaped from nearly all the indolent figures.

"Porcine creatures!" said the leading hero of the show, eying them with loftiness, as though by birth as well as intellect he stood on a higher position. "On what a scene of gormandize, in which they are glutted gods over their own burned meats, lingers their leaden contemplation!"

Then, smiling scornfully, he added:

"And is it to the likes of these that the pearls of the poets are to be cast? Were I old Richie, I would pull up the tent-pegs and start out for a more appreciative borough!"

But, with all his elevation for animal cravings, he had to run a trying ordeal; he must pass along the street lined with improvised bars, tables, sideboards loaded lately with comestibles, cakes, doughnuts, spiceries and little loaves ingeniously filled with sausage meat. Some of the old dames had brought iron furnaces, like tinkers'. These fumed and flared, and from the brazier or kettle over the flames came odors that were common without being any the worse for that—odors of beef boiling with vegetables, of dumplings, and of potpies. Then, too, there were "gipsy ovens," that is, rude constructions of stones and clay, out of which, "ever and anon," as Edmund might say, were drawn to note the progress, platters of pie and pastry, of game which had never been furnished with my lord's knowledge, fresh fish stuffed and baking, and forcemeat balls, in which were hashed up mysterious things; to the beldames considered toothsome, but witchlike—unearthly!

The youth might be sage, but his mouth watered so that he could not utter any caustic comments. He shuddered; these ogresses evidently feared no rivalry; they counted on the feasters coming again just about when his fellows were to begin the combat to win the material creatures from these fleshpots.

He sighed.

"That we do not fare as well as these churls," murmured he, "is all Richardson's fault. Oh, the tyranny of management, which makes even so good a fellow hard in money matters. He wears enlarging glasses; his idea of dividing the spoils is leonine, while his ideas of obtaining them are brutal as the bear's. He starves us, his supports, in all senses of the word! He starves even me, Edmund, who has stayed by him faithfully while all those who had talents, abilities, and even a breath of the divine afflatus, gradually desert his humble colors and struggle along nearer our goal—the capital! Ah, me! the town again!"

His glowing face turned mechanically to the east. London was the actor's Mecca. It has the strolling player's daily prayer.

"Oh, I am a goose! He is killing the goose with the

golden egg. He will repent his short-sightedness when he sees my name 'billed' at 'the Garden' or 'the Lane!' The Hamlet, the Romeo, the Orlando! Mistress Carey! bless her for keeping up my stamina and my ambition! She rates me the ideal Prince of Denmark, since I shall have the requisite youth which the public maintains is his, just as they will not admit he is pursy, mad overmuch, or doing anything but pretend, to overset the usurper! On the other side, old Moses, the prompter, he will insist that Orlando is more my mark at present! Bah! all is one—I can play either—I can play all the round! Orlando or Hamlet, anything not secondary, to appear at the Lane or the Garden!"

Then a glance into a window let him see himself as he stood as for raiment; his pallor changed into a rush of blood, with self-reproach.

"At the Lane," added he, bitterly; "more like on the road, if we fare no better soon!"

More than one gay comedian of the town was wont to talk of "an airing on the road;" in plain English, acting the highwayman, to replenish purse and wardrobe.

Suddenly he reddened still deeper, his hands clinched, and he shook his black locks like a lion throwing back his mane.

His loneliness was broken in upon.

And most disagreeably and gratingly.

A loud guffaw from a group of plowboys, their clogs heavy with clay and redolent of turned-up soil, seemed to indicate that he was being made sport of. His impulse, thought one to many, was to march up to the loudest of voice and dèmand a repetition of the jest at his cost. But, however passionate-tempered he was, he had learned, in his despicable calling, that kind of prudence which checks violence in vengeance with the apprehension that his act might rebound to the detriment of his associates.

"They will mob the theatre if but one of the clowns is pummeled," he thought, opening his nervous fingers again. "Faugh! let the dogs and toads swelter in their congenial mud! Let me hie out of this beer-reeking atmosphere, far from the coarse jollity, as well as from the intoxicated hilarity of their so-called betters!"

But it was among themselves that the joke had oc-

curred, and, if one noticed him hazily, it was merely to remark, with a grin meant to be a compliment:

"That young 'King Dick' be a-goan' fushin', reckon!
If so, be he fush as well as he plays the king and the
leaper, whoy, he will not leave a bullhead in the mill-swim,
sure!"

Attention fell from him entirely, though, for one of his
company, personator of the fools and "horse-player" generally, swaggered up, and, announcing himself as "Yours,
Judy" (truly), let slip more pleasantries in the same vein,
which ingratiated him instantly. Then, remarking that
the sight of others reveling gave him "the collywobbles"
as thick as rabbits after rain, he so imposed on the admiring boors that two of them dashed into the tavern to bring
him out a roll stuffed with minced ham and a tankard of
ale.

Edmund glanced on this seizure of the popular throne
with a pardoning air, half smiling.

"Ribbald is in the proper trim! Oh, lucky for him that
these are so many Touchstones, to whom 'a clown is meat
and drink!' "

Mr. Ribbald took the vessel in one hand, passed it with
mock politeness to the other, bowed to it, and tossed it off
to the dregs with enviable gusto and long habitude. He
pointed with the empty flagon to the sign: "Gnarl, the
Wellpole and Rope!" and said:

"Hip! here, jade! fill again! The master's name is
rough, but he brews good ale! Push about the jorum!"

As Edmund retreated, he heard all following the clown
in a Bacchanalian song.

"Ribbald is a philosopher of the laughing persuasion!
Perhaps it is more foolish to wail inevitable strokes than
to laugh at them! Well, adieu! knots on the fringe!
There is a world elsewhere!"

He left the highway and made for the woods, where his
ruminations could hardly be so inharmoniously interrupted.

The outskirts of the still great forest were romantic.
Trees of fifty years' growth looked not too feeble beside
stumps of the giants, senile after three hundred. Under
the arching boughs, each thick as a hogshead, the check-
ered shadows played and offered the pilgrim relief after

"tiring day and toiling night." Like Ferdinand, he trod upon withered roots and empty husks wherein the acorns cradled. There were the lightning-cloven pines, within which to imprison too nimble spirits, but when he was to climb the trees of the Hesperides, to which his imagination had turned the wood, a placard nailed to a monstrous trunk attracted his attention and drew him back to inhuman earth.

"Men-traps and spring-guns on this ground. By order, NEWELL, per Biggins, bailiff!"

He smiled with scorn; then, his satirical vein inducing retaliation in words, he said:

"Thank you for nothing, Lord Newell! A fine notice to those you take care, by fostering no 'charge school' (free school), should not learn to read!"

CHAPTER III.

THE LEGEND OF THE WELL.

The young actor was seeking solitude where he might count on finding it.

But the uproar along the village way seemed to be envied and imitated by the elves, nymphs and goblins of the New Forest. "The Red King," murdered under one of those oaks, must have altered his hour for careering through the glades with the vengeful arrow in his temple, for his phantom chase was in full height. Instead of there being much to soothe the explorer, there was all to exasperate and enrage.

Edmund heard no stint of sounding horns, baying of dogs and hounds and whispering of setters, halloaing of lusty-lunged boors, whips cracking and whistles blown; while voices rose in jest, in song and with snatches of ribaldry.

Edmund went by a slightly-worn path to a spot where, once or twice, he had nestled down in the brake to study a part. There was a pretty and ancient spring here, at which he had slaked his thirst and softened a hard crust. It had long been welled in, for an iron kettle, large enough for a monastic refectory, held the crystal flow, and let it lap over by a nip out of the brim, on to a bed of white pebbles.

By its vaguely regular shape, a mound of ruins denoted a hunting lodge having been here in time scarcely in mind. It should have been a Rosamund's bower—it was, traditionally, a rendezvous of William Rufus' chase.

Edmund hoped that nothing would entice the wanderers hither; but his wishing day was not this one. A throng of persons had mostly dismounted, and were pursuing their roving on foot, with this as their goal.

There were feminine voices—the feminine voice of the day, coarse, strong, impaired by indulgence in "strong waters." These talked more fluently than the men's, as if the speakers liked to hear their own tones and knew that none listened for sense.

But among all, rather than above them, the actor found one as predominating or distinguished. Psychologists would at once cry: "Sensitiveness of congenial spirits!" Still, it was that same faculty by which, in a chorus a thousand strong, one voice, while accurately in harmony, can be singled out.

"What is this?" murmured the idler, sitting up and resting on one hand. "One could believe in the goddess Euterpe. Or, better, in that maid of Dian's who lured that rash fellow—what's his name?—to his dogs' end. Why, that voice makes those women's rancid and the men's like the orator's before he made a mouth-rasp of pebbles!"

The merry crowd came straight to his repository.

Recalling that his dress was not donned for the gala, he drew back behind one of the monstrous stumps, a hundred years old.

A screen of creepers and sinuous reeds curtained him in.

His curiosity was aroused by that voice still sounding. He was like one of those *virtuosi* who, roaming in the country, hear a milkmaid warble to the kine, with the promise of having a thousand guineas in her throat.

The vanguard were the neighbors of the Newells, at home in the woods, carrying guns, which they well knew how to use; usually limber and supple, but embarrassed to a degree by the guests from town, ladies and gentlemen to whom, judging by their momentary allusions, palaces were open as the day, and to sit at a prince's board as common as the circuit banquet to the judges—to the squires.

Honest, sturdy yeomen, they were like flustered quail before these braggarts, mostly mere "smell-feasts."

These newcomers huddled together by two or three, noisy, self-projecting worthies, like craft of a convoy beside the frigates; these bullies had a military aspect, but were little more than clerks in the victualling offices, and saw no more of the sea than from Essex marshes, and no more of American wars than from Dover pier with a spyglass.

But they were captain and major down here. One

might stand as model to his congeners; red face like his
scarlet coat, naturally padded checks, like his puffed
chest; white or canary waistcoats sullied with dropped
snuff; red sashes with flowing ends, sometimes tasseled
with gold: buff or white breeches, extremely tight; colored stockings, over which some wore leggins against
the brambles; and, if not riding-boots, low-quartered
pumps. As for the hats, three or two-cocked, looped up
with cord, and gilt buttons profusely stitched on, they
needed not the plumes, pompons and cockades to attract
attention.

In full contrast to these swaggering captains was a
man similarly burly and overbearing, but without being
ponderous with learning, weighty with the consciousness
of wealth. It was the illustrious Gresham Danby, called
"the Rigger," out of his hearing, a stock-jobber, who manipulated the reflexes of those deceptions on 'Change
which followed the Mississippi scheme and the South Sea
bubble. Danby had never cringed, but, in his heyday, he
still preferred to be caned by a lord than clapped on the
shoulder by a wit.

In a sentence, he was one of those capitalists who assisted the Prince Regent to live, while awaiting almost all
his life the decease of his father, "the idiot farmer of
Windsor."

Danby had made George the Prince need him, knowing that, when men have no need of another, they hate the
helper if they cannot dispense with him.

He had been introduced at Carlton House, when the
prince of prodigals was on the tenter-hooks, tormented
with the question: Would or would not Parliament vote
him a hundred thousand pounds to clear off some of his
debts and give him a new lease of his capricious career?

Danby had been doubly his supporter. He provided
him with funds to pursue his licentious course, neither
short nor merry, and used all his influence to carry the
Relief Bill. It passed, to say the last word about it, as
all royal demands do in England, pared and insultingly
amended—reduced to fifty or sixty thousand pounds.

On seeing that he had an auditor who might confirm
some of his flights, one of the red-faced captains hastened
to declare, in his dinning voice:

"Mr. Danby will testify that my friend Colonel Hanger enjoys the confidence of his royal highness! It is to Hanger, my friend, that George says: 'Nay, we will not have the earl, for a sandwich will not suffice for a dinner!' Ho, ho! a sandwich makes but a snack, surely!"

As the term was new to most of the audience, the laugh was not spontaneous.

"'And "Sandy" is a heathen'—it is the prince who is still speaking—'a pagan who peppers rumpsteak, to do which is in the capacity of one who would rob a church! Let us have no sandwiches!' That is how it happens I was invited down to Brighthelmstone, and heard the singing of the incomparable La Squarchinino!"

Danby nodded, gravely.

"Not badly told," said a long figure in ecclesiastical black and with a white ruff, cuffs and handkerchief tucked in his fob-pocket, for he took snuff at all times. It was Dr. Caxon, the Newell preceptor. "But I like best your story of the 'Mohocks,' when they took the image of the Highlander from before the tobacconist's——"

"Dugald's, in Hanway street, for testimony!"

"Dugald's Highlander in wood, and jammed it into a sleepy hack-driver's coach, saying, as they clapped a piece in his greasy paw:

"'Hush! It is your chief and commander!' for the Athole Fencibles were on post at St. James' that night, right enough! 'He has been wining out, and fell drunk under the mahogany!' So the trustful jarvy drove off and deposited his precious fare at the palace gateway, where the guard turned out and presented arms to the wooden image—ho, ho, ho!"

The country ladies shrank from this boisterous narrator, preferring a dapper beau, who recited scraps of the aria prevalent at *ridotti* and masquerades.

Another lady, having used her quizzing-glass till tired, said, querulously:

"But what are we waiting here for—a cold collation *à la* Russian?"

"Not at all," hastened to say the tutor, remembering his task. "Only for my lord and Sir Jessamy."

"And Miss Danby!" corrected a satellite of the money-man.

"And Miss Danby! I wish to relate the legend of that well."

All turned to the spring and the square of ruins.

Edmund shuddered in his refuge. None of these antiquated dames or their daughters, too portly or too scraggy, could possess the perfect voice which he had heard.

"O thou thunder-darter of Olympus!" thought he. "Where are your darts now? What a herd! What— 'words, words, words, mere words no matter from the heart!' and these rail at our vapid speech and shallow shows!"

He ceased, for the tutor was about to orate.

Some one, seeing that a couple of servants had arrived and were unpacking a hamper apiece, and sinking bottles of wine in the kettle at the spring, sagely observed that the lecturer need not wait for the lord and his brother, into whom he must have hammered the legend long ago. And Mr. Danby, with his self-sufficient air, added that Miss Danby was too sensible to trouble about legends.

"In the year seven hundred," he began, a little briskly, "here was fought a great battle between the pagans and the converted king of these parts. The heathen were beaten, with the loss of a leader, who was captured, fighting heroically. Life was offered him on condition that he would embrace Christianity. He was sorely wounded. Craftily, he craved a draft of that icy water running there at our feet. And, as he raised the caskful to his fevered lips, he said to the confiding priest who drew it:

"'As long as water' ran, the Cymrians have been servants of Odin, or some god of that kind, and as long as it runs they will live like their fathers. When it stops running, you will govern England your way!' Of course, the perverse sinner knew that, cold upon his heated blood, the drink would be his deathblow! The waters are excellent, but the louts will not drink it, alleging that it would turn them into pagans. That was how the Newell originals displaced the idolaters."

Kean heard this inattentively. He had drunk of that perilous stream, and was not sure that he was not made impervious to pious worship outside of his theatric gods.

The tutor had told his story very curtly. It was time,

for there was a stir. Lord Newell and his brother, with a little retinue of obsequious sycophants, appeared.

The servants prepared drinking-vessels; there was going to be only a libation to Diana.

It was Diana's self who appeared between the two nobles.

The escort being dark, they showed up the fair lady whom they jealously guarded.

Edmund knew who came by the smile of paternal pride on the Danby countenance.

Much of the same pleasure emanated from every eye.

Edmund had feared that Anna Danby would require the glamour of heiressdom, but he granted that he was mistaken.

CHAPTER IV.

TO SAVE A LIFE.

The young woman, upon whom Edmund was utterly absorbed in gazing, was proof that when nature plans a simply delightful creature, she attains perfection. At twenty years, she made one shudder with pleasant amaze at what she must become at the meridian. Somewhat taller in figure, she was quite at odds with the full-bloom, thickset, Hollandish form prevalent and admired by the Court around the Hanovers. But, without being wholly developed, she had not a spice of the ungainliness of the British maiden, and all her movements were in equipoise, like a trained rope-dancer's. Thus was she blest in the most trying time; not a temporary cloud dimmed the luster; she kept animated without making one step to attract attention.

"What a splendid woman!" thought the susceptible actor.

"What a pretty spot!" cried she, in the voice evermore to haunt him, as she turned her eyes around on all the variegated growths in such dells, flowers, herbs, grasses. Glittering newts glided through the trash fallen from over-topping boughs; woodpeckers climbed the ivy and woodbine ladders, and eyes—nothing more—peered out of cleft and riven trees.

"So they set up a hunting lodge here? I should never have credited those Hectors of the ironclad race with enough sentiment to picnic here!"

It was truly that voice, thought Edmund, his ear tingling with the musician's rapture at hearing a gamut run without one flaw or discordant note. How round, ripe, silvery in the high and Corinthian bronze in the lower octave; altogether enticing, detaining and insinuating.

He was too enthralled to be critical. But there was a defect. Miss Anna Danby, from having no cause to select her auditors, was too generally amiable. She was a waste-all of noble gifts; she showered what should have been cherished for the time of drouth, when a loving man pines for affection and attention.

With an object, she would be a great light, to save, like the pharos, but now she threatened to be one of those lures which bring admirers upon the shattering rock.

She had entered into the party like sunshine—it radiated from her glittering teeth and beaming eyes.

"It's a rarity!" thought the spy; then, judging that this near companion to her must be her father, he sneered: "As like as Vulcan and his wife!"

He heard one of the gentlemen, also all eyes to the beauty, whisper to his neighbor:

"She brings live coals in her apron, Mark! See how my lord and his brother are similarly entranced!"

"Yes, colonel! Since Mr. Danby confirmed the plight of Lord Newell and his sparkle of a daughter—this nonsuch—the plight of Mr. Jessamy is pitiable!"

"Pooh, you joke!"

"Not on so serious a subject! Jess does not eat or drink!"

"Eh?"

"He does not smoke!"

"Dear-a-dear me!"

"He does not turn the cup on the dice, or face up a card!"

"This is grave!"

"In my lord's stead, I should not only wed swiftly, but dispatch my brother on a long tour, with that tutor, he who looks like a blackthorn cudgel."

"She does not seem to seek two beaux!"

"No, but there are flowers which the gardeners do not let bloom in a corner, but trim them up, care for them, and place them foremost in the floral show, where royalty comes to view——"

"If you mean that the prince regent——"

"Do you not see Colonel Hanger and Sir John Whipstaffe? They are of the prince's legion. His jackals, they are not here to toss their caps because Newell comes into his own! See how they stare at *la belle* Alba!"

"There are no exceptions to that rude course! I cannot keep my eyes off her! I could not, did I not think of her father's moneybag. That distracts me."

A second corps of the sportsmen came down upon the throng; they sang, with an accompaniment of hunting horns, "With Early Horn!" so that some stopped their ears and others joined in, till the din was terrific.

The glade was filled with the colored coats of the hunt. The cooled drinks circulated.

All at once, vexed that the interruption should have thrust several hunting men between him and the beauty, Edmund had his zealous eye caught by a thin but brilliant line crossing the grass and partly hid in it where untrampled. He distinguished that it was not a serpent, being too long, although quite as shiny and vibrating, but a stretch of wire. On it drops of dew were chance-strung like crystal. From his point of view, the light fell on it, but it was no doubt invisible to all the others. At once, to his memory leaped that notice of inhumanity which reminded him that the lovely and almost wild domain was property to man. This youth before him, to whom all presented their respects and felicitations, owned all, and fenced it in thus.

A deep horror filled him; he trembled, as if it were an adder unrolling for fatal execution.

Death so close to that miracle of health, gayety and liveliness, to say nothing of the youth on the verge of wealth, luxury and power!

The rustic gentleman who arrived gave much heed to the town ladies, particularly Miss Danby; but she was not out of place. From the low garden hat, trimmed with real flowers, fresh plucked, to the thick, strong, and yet not inelegant, boots, she could not be blamed for the milliner's misconceit. Her father had not her sense, or he recked little of comment; as if silk stockings were cheap as wool, he had disdained to put on leggins and protect his breeches with a long-skirted coat. His dress coat, too, was of flowered satin, as if he was prepared already for the dinner. It is true that, being stout, so that few hunters were up to his weight, he was not going to ride to the hounds. Such a neck as his, on which reposed, like Atlas', the world of finance, was not to be broken by a fall off a gibing horse.

Colonel Hanger, the redoubtable, was a coarse, bluff,

pimply-faced swaggerer, who resented an evident move of Danby not to let him ogle his daughter.

"So," said he to Jessamy, isolated by the congratulations concentrated upon his brother, "Mr. Danby is going to give the town the lurch! I hear on the spot that he is buying property adjacent to yours, and so he will benefit the neighborhood by his expenditure here!"

"Yes, he is a philanthropist," struck in the sneering Sir John Whipstaffe, saucily, who, as a gaming-house pilot, lamented the loss of a possible prey; "after doing so much good to the city, he comes here to better your neighbors!"

"To best them, you should say!" said Hanger, spitefully, while pointedly bowing to the plutocrat, as if his name had come up in the talk and he was complimenting him by drinking his long life.

Miss Danby bore the admiring looks commendably; but she was sensitive about this father. She divined most of the sarcasms making mammon their butt; she could not defend one who continued to augment his fortune, and by the same nefarious ways which society reviled, even if it profited by it. She was tiring of being linked with him, and, with a kind of relief, if not joy, she had given way to his desire, that she should accept the hand of Lord Newall. Since the latter, as far as she knew, was rich, no one could style it a mercenary match.

Besides, she saw in this wedlock a silencer to the rumor that the prince had been so delighted at the sight of her, when making her *début* in the West End, that he had pointedly sent an equerry to her father to ask the lady's name. As if the prince, who had the usurers and moneylenders' pedigrees at his finger ends, did not know Danby from a long step into the past.

At all events, to wed, and stay for a space in the country, would let that not uncommon annoyance to contemporary young belles fall to the ground.

Some allusions to her brief but notable town triumph were buzzing about her; seeing that it chafed her, Jessamy, being envious, jealous and quarrelsome, without the prudence to withdraw and let his irritation subside, had the rashness to repeat one of the phrases of praise as hawked about the palace.

Miss Danby had in her hand a rod of flowering stuff, native *spiræ,* or rod of Aaron. On the impulse, never liking this young man, she stopped beating her skirts with it and laid it smartly upon his arm. Jessamy turned scarlet, as if his cheek bore its weal; but he had enough common sense flying to his aid to take the act as a pleasantry. He saw that, under his brother's eyes, to farther tease his intended would be bad policy; besides, he did not want to offend Papa Danby. So he merely sought to keep up the idea that the lady was trifling. He playfully made a snatch at the rod, to disarm her. But, seized with one of those panics which in an instant, in sensitive natures, overrule all habits, lessons and innate decorum, Alba burst away.

"Yoicks, tallyho!" roared Sir John, clapping his hand to his mouth to trumpet the call.

All made way for the girl, turned from quiescence to a romp.

Jessamy followed, after the least pause.

All began to laugh at the improvised race—all save Lord Newell, who frowned, and. by his hands clinching, could be seen to repress an instinct to add himself to the chase and pull down the pursuer.

Two or three gentlemen, not particularly friends of his, threw themselves between, with the pretence of not letting the fun be spoiled.

"The devil mend his manners!" grumbled Danby; but his parental feelings roused, he loudly continued:

"A hundred to ten that she beats him breathless!"

This, falling in with the whim, caused Newell to force a smile, and the mirth to redouble and be unrepressed.

Atalanta kept her lead, because her dress was for walking, and Jessamy was in boots and spurs, while the grass was rank and knotted.

All rejoiced at the agility, speed and gracefulness of the fleeing one.

Edmund was the more astounded at this unprecedented step on the part of the lady, as it was the age when moral ideas bound up the sex like the hideous and antiquated cages about their bodies. It was so violent, brutal, unreconcilable with convention! If a goddess had jumped down from her pedestal in an Italian garden and set the pace for a passerby, he could not have been more pained, as well as confounded.

But his rising indignation and dismay were checked and converted into another mood by his hearing—so strained were his faculties—a faint shrilling in the grass at his feet; he saw, too, that wire thrilling and squirming as if imbued with life.

The vivacious hoyden had taken her course at random —if ever we can take a step at random in this regulated life! But it was traced right across the course of that wire, with its unseen ends. Edmund divined that she had never run a greater peril. He sprang out from behind the tree. His apparition was as startling to all eyes, directed thither, as to Jessamy. If Ariel had stepped out of the cloven pine, it could not have been more out of nature. She did not see him, so swift was her gait by which she had just passed him. He threw up his arms, appealingly, as well to detain Jessamy, whom he already resolved not to let interfere.

His voice was scarcely intelligible in its intensity, as he ejaculated:

"For God's sake, stay! Do you not see——"

In truth, she saw nothing—not even this stranger; as for the almost imperceptible danger under her spring, it was not in the least suspected.

Those who for their first two decades tread the flowery path from which is daily swept all thorns, reptiles and stumbling-stones may disbelieve that there is ruin in any pass they take.

Edmund did not hesitate. He forgot all save that this was an inestimable creature rushing on pain, hurt, death —who knew?

He bounded forward then; he jostled Jessamy, recovering his flight, and, overtaking the fugitive, seized her around the waist with both hands. It was not a tender grip—it was without delicacy, for he meant to save her life, though he burst his heart.

It was such a clutch as the boa flings round a prey— and with such a leap the lion, though laden with a gazelle, overskims the pickets of the Afrikan *kraal*. He saw the wire curve up and curl into several kinks, as if alive, as he and she soared in the air.

Jessamy staggered, stopped short a little aside, confused at the stranger's interruption. The act was so gross that he could not comprehend. All the laughter and mock cries of encouragement were stilled as by magic. But Newell, quivering with rage, indignant at seeing a stranger, and one poorly clad, handle a form of which he had never more than touched the gloved hand, darted forth, and in three strides reached the spot in advance of his brother.

Jessamy cowered, as if he were going to be struck.

It seemed that he would be trampled under foot, but in his blind passion it is a question if Stephen saw him at all. He tottered, for his forward foot was entangled in the metal string; it continued that curling up which is unaccountable and belongs to the category of freaks of which inanimate things are capable at the times least awaited.

He fell upon it, but rose immediately, maddened with shame at the mishap in his betrothed's eyes.

Alba had turned around, burning and stirring with fury at this treatment. An embrace from this beggar! She was about to give him a slash over the head with the rod, not dropped, but she had hardly time to form the resolution, none to carry it out, for a spit of flame and a spurt of smoke, both without a warning hiss, shot up from the side of the group.

And they both came in their direction.

As the actor had supposed, from his knowledge of woodcraft and the gamekeeper's homicidal practices, the wire was attached to the hidden mechanism of a gun. As usual, the muzzle was turned in the direction of the line, so that the person pulling the string would discharge the weapon at his side, most likely. In this case, Lord Stephen faced it. Edmund had fallen upon one knee after the desperately disproportioned bound, but even thus he strove to keep his head and shoulders between his prize and the spot whence he supposed the projectiles must come.

The jet of flame along the grass, firing its dry tops, scathed him—indeed, several pellets tore his clothes, which needed no dilapidation.

It was the body of the heir to the Newells which re-

ceived the whole load, slugs, bullets, a shankless button
or two and a bitten-in-twain sixpence, for luck!

Stephen would have pealed out a shriek of mortal agony
but for the hemorrhage issuing from his lips. Like a
bullrush cleft at the root, he fell, but whirled round and
knocked Jessamy off his feet. The two brothers met
the ground together, and it appeared that they were en-
twined in a deadly wrestle.

Jessamy threw off the burden instinctively, and, as he
struggled to his knees, remained in that position, understanding all, as one sees everything, past, present and to
come in an instant like this.

Thus kneeling over the dying, he seemed praying. No
attitude could be more meet.

CHAPTER V.

A HUMBLE VICTIM.

"The younger rises when the old doth fall!"
—*King Lear*

The smoke had not died away before the spot was covered with the curious, and those purely desirous to lend their aid. Outside the dell, numbers hurried up on foot, or in the saddle, hearing the muffled but significant murmur of the paralyzed and horrible spectators.

These latter thought that it was a bungling shot in the preliminaries to the battue. All were hushed on perceiving who was the victim. It appeared incredible. Even while the supine body was lifted up and a gate, abruptly unhinged, brought to be its litter, all doubted that one could come into wealth and into its utter loss so rapidly.

The most reckless, like Hanger and his colleagues, showed a pale face and tremulous under lip, like one who steps into a church merely to avoid a shower and suddenly hears a sentence from the pulpit deal him a stroke to the deepest, darkest nook of his conscience.

Danby lumbered forward, unable to believe that his daughter had escaped so narrowly.

Without meaning irreverence, he uttered an oath instead of a thanksgiving prayer. No one heeded him. Miss Danby was brave; she pointed to the dead one, as much as to say: "Let all your cares be for him! I am not hurt."

Jessamy let them take the corpse from him, and then trembled, burying his face in his hands. A manservant hastened to lead him apart, and offered his arm.

A gamekeeper, with a guilty air, as if some one had reproached him, hurriedly stammered:

"By your leave, gentlemen, it is the spring-gun—there b'ain't no more on 'em! The master has been and drawed the foir of the spring-gun, but it were set for the poachers, sure-ly! sure-ly, it were set for the night-roamers, gentlefolk all!"

He blew his nose, trumpet-like, in an enormous Indian cotton handkerchief.

The bystanders broke up into two parties; one escorted Mr. Danby, who had his daughter to support. The other accompanied the barrow on which was the extinguished light of the Newells.

Jessamy stood as if rooted, with the menial; he was sobbing convulsively, but in a hushed manner.

Edmund was practically left alone. He was stunned; the girl had not addressed him by a word—had not bestowed one glance upon him. It would appear that she did not like to owe her life to him, as if he were a pariah.

Mr. Danby had not further noticed him, after a long look. His gratitude, probably, was tainted by scorn, like his daughter's.

Jessamy dismissed the servant, and retraced his steps. He had not a tear in his eye; his cheeks were not wet with them. Without fully believing—so great was the stroke —that his brother was dead, he had already realized what an opportunity was almost his. In this moment he was where the cadet sometimes passes his life—at the depth of the river of Tantalus, where he never seizes what he reaches for. His brother had made him kick the beam— a bullet or two on his side brought him down to the level. Still, no actual wish had taken this shape; he had dreamed without dismissing the dream, that was all. If Miss Danby had not come between them, he might have remained unfretting in the position of the waiter on fortune at the table where the next guest must wait for a seat to be vacated.

It was because the woman had become more than all else that he saw in this man of his own age before him, in the deserted glade, not one who had by his silence let his brother precipitate himself on death, but solely one who had the honor, by a superhuman act of quickness, deftness and power, to save Alba Danby.

Jessamy hated the rescuer more for having saved the woman than for letting the man perish, if he had really a power to make a choice.

If the lady whom Edmund had benefited had been his affianced, he could not have shown a more fiery countenance.

A Humble Victim.

"What the deuce!" he began, rudely beyond expectation.

The other put his long, white, elegant hand up, deprecatingly.

"Peace, and list!" he said, suddenly. His low voice had compassion in it—no other emotion. "Do you not hear, sir? That blunderbuss had more than one mission from Fate!"

Actually, in the copse, they heard undeniable writhing, a lashing of the twigs and reeds, a splashing of blood or water, and a peculiar breathing, broken and slackening— all with a floundering on the sod of some stricken creature too dumb with pain to express its misery.

"Your infernal machine has not solely turned on the master who approves of such engines," continued Edmund, coolly. "You have, between you, killed yet another of your kind—that is, a guest—a keeper——"

He did not finish the sentence, for the noble could guess the rest. The close was trite and theatrical:

" 'The engineer hoist with his own petard!' "

Jessamy's heart was not let irredeemably bad. A man unbends when he has narrowly escaped sudden death. He swayed weakly, facing the thicket, which held a mystery; he wondered why resentment had detained him here; it was not his fit place. He ought to be by his brother's side, receiving his last sigh, if a breath were left in him by this time. He should not be wrangling while that poor girl was probably paying with a hysterical attack for her fine calmness. He should not be dallying with this demigod "out of the machine," for he perceived of what tribe he was who had snatched the flower out of the cannon's mouth.

But his curiosity was more than his affection; he was drawn toward the underwood.

Undoubtedly, a body was lying, quite still now, on the broken brake-staff and the cut-up sods.

In great relief, he shouted:

"Oh, a donkey! An animal! A donkey!"

In superior dramas the playwright is held to imitate life most closely when he interleaves his tragic pages with alleviating ones, more or less contrasting, more or less comic. Edmund had found that in life. It intersperses tears and smiles almost regularly among its incidents.

He was also relieved, but he felt some grief.

Certainly the object was a donkey, and as Jessamy gazed upon it he burst into a prolonged and forced laugh. The ass is so unromantic that the noble's terror turned to sport, and he was not much to blame.

"Poor Neddy!" said the actor. "Is it because it is a humble creature who toils in its place without better pay than most of us—asses! More kicks than pence! But I forget; I must not add to your burden when you have to lament the loss of your brother, I think!"

As if everybody did not know the Newells—so this remark envenomed the dart.

"Yes, it is my brother, and I believe he is dead. I feel it here!" He applied his hand somewhat theatrically to his heart.

"I pity you, sir, then!"

"Who wants your pity—anything from you? Pity of the likes of you!" he went on, fiercely, glad to exhale some of his spite on this interloper.

"The likes?" repeated the actor, surprised at the animosity. "I, who saved one whom you worried into hurling herself upon the mine—the masked death! Noble though you are, you are a cipher to one who in the emergency showed he was man!"

"I see that you are going to hang on to those skirts in order to be rewarded! Oh, have no fear, Miss Danby has a rich father, who is fond of her! Besides, if my brother is not dead, as he is betrothed to the lady, you will fare well by your—your heroism—you and your fellows, for I know you now! You must belong to the corps of strollers whose costume—seedy or flowery—you wear! Don't hurry away if there is to be mourning when your fantastic capers go for nothing, for, in my brother's stead, I will behave liberally, as was his wont!"

"I am a player, and I am not ashamed of it! As for strolling, my strolls—this being one—have a gain at the end of them, it appears, sometimes! Indeed, when they took me to London I learned something of the Newells, the two of them! If the tales be one-half true, I give my pity rather to this hard-working beast sooner than to you,

who are a pest to your rank, your country and your hire-
lings!"

"You——"

"Go, while your skin is unimpaired, to mourn over your
brother, or rejoice over your inheritance, as the case may
be!" and he waved him off, grandly.

"Fellow, you shall repent all this!" cried Jessamy; yet,
as he thought he heard steps approaching, he hurried on,
but with a chance of tone and sense, saying: "Not in sack-
cloth and ashes, but in our best wine and apparel, of which
you may not be ashamed! Come up to the house, my
brave man, and——"

A gamekeeper came rushing into the glen at that instant. It was the same who had so awkwardly apologized
for the spring-gun.

"Gideon!" exclaimed the young-man, with a broken
voice, turning weeping eyes upon him, as if anticipating
the worst.

"My lord is no more!" said the man, drawing the edge
of his hand across his eyes. "Dr. Quicksett no sooner
saw the wounds than he shook his head, and said: 'Squan-
tum stuff!' or Latin to the effect that all was hopeless!"
He padded his eyes with his handkerchief. "The whole
country will go into r'yal mourning for this loss, my
lord!"

He was, without innocence, the first to hail Jessamy under his new title. According to usage, the harbinger
should be lavishly recompensed.

"Don't say that! Oh, woe!"

Gideon respected his master's sorrow, for he turned his
face aside, thus including the ass in his glance.

"Halloa!" cried he, for it was gloomy here in the thick
brush; "have they already brought down a deer?"

"Deer, idiot!" interposed the actor. "Like master, like
man! You are all asses alike, to shoot such things as
these! Do you set springs for causing a succession of
succession? And do you kill hard-working and honest
men's beasts of burden for your pampered bucks? Fellow, I am going to get those to whom this poor beast belongs to take their satisfaction out of its hide and hoofs
while awaiting the damages of the county court! Meanwhile," raising his voice and giving it a penetrating and

alarming tone, "see to it that you let it not be moved or touched until they come!"

"Here, here, on this ground!" faltered Gideon, unable to believe his ears that, before his master—the lord now— any one would presume to browbeat him. "Do you, boy, order my master's man about?"

He looked appealingly at Jessamy, who replied, not vocally, but in his own way. It was unseen by Edmund. It was to make off, but on the way to deal the ass a sly kick of contempt.

"But what will I do with him, my lord?" demanded Gideon, in a low voice, for it looked a difficult burr to get rid of.

"Oh, like the ass, shoot him!"

As he was going, he might not have cared whether he was heard or not. He was overheard, for, while his man was touching his forelock in obedience, Edmund said, with defiance and grim humor:

"Shoot me! Would you make game of me, too?"

As this retort conveyed the insinuation, terrible to a game warder, that the marksmen did not know a donkey from a deer, he turned to the saucy intruder, who had become a discharging battery to the electric jars on Newell ground.

"You are sharp, sir!" said Gideon, not knowing how to bring about a result one way or another, but feeling he had free course given him. "I can be as short with you as you with me!"

They faced and glared at each other.

"To-day," resumed the menial, "as it was made free all over Newell and the village, you, and even yours, can go in and out of the manor; so be quick in calling your friends with the tumbrel to cart away this nuisance! To-morrow, if it be here, it will be cut up for our hounds in the kennels!"

Since Edmund was plainly aware that he had made an enemy of Jessamy, and held it as no charge, he might treat his agent lightly. But he was one who would rather "follow an enemy into a fiery gulf than flatter him into a bower," so he accepted this kind of challenge, which ignored the announcement of his own making and his substituted terms. He turned his back on the subordinate, and, regarding the dead body, said, in the half-humorous and half-misanthropical vein of a philosopher:

"Poor Midas! dead on the track of duty! Is it to this final scene your faithful steps on the road to fame have brought you? Is this the *finale* to one who drew off the Trojans and the Greeks, indifferent as fate at our chariot wheels? You have lugged on 'The Merry Wives' for an epilogue! Gobbo has bestridden you to deliver his thanks for his benefit! You have tugged off the loads of treasure which Ali Baba despoiled the spoilers of, in the cave! You, to fall by the slugs intended for the poacher; you who have braved the Peruvian's poisoned arrows! Misery like this to them who level the deadly tube at the thin breast of the cottager who, haply, stole out on the misty moonlight night to procure a mouthful for his wife and the bairns! What loss to the magnate, with his coveys of partridges, one brace of which would have seasoned the boor's eternal cabbage and pork!"

Gideon listened impatiently, yet trying to understand the pith of the apostrophe. Then, learning that this was at least the advocate of the poacher for home relief, and he abhorred all poachers, he blurted out:

"I dare say, had you been civil-spoken, the new lord would have given your friends half a guinea for this carcass, but as it is, not a hair or a bone shall be carried off the premises! It is trespassing after dark to come upon these grounds! You might judge by that 'ere gun how we defend ag'in malignants and non-convormists; and the more luck, since, this night, I shall be almost alone— for you will have seen that all my posse are under the tables at the inn!"

"Then, it is I who will guard this body for its owners! I shall be traced, and then we will take away our own, trespass or no trespass, in spite of your teeth!"

CHAPTER VI.

"WHO SHALL KEEP THE KEEPERS?"

Edmund's eyes and the other's met at this, as the wrestlers' do when they shake hands before closing in the first bout.

At that date the strolling player was own brother to those eternal wanderers, the gypsies; with them they harbored an undying grudge, indefinite yet decided enough, against all authorities. They hated beadles, warders, constables, tipstaves and gatekeepers only a shade less than the gamekeepers, who has not a lover in the country. Vaguely, the people recognize, theoretically, some sense in these being guardians of the property and peace of the well-to-do, but never have they acknowledged, though often beaten on the question, that forests may be inclosed for private gain or pleasure, and that game should be butchered and wasted instead of feeding the needy. So, rarely able to assail the great game-preservers, they revenge themselves by seldom declining an encounter with their agents.

"It is innate," Edmund would say. "As, sons of Shakespeare, poacher-poet in Arden wood, we must detest the keeper!"

He confronted a fair sample of the protectors of lordly pastime. Gideon was stalwart, keen-sighted, quick in action, firm when set going, enduring, experienced in the usual athletic sports. More than all, he had guessed, without having seen the adventure to Miss Danby and the death shot to his late master, that Jessamy and this pretentious young man were foes.

"I do be dubersome that my lord would give even half a guinea as damages for that brute being killed on our land, but I am positive, sure, that he will give I a guinea if he can be told that I licked this spiteful toad in a fisticuff encounter!"

Happily, on account of the feast, he had neither gun nor

knife with him. The actor had dropped his cane somewhere, so that they were equal.

"Now that you boast that you will stay here, wolly-
bolly, we shall see about that, Don Pomposo!" cried
Gideon.

"To it!" returned Edmund. "But, whatever the out-
shot of our encounter, remember, it will not affect your
new lord's having to set off the score! My employer, Mr.
Richardson, will demand and insist upon having full com-
pensation!"

"Yes, I knowed you to be one of Muster Richardson's
croaking crew! Ah, crows have been shot for calling out
less sweetly than you!"

This young adversary was slight as compared with Gideon, but the horse-copers, the swarthy vagrants, had char-
acterized him as a "colt of promise." As for the prize-
fighters, who pitched their marquee next to Richardson's
Temple of the Drama, they had often praised Edmund for
his dexterity, endurance and inventive ability. As well
get an eel pinned up in a corner of "the round square!"
they said.

"You have lost your only chance," went on the young
man, taking off his coat and tightening the strap to his
breeches. "You might have been none the worse for
keeping watch over poor Midas till the relief came, but—
but your hounds shall not fatten on it! Either I stand
guard here or you must come along with me, if I have to
take you by the collar! I promise that this carcass shall
not be handled by any but those entitled to it!"

"You take me by the collar, you 'natomy! A body
nigh so thin, with want of proper nourishers that it's a
miracle you can draw a breath without bursting your
skin!"

"My arms may be thin, but they can reach as far as
your insolent tongue!"

Gideon felt, rather than saw, that a conflict so recklessly
accepted would not be child's play, and he dismissed any
idea he would otherwise have entertained of "letting the
boy off light."

He looked merely for one of those brief but rough col-
lisions common on the village green, where the rustics,
after a little clawing and wild striking out, close and tug

till one or both is tripped and they fall, so nearly winded that the struggle is not renewed.

The noble game of fisticuffs had degenerated into wrestling.

When Richard the Lion-hearted stood up to Friar Tuck, in a forest like this, they gave and took blow for blow until one cried the talismanic words: "Enough!"

Edmund had studied the matter while learning the classic plays of Shakespeare. He knew that the pugilists of the amphitheatre had their arms and hands bound up in leather, or even plated with metal, a sort of clumsy boxing mitten. But the gypsies, who cherish many a variation in ancient usages, taught him that this test of strength and endurance had been modified by those who saw an opening for skill, nimbleness and cunning to obtain the meed.

Again, Moses the Prompter, a Jew proud of his race, recalled the Maccabees, and insisted that they had a certain prowess with the bare hands.

Between them, gypsy and Jew, Edmund learned that a man in the fistic arena was to win at any price, by any means not actually precluded by rules.

Therefore, Mr. Gamekeeper, thinking to settle all after the first bearlike embrace, found that this conclusion was remote. Meanwhile, puzzled by the young man leaping to one side, leaning back, shifting his positions and altering his pose, he could not get one blow to tell; as for seizing this puppet of quicksilver, as well clutch the Jack-o'-Lantern in the marsh. But, what was worse, taking advantage of this bewilderment, Edmund, who had learned to make a blow with his arm becoming rigid and as one with his body at the shoulder, struck him seldom, but always to make impression.

In a few words, Gideon was beaten to a stand, and that stand was unstable. Tottering, blinded, humming in the skull, he muttered, with a kind of dubious congratulation, at such prowess:

"That's a black ace for you!"

A second blow set his forehead aching anew.

"It's a pair of black eyes," said Edmund. "Will you never know when you should cry 'Enow!' according to rules of the game?"

"Game, master! I own up that you are game!"

"Then, without insisting on your being more open, let it rest here. And you rest there!" leading him to the springside. "It won't make a pagan of you to wash your mouth out and bathe your numbskull, while doing which I will go to my friends of the theatre. I am sure now that you will not run away with our donkey!"

He stalked away, feeling shaken, but determined not to show a pang, while repairing ineffectually his disrupted apparel.

He was not overproud at this kind of brutal triumph. He reflected that it was not a conflict over which he could wish Miss Danby to be queen of the lists.

"She is not that kind. She is, as far as that peep at her lets me pronounce, a connecting link between woman and angel. She would repudiate the hands which saved her, since they are dabbled in the gore of that ruffian." He strode on. "And yet, is it not pure prejudice, that shifting of tastes? In the days of the Roman Empire, I dare say such dainty darlings would have curled the thumb for a craven to be given his quietus, or tossed their jeweled fanheads to the victor. If we had stood up with pistols or swords in our grasp she would have clapped her riding gloves in twain! It's prejudice! Her paltry glance at me showed that she was all that—and she only a *parvenu,* at the most!"

Fox decrying the grapes out of reach!

When Gideon had laved his bruises and vainly slapped water on the twin "mice" swelling under his eyes he began to consider his position. This was not the visage, woeful as it had become, to show at the festivity turned into wailing; his first act under the new ruler to be ineffectual—a failure was a bad overture. Far less could he show himself to the dashed carousers, dolefully wending their homeward way from the untimely-ended "wassels" (wassail). Reckoning that he would not be missed, chuckling at his having been paid in advance, he expected that this levanting would be set down to fear of being included in the call for witnesses as to the planting of the manor with hidden homicidal devices.

Knowing all the byways and wild-dog paths, he sneaked out of the park, and plunged into the forest.

So vast was the domain of the Newells that the shoot-ing parties were well apart.

Some executed their first bout and returned to environs of the house without any idea of the important mishap.

One was composed of a number of Londoners, in whose midst was the rising comedian, William Belliston, of his majesty's "patented" theatres.

These cockneys had flocked together in awe of the local Nimrods. They had toyed with their new guns with much grace and many flourishes, but they were going elsewhere, with hope of no longer being "empty-bagged," when Bel-liston, wishing to dye his maiden suit of sporting clothes with indubitable deer-red, spied a target in the copse. He waved back his loader and beater, with an imperious ges-ture, brought his fine gun to bear, and fired, as he vocifer-ated :

"A royal head! A stag of ten !"

"Did you bring him down?" queried all, as there was no leaping away of anything maimed and fleeing.

"I wager !"

"Down or feather?" queried a wag.

This shot had been fired just a little after some men from Richardson's show, warned by their tragic actor, hastened to the spot. They were about to hoist poor Midas upon a bed of stakes, fastened with the woodbine. It was the animal's long ears that the amateur marksman had taken for antlers. His mistake was plain "buck fever," and pardonable. But, on advancing with his friends, and perceiving the ludicrous error, he felt like the bowler who casts the ball too soon and all but kills the setter-up among the pins.

The theatre men were white as he, for the shot had whizzed among them. Belliston would have fled, but his companions would not allow that until it was ascertained what hurt had been done.

The showmen bore the attack pretty calmly, for Ed-mund had notified them that he had had a collision with the gamekeepers, and that they had best perform their commission briskly. They took the volley as a reception, directed by the lord of the manor which the donkey had invaded.

As none of them could show a graze, and a clip or two

of Midas' forelock could not well be charged for, Belliston
did not have to draw on his purse-strings or his compeers'. As all had gone off harmlessly, all that need be
done was to pull out the pocket pistols and shoot one another in the neck—to make up the abrupt introduction.

On hearing that the envoys came to bury Cæsar, while
praising him, Belliston pressed a guinea on the under-fol-
lowers of Thespis, and begged to have his compliments repeated to Mr. Richardson, under whose colors he had
served in earlier days.

As Midas had played *rôles* on the stage, he sprinkled
him with snuff and uttered a mock epitaph, which con-
vulsed the hearers, glad to be relieved.

When the stable helper came, with cart and horse, to
carry the carrion to the dogs' quarters he was out for his
drive.

Meanwhile, the direful news had penetrated every corner. The departing guests carried it homeward in many
directions.

All gayety vanished, except among the nearest to Belliston, where, with that tenacity in "chaffing" characteristic of the Londoners, jest after jest bid fair to perpetuate
the fame of him who killed the donkey for a deer.

It was all the regale the disappointed locusts chewed as
they turned away from the house of distress, where the
bottles were opened not to flow.

Few things irritate a table-lover as much as the loss of a
fine dinner. In Belliston's case, he had prepared several
toasts and neat repartees, which would have to be stored
up for a fitter occasion. He could have likened himself to
those pasteboard monsters of Chinese holidays, stuffed
with firecrackers, which, deterred from explosion, made
the bearers sick with the load.

Belliston, too, being comedian and a fellow of mirth
withal, was not alleviated by seeing the materials for
tragedy in the day's incidents; "the younger rising when
the elder fell;" the fateful employment of Miss Danby as a
decoy toward the secreted gun; the cold reception to the
shows, and the vexation to the hundred invited ones to the
manor.

No one could say that the fair heiress was the lure, but
the malevolent winked and cited Scripture and later prece-

dents for the rule of a brother carrying out his elder's love pledges at his decease. Besides, whatever the inheritance of Jessamy, it was understood that by loans from Danby to both sons of the house during their minority, he was almost the real owner of the Hold.

Danby was in acute dudgeon; the stroke had upset his plans; he was a man who, having toiled to amass his wealth, looked forward to being alone to enjoy it. His daughter wedded, he would be free. Now, she was still on his hands. Besides, the death placed the distribution of accumulated moneys in Jessamy's hands, and he well knew that this was the wily, slippery spendthrift of the two, over whom he had not the control favoring him with the other. It was premature to set any plans, but Jessamy, more or less hypocritically, hinted that he would go and pass the term of grieving in Luxembourg.

This out, Danby, masking his spite badly, ordered his landau, to be conveyed to his house in Russell Square. His daughter's dreams of the county ball were faded, as well as her prospect of adulation and felicitation as the bride of the best match of the county.

To relieve the monotony of traveling, Danby, delighted with Belliston, begged to have his company up to London.

As this fell in with the comedian's project of securing a financial backer to his ambition to rule a town theatre, he accepted, gladly.

CHAPTER VII.

THE FORCING-BED OF TALENT.

Mr. William Belliston, while an actor in London, became, during his holidays, as was the tacit custom, a gentleman at ease—never ill at ease; always at home.

He had few enemies, except those antiquated persons who believe in debts of honor and assert that loaned money should be repaid before all, and at call. Even these did not dare say that he could not ingratiate himself with any, even the most obdurate.

This little weakness of William the Silvery, his first nickname, would have caused him to choose the Continent for his vocation, since he owed a pretty sum here and there, indiscriminately, over England; but this time he had not the faintest alarm about meeting the stragglers of the drama down at Newell in the great house.

He had higher aims than in the old times; he disdained wielding the mace for a petty "pool," while he could probably "let in deeply" those who, in the slang of Cornhill, "ran rigs on the loobies." He had seen, after a slight acquaintance with Drury Lane Theatre, that it was in the slough, and that the gilded lever of "the mushrooms," spreading on the mounds around the new bank, was very much wanted.

He could not but be delighted when the manipulator in gold offered to place him in his ample carriage for the return to town. But one thing marred his pleasure. The sportsmen could not refrain from "snickering" every time they caught sight of him, and the very tapestry seemed to echo with the awful query: "Who shot the donkey for a deer?"

The comedian might live on ridicule, but this could kill him.

A boisterous wit, very bucolic, must repeat this tale as a send-off to the plutocrat, and perhaps add that he supposed they would carry "the game" in the boot!

Danby was of the class of non-inventive men who wring

a tale like a young terrier its first rat, never knowing when to leave off. So Belliston, who read him like a book, was fearful that he would have this donkey dangled before his eyes all the road, not even Miss Danby's company being a check. In consequence, he excused himself at the last moment, with poignant regret, his vanity ruling over his self-advantage.

Being a kind of butt, he walked into the village, expecting, without any difficulty, to hire a conveyance.

He reckoned without his—post. Those who had come to Newell hoping to hang on for a week, at the least, but not finding any attraction in the obsequies, were eager to get away, fleeing the place as unlucky. Everything which went on wheels, or legs, was pressed into service.

Belliston knocked at a tiresome row of doors until desperate.

In the street and on the green the nomads had struck their colors and carried away their canvas roofs. They had been paid to give three or four days' entertainment, and were a little timid about the death in the family leading to a hint that they should refund—to the steward. So they yielded to an Arab-like *hegira,* carrying the dread tidings to all points of the compass.

Richardson's Penny Show wagon alone remained, lighted up fairly, but not according to its degree of effulgence, if the performance was "on." Better than lights. Belliston heard horses neighing.

Since business was suspended, the platform before the inn led no longer into its interior; all the apertures were shuttered up. But it ran on unimpeded to the front of the living-wagon. Here was a door, with a real knocker, memento presented to Richardson in a college town, where even his exponents of the drama had been welcomed by the youths as "a devilish recreation."

As Belliston held on to the knocker, hearing bustle within, as if the company were condoling over the quietus to their hopes, he also heard hard breathing behind him, and a heavy step.

He might have thought a pavior was leveling the street after its plowing up with iron-shod shoon. He turned on the planks of "the parade," to which his foot, though in varnished leather now, warmed with renewed familiarity.

The figure he saw on the street was imposing, for its bulk, if not for any majesty. It was the proprietor, coquettishly eying his own "outfit," who lorded it over the mock monarchs within without having caught any of their airs and attitudes.

Unaware in the gloom that there was an applicant at his door for admission out of hours, he continued a soliloquy.

"Do no' talk to me of there being no sech a thing as judgment on the antagonists of the stage!" said he, growling like a bear. "No sooner had that booby, the steward, given me the cold chuck-out than lo! and behold! down goes his lord with a dozen plumpers in his back! I hurry here, look you, to this dissignificant Freefolk, where the folk b'ain't free of their money, scorning the trial of cart-hosses and the all-the-county plowmen's match at Latchlea, which it is worth thirty pun' the three days, and no 'kidding!' And what do I bump up again'? Whoy, a bier like that of the owld Dook of Double-Gloster! A black lookout, a total upset of the applecart! Billy Fairplay is tied down with golden threads! All the attractions are sweepingly boughten out, and 'cause I came at my leisure and were late, they would not pay me for free exhibitions, which I never agreed to yet! And thereupon my lord's high cockolorum, the carrier of the bag! Judas Fishchariot, to .be plain with you, a Master Biggins! Fobus, what a name! He would not level up to my terms! I stood on my dignity, and why not? He drew off with the bag, and here we are like porpoises, stranded, out in the cold, and dark, like gypsums at Pharaoh's table! What time they drew the gauzes close, and there was blackness on the land! The drama at one penny, with all the other shows wide open for nothing at all, would not have fine-tooth raked in a doit! I know the public! And, when we shall have shook off the dust of Freefolk from our anklejacks, look ye! No crumbs will fall with it; no drops of even a parting cup! Not a loose coin! Not a dump! Not a tongueless button!"

Mounting the steps, as if he were going to be beheaded at the summit, poor Ritchie collapsed, and sat down at the apex. What was his amazement to feel that another sat himself down beside him, hip to hip, and a huge sheet of cambric, after a grand flourish in the air, was waved before another lugubrious face. He looked under the broad-brimmed and curly-haired beaver which darkened the blank visage, and listened as if the victim of an illusion, to the cooing in a voice which would have softened granite:

"Cheer up, old cockywax! We have seen weather more calculated to take the starch out of a collar! I ask your pardon, Daddy Rich, but this is a companion in dolor! William Belliston has no more grounds to bless the house of Newell than my old general!"

"Now comes my lucky! My old pupil—why, you dog! Send me a new pair of ogles if I do not reconnoiter some of you, though the feathers are new! It's your v'ice!"

"Many a man is betrayed by his v'ice!" responded the other, merrily. "Blame the dark! You must know your best cream-faced 'Mercutio!'"

"It's Billy! it's Bill Liston! Dough-face, with such a trumpeter's puffed and scarlet cheek! You have been at the bottle, sir!"

"It's modesty's own blush, daddy, positively!"

Richardson's joy was sincere. He clapped the other on the shoulder, and blubbered.

"Little Whitey Bill!" snuffled he. "An' turned out a prize for the 'cruetting sargeant, at that! And a beau of the first brandy-and-water, too! In the lamps turned 'full on,' you would be a dazzler! I declare! None what knowed you in my wardrobe, as that snipe 'H'Osrick, would see the same stripped-ling in you—lace above and fur below, and di'munds on your garters, like the king at Windsor! Eh, man, how all my pupils get on!"

Belliston tendered him his snuffbox, painted and set with brilliants, as to an old crony.

"You will say that, when you hear what I have got on to, old 'un!" said the comedian, chuckling, unctuously.

They had risen, finding the plank seat damp.

"On my front stage—on 'the walk,' certain sure, again! I see that! Haw, haw, haw!"

Belliston drew off a little, stuck one hand in his bosom, posed the other on the slight hand rail, and replied, much as the disguised sovereign in a mysterious piece announces his rank:

"I am a son of old Drury, by eager adoption!"

"What! old Dr. Drury, of Exeter?"

"Pshaw! Drury Lane—the theatre of the world!"

"Lor'! have they made you master to the king's devils——"

"One of the king's revelers, Mr. Richie—revels, not devils, sir!"

"I won't culminate (calumniate) the owld king, but I hear that his son, the prince, is the associate of devils!"

"George and I have danced 'the Hay' together, I confess!"

"Honest? You don't mean for to say you dance in the r'yal palace! Never!"

"In the adjunct—the pavilion at Brighton, sir! I could show you the diamond ring, token of his favor——"

"No; I know where it would be—show me the pawn duplicate, if you like!"

"Richardson, times are changed!"

"Well, they have not changed some I. O. U.'s which clever members of my company induced me to cash for them when you levanted! But sink that, Bill! I burned them to light my pipe long ago! So, you have the pavilion palace doors open to you?"

"From ear to ear! But, as for Drury Lane, I want palm oil to anoint the hinges! I make a clean breast of it to you; I am on the edge! I am in the gap of the door!"

"Yes, I reckon they would put it on high to sell a share in a patent theayter! But you have time to save up! How young you are?"

"Dear old master," said Belliston, fawning on him, "I have found the secret—not of being ever young, but of looking so! Look always at 'thirty-year'! It's the talisman!"

"Oh, if you have squared it with the tallyman, old Time, you are on the tiptop! You handle 'the coin of Wantage,' as the bard says, eh?"

"A little more coin, and I shall control Drury Lane!"

"So well up?"

"My conditions stipulate no going down traps—no blackening my face!"

"I thought you would be always proud to play the

ghost of Gimblet's father! 'Anglers and Scimetars of Greece,' or yet 'the Moore of Wenice?'"

"Perhaps, but I eschew tragedy! The people, sir, the enlightened mass, are wearied of the butcher's bill, of war and slaughter, sir! They lean and cleave to Momus. I am the leading light comedian. You know that Mr. Garrick said——"

"Don't tell me what Muster Garrlick said!" interrupted the old crab, shaking his head. "Muster Garrlick were a rank outsider! None of mine true-breds! He stepped on to the stage out of the manager's office! Quite on-regular and syruptishiously!"

"In any case, Garrick would say to a theatrical aspirant: 'You may humbug the town in tragedy'——"

"As he did, the humbuggist!"

"But comedy is a serious thing! I am, sir, I repeat, the favorite London comedian!"

"You make fun—good fun? You that I used to say was cut out of weepin'-willer to be a wooden image in a pulpit! Well, tell me, Bill——"

"Ever your Bill at heart, but let it be 'William,' and I will answer you freely. Call me Belliston, and I will answer you gladly!"

"Sly droll! be it Muster Belliston! I b'ain't no scribe, but I likes my bills to look their best with curlycues and flourishes! To near-by get 'the sack' from yours truly, and hold 'the sock' now!"

"Mark, I only wait to secure a capitalist 'angel,' with golden wings, you know! And, when you drop in upon me in my town lodgings, you will be guest of one of his majesty's servants! Ah, my ancient pistol, we will go off with a bang then. To tell truth, I find it hard to slip through a sheriff's fingers! We will dine at the Savoy Broiled Bone rooms, dine at the Stag-and-Hounds, and round off with steak and oysters at the Coronation Tavern!"

Inspired by the prospect, the good fellow caught Richardson as if he were a Dutch waltzer, and spun him round dextrously on the limited platform, singing and making him sing, too:

> "We went strolling,
> But still caroling!"

Till between the footfalls and the loud voices, not very concordant, the inmates of the traveling playhouse must have dreaded that the dull lookout had turned their manager's wits.

"Meanwhile," said Richardson, as soon as he had regained his breath after this unwonted gambol, "come in and peck! They are but crows and daws, but you shall be the parrot!"

"Parrot!" said Belliston, cooled by this misnomer.

"Ah, my boy, it is I who reserved my eagle!"

He opened the door, at which, indeed, impatient hands were rattling.

"You are daintily got up for a banquet—not for a tramp!"

"I was a guest at the great house!"

"Lor', were they going to give a show there?"

"Invited—a guest! I am a gentleman by birth and connections!"

"So the poor young lord's sudden taking off has left the head of the table vacant? Sad, sad!"

"Yes, the baked meats will coldly furnish the funeral tables," quoted the actor, carelessly.

"Well, I am independent of them!" he snapped his thick fingers as carelessly. "It is potluck here, but times is not what they used to was! The patrons want all the London novelties, for the newspapers bring the kittikisks to their breakfast table within a week sometimes! We are stragglers still, but strugglers—well, no! In your time, ay; but, since, the carrywan contains a larder!" He sniffed. "Him what is cast for the 'poticary in 'Rumble-low and Jubilate' is obleeged to fast, for true, the day he goes on to sell the dose of cold p'ison!"

The door being open, he locked arms with his new-found adept, and marched him down the narrow aisle in the "hall" of the "carrywan."

Any one would know that the newcomer was experienced by the "knowing" duck of the head, not to have it soundly boxed by the rafters. Yet he had to confess that the march of improvement had penetrated Richardson's.

The gathering under his eyes would no longer form a group for Hogarth or Churchill. Men or women, they were tidily garbed and carried themselves with as much self-respect as the legal or clerical underlings whom they ranked with. Their hands, hair and footgear were as the gentlefolks', and they offered, on the whole, a picture of the acme of English commendation—respectability and comfort.

"Quakers' meeting," said Belliston, in an audible "aside," for his strangeness had daunted them; "only, the sexes commingle!"

He was being scrutinized finely. The true actor is always studying character and characters. The ordinary ones go by the externals only, since that is about all they can represent. But the extraordinary—and the tragedian, Edmund, was that one—examined Belliston penetratively.

Like them, he knew that this was a "theatrical." A sort of continuous bidding for notice betrayed that. But his apparel, to a seam and stitch, denoted that he rubbed elbows with the highest flyers of dandydom.

"A former imposter of mine!" said Richardson, waving his hand.

He meant to say "apostle," no doubt, but they understood him.

"He has arisen! So, to him the seat of honor!"

Belliston made the recognized triple salute to the company; that is, a bow to the right and the left, and one centrally to the ladies.

"The spirit of appetite rather than Apollo pushes me to the stool," he said, genially, and beginning to charm them with his smile. "My amble—from the manor house, where calamity claims all as her own—has marred my friends' banquet. I shunned the cerecloth, and had the happiness to fall in with my mentor! Still," he went on, with the heartlessness of the beau on the stage, and, perhaps, in real life, which pains us in tales of that day, "it is not in our family!"

Like the thieves—ugly parallel—the actors consider themselves as one family.

They accepted him now freely, for here was one of the arrogance they had feared, from his fine clothes and graces.

In fact, Belliston, who might have imagined he could awe the high and mighty potentates, with his humbler brothers at once drew in his plumes. Richardson, who

had attained a well-deserved repute for honesty and giving full pennyworth, insisted on his company dressing
well "on and off." He allowed none of the begging for
charity under the guise of hawking tickets, which dis-
graced the players not so many years back. He would
probably have cudgeled any member caught "finding" a
clean shirt on the hedge, and he went the rounds of the
taverns before he quitted a "regular" town he visited, to
be sure no score was left unliquidated.

Edmund silently approved of this keen change of intention, which he had hoped for.

By intuition, he knew that there was the perfected comedian, the idol alike of Fribbles and learned critics.

The man destined to be tragedian always envies the
sprite of levity and buoyancy and elegance just the same
as the latter would give ten years of his age to wear for
an hour, only, the wild-flower mock crown of maddened
Lear, the toga of Cæsar, or the turban of Othello.

Relishing a dry joke, Richardson presented him merely
as his old disciple "Williams," adding that he was in a
fixed capacity in town. Had he been but the candle snuf-
fer at a royal house, he had glory enough. Imagine a
castaway crew, from whose forlorn midst one had been
blown away on a raft, and the news came that he had
reached land, was dressed, feasted, toasted by the king
and court of the far country! Thus might it be with all!

Then, assured as to his excellence as an actor, Edmund
watched his table manners. They were good. Belliston
had heart·enough to understand true gentlemanliness not
to disturb society.

He did not, by any sign, express the want of customary
table appurtenances; he adopted a free-and-devil-may-
care way, admirably, revealing that he no doubt belonged
to "the Bohemians," who mostly possessed, by right of
rank and inheritance, the shares in the king's two playhouses. These "original boxholders," including the aristocracy, had "adopted him," and in return he aped "the
first gentleman of Europe."

"It's a real gentleman," remarked Moses, the prompter
and wardrobe-keeper, supposed to know uppermost life
in town from one of his multifarious occupations. "Note,

he would bear himself alone as if John Footman were still in the dining-room!"

The chair of honor was that in which Hamlet's uncle gnaws his nails and fidgets at the mock-play, and the same in which Macbeth alone sees Banquo's wraith. The visitor occupied it without misgiving, and on his nobler hand sat the "persecuted maiden" of the stage. Mistress Carey, very faded and washed-out by day, was one of those creatures of hard, marble-like flesh and elastic bone, who outlast, with their ephemeral aspect, the burliest and sturdiest of men. She had never once "disappointed her audience"—that was her boast, and it retained her in the company after her youth had departed. She flattered herself that she had an aristocratic profile, and in consequence the audience rarely saw her, except as what artists call "half a face." She hazily attributed this trait to kinship with the Savilles, of which family her name of Carey reminded one of the hapless composer of "Sally in Our Alley."

However true a gentleman Balliston was, he would talk of women when the wine was in. So, without any prelude, having had a welcoming glass, he burst out:

"Lucky old badger—that Danby plutocrat! One is never blessed with one slice of cake; he gets all! This mammon has one fair daughter, whom he loves next to his pile. Fair? How she would be *fêted*, admired, ovationized, if only lack of affluence influenced her to embrace the stage!"

He was heard without any emotion; these here, given a tithe of Miss Danby's expectations, would not have trod the boards' two steps.

"Oh, Miss Danby?" stammered Edmund, feeling warm to the roots of his hair.

"Miss Alba Danby—the dandy! A young woman, Mr. Richardson and gentlemen, woman to the tip, and magnificent creature! An ideal of Imogen—ay, and Cordelia, if she could be given a few acute twitches at the heart-strings! Yet, while now touched with the icicle, she needs but little coquetry, innate in her soft sex, some intrigunate spirit, and the desire to be the admired of all admiration, to be Lady Betty Modish to the life. Mrs. Pritchard's 'business' would fall to her as the iron to the magnet. Mr. Edmund, it is a beauty pre-eminent! What a godsend it is to vulgar gold that it has a beauty to wed into the aristocracy!"

"You are a man of taste!" said Edmund, "and with the Danby cash you would make your theatre a temple like the Ephesians'!"

CHAPTER VIII.

"O like a book of sport thou'lt read me o'er,
But there's more in me than thou understandest!"
—*Troilus.*

Having enjoyed their look at the guest to the fill, the party set to listening to his speech. He had a pleasant, round voice, clinging and almost cloying with its dulcet notes. He was "Sir Oracle," and the voice little mattered.

He told of the town, and his stories, with illustrations and imitations, where thoroughly commended by the fit congregation.

"Lon'on is not gay," said the showman, for once animated by the prattle, and as if to palliate an inattention caused by some rising anxiety. There entered into the room and penetrated every crevice, after the manner of quarantine fumigation, the savory odor from a kettle—the identical caldron in "Macbeth" which contained the crowned heads of Scotland.

"It is in glumness!" was the reply. "They have lost Parsons' strong misnomer! 'But what is in a name?'" he went over to the Majors', to repeat Sir Blunderby Wrongside, or 'to the Coventry,' as says Monsieur Coquett. Neither 'Garden' nor 'Lane' with a laughter-raiser. Suett is not 'up to Dick,' ha, ha! What is looked for is a versatile leader of the diversionists; another Garrick, powerful in tragedy and stirring the risibles in the comics."

"Don't taunt me with that red rag again, Bill! That is, my William!" uttered the showman, fiercely. " 'Don Choleric' should never have been let climb out of his wine cellar upon the stage! Hang me! In my time actors were actors, and, as the admirals were seamen, no one got in but after l'arning the ropes. Bettertons, Booths, Burbages, they went through the whole course of sprouts, bough and stem! Garrick? A ficc! He studies

me our Shapeskeare in his study—in his lib'ory, forsooth!
practices to his bust on a marble pedestall; spouts to a
gown on a cloak rack, and goes straight upon the boards
as 'Gambrick;' no less will content him, egad! without
having tried his hand as Laertes, or doubling Rosencrantz
with Francisco, which is riglar! Oh, you want actors,
the jinnywine thing, in town, do 'ee!

"Well," suddenly fixing his eyes on Edmund, and holding him by the gaze, as if the ray pinned him like an in-
sect under the microscope, "your managers seek for the
loose us naturalibus in a 'varsity lib'ory, in the ammytour
clubs, in the lyceums! Bah! And, likewise, pooh, pooh!
If the Board of Drury Lane came to old Richie, he could
lift them out o' their quorn-dairy! He would p'int, as I
am p'inting now, and say:

" 'You are looking in the dusty, fusty museums, in the
precise flowerbeds of my lord's French garden, in the
antechamber of my lady, for an actor truly a "draw!"
That is, choke up your theatres, from the scenery to the
outer doors, with all sorts of people, but all actuated by
the same impulse, to see novelty, hactuality, and all the
other 'alities!'

"Well, my brother-managers, you have turned your
back on the hollow places to land on the right spot to find
talent—ay, and genius! for all your stars have come out of
the unekalled and rarest Penny Show! All your flowers
are out of my hotbed! Whoy, I ha' gotten an actor here
who has all Bully Henderson's affectedness (effective-
ness), and, like that raging old Turk, he has some of those
fits of 'fetchingness' which are too much to bear. But
the public likes to be friz to the core, and enj'ys a shudder
up and down the backbone.

"He is dainty and airy, like diverting quick; fantastic
and wayward as a woman! Terrible as the sea rolling in
at the bore of the Severn! Poetical as I judge old Shape-
shears was when he showed 'em how to do the ghost without slapping his cuishes with his trunch-horn to raise a
laugh! Ah, he can wear you the royal robes as naterally
as the rags of Edgar! All the real gentlemen, l'arned
ones, deacons, deans, doctors of the law and divinity and
med'cines, too, they will say that he gives every mortal

part he undertakes a new and original phase, and makes 'em immortals, into the bargain!

"Whoy, he will take his ordience along with him! H'ain't we all seed some of the same folk go in every turn until they had not a penny piece to try it ag'in, and I have so took pity on them, true lovyers of the drayma, that I have winked to the tickettaker to give them 'the blind eye!' And then, again, some of them that had good underpinning, or got a lift on the carrier's spare hoss, they 'companied us to the next fairing, when the willages was not too far apart, and wanted to see Edmund's Gaffer (Jaffier) and Bag-o'-jet (Bajazet, bless his blundering soul!) Ain't that proof possitive? And you can't work that kind of wonder to death, though you might to skin and bone! All the nourishment he takes goes to brains and ardor! He will play you all the rippertore, from the moss-grown 'Cato' to 'Scrub!' Then, you managers can let him play every noight of the week and roll out to Greenwich for the Whitebait dinner in your curricles, sure that the crowns are piling up and that one man is doing the mission of ten!

"Edmund, make your bow to the gentleman!

"Mr. Belliston, as soon as you are Huggermugger-pontiff at Drury Lane, communicate with this spirit of marvels and your committee will think you the finder of the rarest jewel since the Saucy Diamond!"

For an instant the young actor and the passed master in comedy looked at each other. Belliston knew the old showman so well, believing him selfish, that he was perplexed at this revelation of the performer of many sides, the very *desideratum* to a traveling show.

But the one was prevented promising by a confused noise at both front and back doors.

A stableman, with a pallid face, equipping him for the messenger whom King Richard the Third addresses as a cream-faced loon, gasped out:

"The red murrains on us, measter! The constable! the constable, wi' a warrant to incriminate the hull troop of us for stealing of a dead deer out o' Lord Newell's paark!"

All rose in agitation, and some in trepidation.

Mr. Prettiman, C P., was ushered in between two surly

stablemen, much more resembling his jailers than his ushers.

"How d'e do, Master Prettiman!" hailed Edmund, nodding; "welcome in the sanctum of the Temple of Folly! I hope you appreciate the honor of being let in, without paying at the door, although the master recognizes the setting apart of the officers of justice from the common herd; and you are allowed the 'deadhead' privilege! I know that you make proper return for the courtesy—that you are not one of those boors who rate the Swan of Avon as a Michaelmas goose, and take their fill in staring at the outside show, and, at the pay place, stop as if *ne plus ultra* meant 'Thus far, and no farther!'"

Mr. Prettiman had spied the comedian in the slightly-known concourse; he bowed to a guest of my lord's. He altered his tone from what he had set his mind on, and, in replying, contrived to address the young actor, the showman and this gentleman from town.

"Sir, and gentlemen all, likewise the ladies, to whom I kiss my hand! I am constable of Freefolk Hundred, and, as the deputy of the lord of the manor, I beg to relate the mandate of the said Lord Newell, sitting as justice of the peace and *cuss'us cockolorum!*"

Richardson saw that there was more apology than menace in his overture, and he tendered his mull of ramshorn, and said, with bluff amiability:

"We are friends, then, at a pinch, Muster 'Pincher'— have a snuff!"

All waited till the inhalation was followed by the sneeze, when the functionary resumed:

"I have my orders, seeing that deer's carcass has been secretively and of malest-pretence abstracted from the ground of Newell." He showed a folded sheet of blue foolscap, without flaunting it. "To apprehend the Culprits, and to get a cat——"

"A cat! You mean a deer?" said Edmund.

"Oh, no, sir; it is writ down a cat!"

"You mean," said Belliston, "it is you are writ down an ass."

"No, no, sir, a cat! I am to get a cat and tie a knot in the tail!"

"Cruel!" said Mistress Carev.

"With which cat I am to chastise the purloiners of the said deer carcass! The offenders are, in a word, to be whipped off the parish bounds!"

"Whip? Master Constable, did your lord say you were to whip the stealers of the game!" cried Belliston.

"With the aforesaid cat!"

"Then, I repudiate his hospitality. I will cut him dead as nail in door if ever he presumes to speak to me in town!"

"And he said, my lord did, as the *Pee-Ess* to his warrant, if I did not draw blood he would send me into quod and ruin me!"

"Let him ruin you!" said Richardson. "I will put you on as a—a——"

"Let me be an actor?" cried Prettiman, revealing that he had an ambition above writs and processes.

"Lor', no; but as a hostler!"

"And, if you come to Drury Lane Theatre, London," added Belliston, "I will put you on the list to be assistant stage doorkeeper!"

"And," subjoined Edmund, seeing that the officer was yielding, "I will teach you that trick of boxing by which a man may cause one to knuckle under in two rounds, though vastly inferior to his antagonist."

"I thank you, one and all, but——" he sniffed, as if snuff were again under his nose; "but, in the air—it is a smell from the kitchen, alas! There is no hiding that under a bushel! It is——" he ended his regretful plaint in a whisper, "it is wenison!"

"You are wrong to follow your nose," said Edmund, sharply. "It is no search warrant!" He looked toward the outer door.

At this juncture a man in a white apron, and looking greasy and hot like a cook, cried out, enigmatically and apropos of nothing, "John Orderly is in!"

This is a talismanic sentence among the strollers. It implies that it is time to break off the hearing.

"What you fancy is the odor of venison, I, who am little familiar with venison as daily dish," continued Edmund, "maintain that it is donkey meat!"

"D-d-donkey meat!" said Prettiman and Belliston in the same strangled voice.

"Jack! Ned! In with the dishes!"

(See page 65)

"Certainly, a donkey—our donkey—which, straying into the park since the festivity took down all barriers to peasants and asses, got in the way——"

"Oh, yes," said the constable, quickly, "he knows—that gentleman, for they say that he shot it!"

All looked reproachfully at Belliston, whose crime had followed him here.

"I protest!" cried he; "I shot, but the donkey was already dead by then, I am accurately informed!"

"You are correct, sir," suddenly struck in the young tragedian, "for it was pierced by some of the shot which disdained to find a lodging in a noble's flesh. The same hidden machine slew donkey and peer!"

In his relief, Belliston seized and wrung his deliverer's hand.

"My arms are open to you—as are the doors of the Lane!" faltered he.

"But—but," pursued Prettiman, willing to be convinced, but there were his men without, volunteers, who wished the pleasure of hailing the play-actors before the magistrates, "it is alleged that your men carried off not the donkey, but the dead deer in question."

"To send you away on our simple affirmation is weak," agreed the spokesman, unembarrassed, "so we will let you go back to report not only with your eyes filled with conviction, but your mouth!"

"Eh?"

"Certainly, your mouth! To supper with us, Thomas the Doubter——"

Not Thomas—Dobbin, sir, Dobbin Prettiman!"

"Make room at the board for Mr. Prettiman, the tipstaff! Jack, Ned! in with the dishes!"

There was a burlesque flourish of trumpets, an alarum of drums and an invisible chorus as to a boar's head borne to a royal sideboard. Supplied with large, drolly hideous pantomime heads over their own, concealing the mirth, several men marched in after the mode of demons and goblins, bearing head high enormous salvers and platters of gilded and silvered pasteboard, with covers large enough to be a Goliath's breastplate. They placed them on the void places on the table, and at a signal from a

major domo in Satanic red and black, whisked off the
lids.

On one broad plate appeared four hoofs, interlaced with
blue ribbon and smothered in gelatine, after the manner
of sheep's trotters *en Daube;* through the transparent jelly
gleamed the silver of the worn shoes; on another, gobbets
of very lean meat pierced with silver skewer, was a tidbit
for an ogre; on the largest tray grinned complacently,
with closed eyes, a head such as Bully Bottom unwittingly
wears after being "translated."

"Oons! it is the donkey!" cried Belliston, starting back
with the gourmand's qualms.

"Donkey, and not deer!" said Prettiman, shaking his
head with belief.

"You were forced to give your old friend a supper of
ass's flesh?" continued Belliston, reproachfully, to the
showman, "and I had two gold pieces rubbing each other
in my pouch! I would have walked back to Westminster
Bars rather than that——"

"Hush! you are making the constable pity us!"

Indeed, the officer, twitching his nostrils as if about to
snivel, buried his face in his bandanna, and through it
they heard him softly blubber:

"Poor hartists! If I had 'a' knowed that in consekence
of there being no money circ'lating in Freefolk by reason
of the shows being bought up, I would have——" Edmund held him, so that he could not withdraw his fat hand
from the pocket into which he had charitably thrust it.

"Spare our blushes!" said the young man, sobbing
"You see to what complexion we have c-c-come! But we
must bear our degradation to the utterance, I suppose!
Call in your posse—to the least boy of them—and let them
behold that we eat donkey, and not deer!"

Prettiman was delicate; he drew the line of humiliation
at calling in two of his janissaries, to whom, with a gesture of compassion, he pointed out the mammoth dishes
and their unusual garnishment. He must have comprehended that there was a hidden joke, for it was in a voice
worthy of Mawworm, but with a false twang, that he said,
wailingly:

"Hob! Lance! see what a mistake—steak of Neddy,
and not of Reddy! The writ no farther runs!" He

pressed the paper into his pocket. "You can hie home! I must stay a bit to—to—what the deuce am I to stay for?"

"Why," interposed Edmund, "to arrange with Mr. Richardson what indemnity must be paid him for his beast being shot to death on grounds thrown open to the public, mark you, on a proclaimed holiday! The simple creature, deluded by the signboards that the ordinary warnings against trespassers were in abeyance this day, confiding in his fellowman, he walked into the mouth of destruction! And, alas! he falls victim! As master, and losing the services of his servant, you will, as man of the law, acknowledge Mr. Richardson is entitled to substantial damages, eh, eh?"

"That is it! Good-night, Hob, and Lance! I must arrange about the damages!"

The showman had been given a tankard of ale, which he held out to the constable as soon as his myrmidons had withdrawn, to retail that the poor strollers were "devouring their Neddy!"

There is an old saying that the cottage rests nigh the castle, but there is distance between them; indeed, while the manor house was plunged into the extreme gloom of mourning, a hilarious crowd might be easily heard in the village. They were roaring the popular "topical" song, which the guest of the evening had taught to the rustics

> "How folks will stare,
> As I go by!
> Hark, hark, they cry!
> His jaunty air!
> And the trolls will troll: 'Dear heart, what a flash!
> Look at the new warder in his silken sash!'"

During the prolonged revelry, Belliston, who could stand his cups, saw the young actor perform by snatches a string of impersonations which Proteus, had he been of the stage, would have granted exhaustive. He was prepossessed, and indorsed the old showman's eulogy.

But the liquor had made Belliston fancy his own vision realized. He thought he was manager of Drury Lane Theatre.

He took Edmund's hands and shook them effusively.

"Come to me, to me, Billiam Welliston, at Lury Drain;

there is an opening for you! Meanwhile, study Shave-
steare! An old divine said: 'Beware of the man with one
book!' The old solon was correct as a die in the royal
mint! The actor who knows his Shakesclear is to be
dreaded! He will sweep the table all before him!"

At which, too literally suiting the action to the word, he,
reeling and snatching at anything for detention, clutched
the tablecloth, and he fell amid the wreck of the not sumptuous garniture and plate.

"E'mund," hiccoughed Richardson, unconscious of his
old friend's downfall, "I have made your fortune! Your
next step will be on—what's the thingumy's blessed name?
Oh, on K-K-Kembull's head!"

CHAPTER IX.

"THE LITTLE MAN IN THE CAMLET CLOAK."

At the close of the year, a man who seemed prematurely aged, back-bent and brow-laden by disappointment and despondency, was to be seen dolefully pacing the street adjacent to the then much-traversed district between Temple Bar and Charing Cross on one side and the Strand and St. Giles' Church on the other.

Here Covent Garden Market, surrounded by life, offered in more than one street a double hedge of pleasure-houses, gaming, coffee, tailors, milliners, haberdashers, perfumery, tavern upon tavern. Gallants strutted with cane and snuffbox among flower-girls and orange-sellers. News-sheet and flying postmen dashed aside beggars of the sturdy sort; tricksters sought for prey; petty peddlers offered wares upon trays slung before them, under which they cut watch-ribbons and relieved the bulging pockets of their silk handkerchiefs.

After the industry of the market was swept away, the whole world here was of spending and seizing.

There was true gold and much tinsel; real diamonds and huge paste brilliants; stained hands in dainty gloves, aching hearts under costly plumes; but even the masked grievers gave a glance to this woefulest-looking object that ever roamed "the pavement of gold" and murmured:

"Stab my vitals! what a poor creature!"

Daily Edmund Kean made the rounds of the theatrical aspirant; from the sordid lodging in Bloomsbury to the stage door of Drury Lane playhouse. His retreat, baffled, was ever in misery and mourning, which ought not to be shown to the general eye.

Worth feels that the coming generation must not perceive that it was long unappreciated.

Belliston had bragged; at least, Mr. Danby had not concluded the pretty arrangement of furthering his desire to be a partner in the theatrical management. Though his abilities were proven, there lagged on the stage some superfluous veterans, who would have played Chamont, the juvenile fop, after seventy, if they had to be rolled on in a goat-chair! So he had gone on what would be called later, "a starring tour."

To the penniless youth in London, a man at Dublin or Edinburgh was at the Antipodes. One could not afford to pay a letter.

Thereupon the man who had trusted too fully and staked all upon a place in London, and the first place, too, was reduced to extremity.

Fortunately Moses, who was pained at having heard nothing of him, and, then nothing from him, hastened to town and discovered him, by his despair, without difficulty.

The stage doorkeeper would grin when he saw the shabby seeker coming up the lane. As an echo of the manager, which the Cerberus theatrical is, he would call him "the little man in the camlet," a quotation which Arnold, the manager, had resurrected out of "King Henry VIII." Moses had lent his name after lending everything else possibly helpful, and Kean wore, to cover his misery, a cloak of camlet, though it was the wet and dismal season.

Moses fared better by a shade. He stepped into the prompt-box when the prompter was having a night off at the two great theatres or the little one in the Haymarket. He copied music scores and actors' parts; he was one of those factotums never idle while a playhouse keeps its doors open. But half a loaf is little for two men.

He heard his *protégé* rehearse; they went over old plays together, and he encouraged new "readings," without comprehending more than that the world must be blind not to adore this wonder.

He would say, with an oracle's steadiness: "In the lottery of destiny, you will inevitably draw a prize! It will be accumulative, too—the longer it is deferred, the greater it will swell!"

Kean sighed, instead of being cheered.

"But I shall not live long to enjoy so belated a triumph!"

To be sure it was the curlish age when a Chatterton

died blighted in the spring. On the other hand, a Byron sprang into fame in a single day.

So, received every night with Moses' intelligent faith and delicate care not to put a wounding question, and sent off of a morning when his writing did not let him accompany him, Kean persevered in calling for the letter out of the country, which did not come, and asked in a stereotyped way if the management had not left word for him?

Ambition is the player's staff as hope is the lover's.

As he became less presentable, even at a court of St. Giles, he refrained from those journeys to the park, where he had the pleasure of seeing Miss Danby in her carriage, drawn by a matchless pair of bays or grays.

Danby he had seen on the Oxford road, going into the city, but if he had ever known him he would have avoided him now. To have introduced himself as his daughter's preserver, after neither of them having tried to seek him out, was a step to which he would not have consented.

Moses had not dared to urge it; on making very cunning inquiries of the rich man's servants, he learned that the master was peculiar in his charitable acts.

He resented any one pricing the deed, and wished to value in his own scales. Then he acted munificently.

These glimpses ceased, however, when Kean was ashamed of his garb and unhappy mien.

As for the news about her, which he gleaned from the news-sheets picked up by Moses in the coffeehouses, Miss Danby's suddenly broken-off engagement with Lord Newell was still on the stocks. The event compelled a little respite before the new lord followed patriarchal and royal precedent in marrying his brother's widow. So the derided and neglected tragedian kept on, without any side ray of relief, such as even a desperate love would have been. Like the horse in the cider mill, he was unable to snatch even a scrap of comfort in the cores he crunched under foot.

He often crept to his lodgings with fear that his "duds" would be at the door with Moses sitting on them, for the rent was in arrears despite the latter's Herculean exertions. He knew every stud in the stage door; every door and window in Drury Lane itself, from the White Star at the Strand to the Three Casks at the top. He was glad that the hackney coachmen on their stand deigned to exchange good-day with him from seeing him so often, for they could not expect he would be a fare; indeed, it was kind of them not to jeeringly wave the whip and cry, "Coach, your honor?" in playfulness.

At last there was a gleam of light.

Belliston had excited so much enthusiasm and pocketed so much money in the circuit theatres that the petty band of controllers of the players in town united to recall him.

Belliston opening the merest chink, Kean believed that he was the wedge of adamant to widen it.

"And I heard, too," remarked Moses, "for I am making a coat for Mr. Arnold, that he and his partner, Raymond, are at loggerheads. The theatre is no longer in Great Russell street, but the street called 'Queer!'"

"If Belliston should be returned with enough gold to buy one or the other out!" suggested Edmund.

"Belliston is too friendly with every one!" said the man of many trades, and also of phrenology. "He is a watering pot with a fine nose, not a bucket; each flower gets a drop or so, while they die for want of a thorough soaking!"

"My friend, to restore me, I need a deluge!"

This time Belliston was rooted in the playhouse; he had rooms of his own, with a bed in them. "Useful in case it became my jail," said the comedian, blander and rosier than ever, but deftly dodging any very timid overture toward financially assisting. "Sir, we are going to light up a lamp which will throw the sepulchral beaker of the Kembles into the shade."

So Kean was retreating homeward with something like good news; his bosom was buoyant for once, as he dived into the dark, vile street which, on account of a brewery's dead wall, spoiled the property over the way, where dwelt the poor and wretched. Now this dead wall, with all its dinginess and blankness, offered a wide canvas for bill posting, and police, auction and theatre bills illuminated the bricks.

Kean always perused what attracted his eye.

Like the dullard who reads a journal from the advertisements to the "Printed by——" he lingered over these lines, epitomizing the times.

Rewards for "Villains who knocked a gentleman down on Cornhill in broad day, necessitating the constables going on duty before dark!" "Cause of the scarcity of corn," "Suggestion on the use of Indian corn," "Bounties for volunteers in H. M. Navy," etc.

He cracked these dry morsels before the toothsome ones, the bills of the play. These "sweet scrolls to fly about the street" were beginning, thanks to Belliston and other florid penmen, to be worth reading. But the words cited were of magic to the tragedian; they announced that still Shakespeare ruled. At Covent Garden, with the Kembles, familiar names, met his eye. At "his" theatre, Drury Lane, modern plays filled out the weekly spaces.

Then he gave a great start. If ever a human heart may stop short and go on again normally, without hurt, his did so that instant.

" 'Othello!' up at the Lane!" he ejaculated, frightening a miserable foreigner who, while facing a bill and pretending to read, was devouring secretly out of a strip of writing paper one of those concoctions in the way of a half-cooked sausage called locally a saveloy. This Londonized version of the Italian brain-sausage, *cervellata,* originated the quip, that he who ate of it, as the mysterious bag itself, had "neither brains nor taste."

At another time Kean might have envied the lucky one who was eating with such evident relish while hoping not to be noticed.

" 'Othello' on," repeated he, not believing his eyes, especially, as looking farther to confirm his hopes, he saw this line:

"For the first time, by Mr. Edmund Kean, from the principal provincial theatres."

There could be no doubting this! He was too poor a mark for any one to "hoax" him with a specially-printed programme—not an unheard-of mystification! Belliston must have known this; yet he forebore to let him into the tremendous secret. He saw that the sly dog had something on his mind—if nothing in his hand. Never mind, he would forgive him all—even this hour or two of waiting still to be undergone. His heart had been light—now he seemed to have none at all.

He could have called back the starving *emigré* and wept on his bosom. Oh, if Moses would only stray along at this nick!

He could have knelt in the refuse and prayed his gratitude.

His eyes cleared of a veil. He felt the transient giddiness of enormous joy quit him. He had the revived power from those few words to cleave this wall with his fist.

Who had revolved the wheel, on which he had been racked like Ixion, but so that, at the height, he was in the sunshine and the genial breeze? Belliston? The others, abruptly convinced of his merits? Or was it one of those unholy pranks to bolster him up with mock support and let him stand, like certain amateurs, the "guy" of the fun lovers?

No, they dared not do that—could not think that.

"I am the newcomer, then! for whom the *cognoscenti* have looked since Garrick!" he murmured, with his voice becoming sweet. "The cup will not be tantalizingly snatched from me!"

Still he trembled with the sudden unstringing of the cord. But a glow of extreme pleasure was replacing the weighty chill of balked expectation, when he heard a whinny of horses.

Afraid of being crushed, for there was no separate pathway in this lane for men and beasts, he flattened himself against the wall. Coming toward him he saw a pair of splendid horses, attached to a carriage equipped for a long journey. It was called a "Berlin," after the place of original invention. Only a wealthy person could indulge in this luxury, with its glass windows, protected by venetian blinds.

As these blinds were of steel, serving to prevent a bullet making undesirable intimacy with the insides of the "inside" (the jest of the period), the people seeing them when hermetically closed, termed them "cages."

Not to arouse too much notice, the leaders had been led away under their rider into an alley, but, after all, as this dirty byway was at the back of the fashionable lounges, Kean need not have given the matter second thought.

Sitting on a stone post, or on the doorsteps beside the vehicle, were some stalwart rogues, looking like servants, over whose liveries, turned inside out for precaution, were huddled great Irish frieze coats. Kean thought even at the casual glance that he saw swords under these outer wraps.

The canes which the footmen carried might also be sword-sticks, if his surmise of evil were well founded.

Kean felt that now his immediate future was valuable to others, and he crossed the kennel to give the conveyance and its numerous attendants a wide space.

This step was like steering from the rock into the whirlpool. For, set against the wall, without a care of the foot passengers, stood a public chair. The porters had been given "garnish," or drink money, imprudently in advance, and they had set up their poles against the latter and took themselves to the beerhouse at the corner.

This forced Kean to proceed in the midway. One of the guards over the coach noticed him as he approached and hailed him in a perfunctory manner.

" 'Nanny, wilt thou gang with me?' "

This snatch of a popular song was clearly a catchword, a sign of recognition. Under the rough coat the actor spied a satin waistcoat and the chiseled hilt of a rapier. But above all, he knew the voice, which the owner had not taken pains to disguise.

"Lord Newell!" muttered he, surprised at this man again in his path, as if it were a bird of ill omen just when the sky brightened.

With any other he might have believed that it was a matter which would not much disturb the public peace or cause heartburn to any decent person. Some trifling with an "actress," whose acting was most known off the stage, or a divinity of Wells street, one or the other, no occasion for him to risk a finger.

He would have gone straight on, but the person, barring the way more than heretofore, vexed at being misunderstood, but persisting in believing this an ally, said curtly:

"Is she not coming out soon, you dullard?"

CHAPTER X.

"She?"

This was not a political stroke, then, or the ear-clipping of a satirist. It was a woman expected from one of these houses.

Kean was a youth nourished on romance and heroics; as he arrived toward manhood all latent gallantry had been kindled and maintained by his life, and, since he had rescued Miss Danby, he had an ideal for the sake of which he would be champion for her sex.

At this point the half-dozen waylayers, tired of the waiting, left the cover of the coach. Their disguise or usual dress was concealed by the overcoat called by the elegant "Roquelaures," after the French beau, and wraprascals by the low English, as denoting the evil wearers. But if nothing else had enlightened the tragedian, he would have pronounced them of the gentry, since they came on at that halting gait due to extravagant use of high heels.

Such an array of gentlemen, trained in the fencing-schools, or the military colleges, would have daunted a hale and skillful swordsman, and Kean, enfeebled by want, had no wish to become their football.

In making a not too marked essay to circle them, one of the fellows in the rear, a servant, yelled:

"That's not one of ours! Roll the rogue in the channel!"

The voice stung Kean as poignantly as the nobleman's presence. This was the gamekeeper to whom he had given a thrashing.

The recognition was almost simultaneous, for this giver of good advice advanced quite joyfully and added, to his master:

"By Bold Robin's bow, my lord, see this! It's that strutting player of the Penny Show; the black imp! He saved Miss Danby from the spring gun! and," in a whisper, "let your brother meet the shot!"

It would be hard to tell which of the two reminders was the more sharp to the hearer.

"You puppet, you!" he screamed, in his heightened fury, to the interferer, for he surmised that he was there to interfere; all his features working and his eyes snapping their lashes, like a man whose conscience was never at rest, so that his agitation at being presented with images of the occurrence at the New Forest was manifest.

Just then a whistle was blown at a little distance, apparently in one of the houses, at a window high up.

Immediately, on the high outside stoop of a tumbledown house, seemingly carved out of the brewery wall, three women appeared. One was old and bent, in a ragged shawl and odd shoes, shivering with palsy or pretense of it, and redolent of malt; next her was a kind of lady's maid, who perked up her nose as though disgusted by this odor. As for the third, in cape and hood, her mantle hid her dress, but it was clear from her stately carriage and fine countenance, though shaded by the cowl, that she was merely a transient visitor to this slum.

The old hag seemed mumbling thanks, and in her skinny hand held what was probably a purse; she was the recipient of charity from the lady.

Of all the beholders, Kean was the only one taken by surprise on seeing that this angel of benevolence was Miss Danby.

"Miss Danby!" stammered the actor, his heart beating madly.

Newell was pale under a coat of cosmetic and powder. But he flushed up to the eyes with pleasure at the nearness of the critical moment, when he should seize his affianced. Yes, it was droll, but he had marshaled his friends to perform the abduction of his own betrothed and force her to go through the marriage which nothing but her obstinacy had prevented being enacted some time since.

After her escape in the New Forest, she had offered an opposition which her father could not lessen, and Newell could not remove.

"Yes, there she is, at last!" cried the noble to his party, whom he had had some difficulty in keeping together. "Into the coach! bundle the baggage! May I perish if I am any longer to have my engagement set at nought and the appointed day adjourned to the Greek kalends!"

As if concealment were now useless, the accessories to the noble plotter threw off their outer garments and drew their small swords. They appeared, like their leader, as for a wedding; in luxuriously embroidered coats and undercoats, velvet or satin breeches. Buckles sparkled and lace flowed snowily. Their swords were sharp and deadly, while pretty, and these formed a half-moon of steel at the base of the stoop, where the three women stood.

As though frightened—but it was a more likely part of the scheme—the old witch, dropping her palsy, but not the purse, sprang like a cat into the house-passage, slamming the door, and a bolt was heard to be shot. The maid leaped down into the area with the precision of one who had executed that act previously. A door was heard to close under the porch, proving that she knew the house well.

Miss Alba Danby was left wholly alone on the high stand.

She could not fail to be startled by the storming party and the desertion of her attendant, but it could not be said she was appalled.

She quivered with commingling emotions, while blushing intermittently, like a rosy veil drawn at intervals over that blonde beauty of hers which charmed all men. With this flitting aspect, she presented herself like a swan seen on wavy water.

Courage seemed hers, along with the pride that is foremost of Eva's legacy to her favorite daughters.

Her fright had been so soon overcome that a casual observer must have thought—though the site was bizarre—that she was to descend according to a dance-step of the day, to pass under the arch of steel, borrowed from a secret society ceremonial.

She did not even try the door or make any backward step.

"Gad! if I did not admire that woman already, I should worship her now!" thought Kean.

The pose was so theatrical that he could have shouted a lusty "bravo!" but there was a good deal yet to do before it was the time for the cheering. Those real swords flashed, and Newell's eyes showed hatred and revenge against the beleaguered lady.

"Bring her down!" cried he making a mock bow of recognition to Miss Danby, as much as to announce that the movement was officially authorized, for the allies hesitated to climb the stairs. "Leave it to the grooms and the lackeys, then! Hey, you! but with care! She is tender as the overripe mulberry, which will not stand the handling!"

For this gloving the hand or, rather, substituting vulgar cat's-paws, the gentlemen opened out so that Gideon and another, a footman, might run up the rickety steps.

Kean, infuriated and scandalized as a man at a bridegroom making a public spectacle of his future wife being roughly handled, growled like a hungry beast, and this threat being heard, the hot-bloods spun round on their heels, glad to have a man to deal with. They turned their points upon him with dastardly impertinence, as if he were a dog to be stabbed.

"If you are a player," said Sir John Whipstaffe, man of the court, and the debtors' court, "make your exit!" He said it with sham courtesy, but with something like good humor.

He did not relish this scene having even one witness.

Convinced that the gamekeepers and the varlets would obey orders and that the prize must be dragged down from the stoop if she resisted, Kean would have thrown himself on the points in the hope to seize Lord Newell; but if he were impaled on the skewers, that would give the dastard time to execute his purpose.

"A weapon! a weapon!" he groaned, much as King Richard howled for a battle-horse.

At the same moment, to clear the way to the coach, the gentlemen came on regularly as a file of soldiers, with their swords aimed at his heart.

He recoiled instinctively, for to the intelligent, it is

not the wound but all the possibilities of the weapon which causes a shrinking.

But, partly across the street, the sedan chair brought him up to a halt, with his calves against its side.

He stood between the two poles, on end, also leaning against its doorway.

"Heaven has heard my prayer!" he fervently muttered, as his hands on either side touched the ashen staves.

At this eminence he could easily see Gideon grasp Miss Danby's wrapper with both hands, to roll her up in it, as he called on his reluctant comrades to lend their hands and carry her down in a body.

More than for his own safety, Kean clutched the pole on his right. He took it up in both hands and with a sweep, called "the mill-wheel swirl," in cudgel-play, with which he was luckily familiar, he broke in halves four of the swords threatening him. With a prod he hurled down Sir John, and, striding over the squirming body, was at the stoop-bottom in a moment.

Newell stood petrified at this apparition in the midst; a bear had broken its chain and was flourishing its dancing-staff.

"The mummer! the player!" faltered he, holding his sword on guard, but with a trembling hand.

"Ay, the mummer! the player!" responded Kean, pre-paring to fell him, sword and all, "and his enter and exit shall be smashing a snake!"

In this instant the pretty plan hitherto running on as smoothly as well-oiled clockwork was upset.

Instead of a single man overawed by murderers, the swordsmen were discomfited, disarmed and receding to rub their aches and bruises. Instead of Master Gideon throwing down the captured lady to his employer, he was beset; at the bottom of the stairs, like the angel with the fiery sword, stood this transfigured starveling; David cast in the colossal mold, brandishing that terrible mast which seemed plucked out of a ship's deck.

Nothing but the likelihood of the blow striking the woman prevented the gamekeeper's brains showering that door; but in his place the footman, thinking he could run the risk with impunity, leaped forward; he encountered the pole and was swept into the street to the feet of Lord Newell.

The impetus and the weight of the pole made the wielder describe half a circle, and the way was open to Gideon had he relinquished his prize and been bold.

But he was no sooner freed than he bounded down into the area, where, probably, the accomplice maid was anxiously waiting, with her ear or eye to an airhole. For she helped the fugitive to his feet and drew him into the den of treachery.

Nobody hurtful was before Kean; with one step or so upward he might release the captive. He did this, having dropped his great instrument of defense, but setting his foot on it to frustrate any attempt to turn it against himself.

The shaking of the old stoop made it less certain; it almost flew asunder as Kean descended with the lady.

He pushed her behind him, expecting a renewal of the attack.

But two of his friends had cleverly assisted Sir John to rise, two of the lackeys hastened to rub the mud off him, and all four, with touching tenderness and prudence, carried him off to the nearest coffeehouse. They deemed hot drink would do him more good than a lotion at the druggist's.

Thus losing his forces, Newell saw that the fever of battle had become lukewarm on his side. He lost all hope of making his intention good.

He did not have the impudence to offer either apology or excuse; he had mortally offended his intended—who would probably prefer the scaffold alone to the altar with him beside her.

Gideon, safe in the kitchen floor, was at the peephole.

"If master had the pluck of a mouse," he said to the maid," "he would plunge his sword into him while the rude rogue has let down his rod—that rod a rod long! "Well, he has sown cockles and he could not expect corn!"

Ashamed for their superiors, the footmen clubbed together and came on as if to overwhelm the defender by numbers. Kean gave a growl like a lion that, after one bout, sees with unglutted fierceness a resumption of charge. He poised that formidable lance and ran with it against the serried ranks. Not to be pierced, the two most menaced broke, dodged and ran. The others withdrew to the coach side, and shouted madly for help.

Kean flung the catapult at the fleeing ones and picked up one of the fallen swords.

He looked about with bloodshot eyes for the moving spirit of the outrage, Newell.

He saluted him, retiring in a panic, as duellists do before the meeting. Newell stopped but only to hear, in a sinister voice, which was a foretaste of "King Richard III.," homicidically bent:

"My Lord of Cowardice, but for the lady on my arm, I should not spare you! But you shall hear of me again!"

"Master has bolted!" whispered Gideon, to the maid; "oh, hevings! if that devil let loose should hark back to this house to see what became of me? he gave me a one-er once't, and I don't want no punching with that splinter besides!"

At the threat, Jessamy felt chill, but it was not the chill of numbness; never had he felt more brisk and with a greater desire to be in a far-off country. But before his servants, his friends' servants, and the young lady, he forced himself to overcome his dread.

What could the stage fencer do against one who had "pinked" his antagonist more than once, for there is all the difference in the world between an impromptu encounter with a stranger in the vulgar street and with an acquaintance in the fencing-hall?

But he had hardly taken three steps toward his confronter when one of the gentlemen, who had investigated the neighborhood or knew it, cried in his ear:

"What fly has bitten you? Have you not had enough to know we are beaten, and plentifully! Put up the prod!" He seized him around the waist and dragged him up to the coach and shoved him into it.

On hearing the tumult, the postboy brought his pair of horses out to the vehicle to which it was attached by the pole-hook.

All was ready for the flight.

"We shall go the lighter," remarked the gentleman, who was witty. "For we shall go empty-handed!"

Another popped his head within, saying, with his teeth almost chattering:

"And get away smartly, for can you not hear the buzz of the wasps? Do you know, friend Newell, you have roused all St. Giles! They will not leave a spangle on our coats, a prong in our buckles or a hair on the horses' heads, if they come in their masses hot for robbery!"

Indeed, there was that overboiling of the caldron denoting that the volcano, though adjudged extinct, continually gives a "last" effort.

Perhaps, if the true account had circulated in the drinking dens, from Broad street to St. Clement-Dane's, that a lady was being compelled to go to the altar with the man chosen by her parents, not a cooksman would take up the spare steel spit, nor a charwoman arm herself with her broom, and not a hammerman sally out of the forge like a new Wat Tyler. But they heard that an orange-girl, while making the rounds of the coffee-houses, had been prevailed on by a gay young spark to enter his coach and was being driven off hurry-scurry!

So the cellars and the attics mingled their noxious streams, and the brewery-passage, indicated as the scene of the kidnaping of a "daughter of the mob," was being filled up at either end.

The postboy snapped his whip; the coachman lashed out; the four superb horses strained at the pole and traces to start the vehicle out of the bed of mud. Then the Berlin rolled off amid a hollow cheer of the servants, who could not leap on the footboard behind. Then, they, too, ran after, splashing their stockings, but afraid of the demon whose name was legion.

Thus Kean remained alone with the delivered and puzzled lady.

"That's the mob coming," said he, quickly, to prevent her uttering her thanks. "By my little life! for your own sake, hasten away!"

"Oh, I remember you, sir! Your avocation is being of the first utility to me! I must see you to explain—my gratitude is ever yours! Soon, soon! Your address?"

She scarcely knew that she was speaking very conventionally. But she did not feel pressed to go.

"I am Edmund Kean, tragedian, and my address is— the Theatre Royal, Drury Lane! I am going to make my first bow to the London public as 'Othello, the Moor;' at your pleasure!"

"To my pleasure!" she could not forbear amending, roguishly. Then reflecting that as this mob was peering, but with some timidity at each passage, she was not very safe as a well-dressed lady. "But how will I get hence?"

"You are forgetting yourself!" said he, and picking up the pole which gave him the air of a knight, dismounted, and shouldering his lance, he ushered her to the handborne vehicle.

The delinquent chair men, whether bribed or not to hurry their return, were borne on the front of the crowd and were glad to be met with a welcoming mien. They displayed astonishing alacrity, therefore, in replacing the two poles in their slings, and awaited orders without any inquisitiveness about the tatterdemalion cavaliering for their fare.

He looked one of the hundreds running to and fro, trying to discover anything like the kidnaping affair going on. The foremost had barely a peep at the fair lady. As for her companion, they saw him make her a bow as she was shut up in the box, which would have been a model even to the Prince Regent.

Suddenly turned mute, sad and depressed so soon after his pride and ecstasy at fate again bringing them together, Kean watched the sturdy Irishmen carry her away.

"By the memory of Garrick, the One!" he murmured, as he walked through the increasing turbulence which respected his humble garments, as their own uniform, "what a cordial charm that woman has! She has not properly thanked me, not even by an eloquent look, and yet she seems to have unfolded a volume to me. It has carried undiminished warmth to my heart, which wanted it. I began to hate my kind, and yet, lo! I now love my kind—at least, the other kind—one of them absolutely! Upon my ambitious soul, I do not know whether I would not have given the blessed sight of my name on the announcement bill for this sight of her, rescued by yours and hers faithfully ever to serve! But what a despicable crawler that Lord Newell must be to skulk away under her eyes after having irretrievably damned himself! I would have preferred to die under them, with my own sword stuck through my lying throat!"

After he had gone Gideon came out of his lair.

The false maid was sharing the purse with the beldame, a kinswoman of hers, and Gideon received nothing of that plunder.

"That woman expects me to marry her!" thought he. "Catch me! that's all. A woman what won't shell out half a crown for one to wash the nasty flavor of this adventure out of his palate, is not for Mr. Gideon's home! What am I to do now? Master will be in a tearing humor. I will wait a day or two before I face him and, then—any go—even to selling him out to the lady and that actor, if he proposes a new attack on her or, in revenge, on him!"

CHAPTER XI.

"Since you will buckle fortune on my back, I will endure the
    load."
                        —*King Richard III.*

When Miss Danby left her second-time reliever to himself in the dark streets he felt it as a ray of light with-
drawing. There remained to him that "radiating," so
to word it, from the theatre bills. But this was imma-
terial; it showed him his desperate straits connected immediately with his prospective essay on the London
boards.

To the miserable but persistent struggler against all
that was detrimental, to have met another disillusion
would have been next to fatal. Unconquerable faith
in his "star," that fetish of uncommon men, would have
still moved him to carry on the one-sided war, but it is
hard to climb a slippery hill when all the stones hiss or
howl against one.

At the verge of his great dream becoming real, as one
stands before the black frame traced by the cases of fire-
works and, doubts that, after all, one spark at the right
place, at the right moment, too, will convert all into a
sheet of splendor, so he hesitated.

Kean had vaunted to Miss Danby that he would make
his appearance in Drury Lane, but yet without intending
to plead for her watching his trial.

But now, if he could trust to her coming, he was more
than ever determined that he should not fail. He even
set his aspirations farther.

"There is no peak—no point in the azure to which such
a soul as that has not flown! To such a woman we owe
the model of Will Shakespeare's muse. She will, to me,
be the first in the house—the one in the boxes! I am
going to 'play to her!'"

Yet he blamed himself, a young woman renouncing
her patrimony, her home, such as it was without a mother
or a confidant, betrayed by her maid, cutting herself

perhaps to a pittance; the object of Lord Newell's ma-
lignity and jealousy, a man who would not let her repose, if he could worm his way to her retreat.

Fortunately the current of cross-purposes stayed; there
was no deception about his being "billed" to appear as
"Othello." It was no mean honor to be selected by the
Drury Lane Committee, lords, senators, poets, historians,
orators, legists, generals, to wrestle with that character,
which has overthrown, oh, so many promising actors!
He could cite many who had scaled that eminence, only to
be hurled down into impenetrable obscurity.

The pit presented no terrors more dreadful than
Newell's straps; the great gun of the leading journal was
surely not as mortal as a spring-gun!

"I shall not be small," he consoled himself; "a dry
kernel in the vast shell—in the spacious arena of the
metropolis!"

The minor performers, at the first "reckoning up," regarded him as the veritable Hagar of the profession, in
breeches. Consequently all treated him coldly because
of his sorry attire. They reproached Belliston, indirectly, for unearthing this "barn-brawler with his raven
locks and raven voice."

The stage manager had said, and in no undertone:
"This young man will not do for The Lane!"

The one or two old employeés who had heard the
players styled "Gentlemen of the Grand Royal Chamber"
and seen them arrayed like unto the peony, in scarlet
cloth and real gold lace, the gift of the king, out of his
wardrobe, also protested against this scarecrow.

Some suggested a petition to the Prince Regent, to revive the usage of the sovereign settling all this playhouse
dissension, and quash the scandal of this inevitable fiasco.

The governors accorded the stranger a single rehearsal
for a piece so stupendous as "Othello!"

But he bore this and the other slights like a martyr,
sure of his crown some time—somewhere. They took
this determination as torpor, bred of debility.

But one or two noted the simmering of boiling passions
under the cold surface; now and then they caught a
glimpse of magical eyes irresistible in wrath or in love-
making.

"Hark 'ee, gent'men, all," ventured an old John Blunt, a stage carpenter, "him does not want more nor one rehearsal, he don't! 'Cause why? Can't you blind mums see by the way he threads Old Drury behind the scenes, with all its pitfalls and treacherous traps, that the stage is a playground to him? Why, the Spouters' Club— which it holds forth at the Black Lion out there, in the market—it has old members who remember this here Mr. Edmunds as a finder of a child, but a child of the stage!

"You say!" continued the old oracle, hot to the last, "you say he walks about on the foxy pad, and don't stamp like Booth and Betterton! wait! there will be paving (stamping) and lots; but it will be out there (meaning the pit), and up there (the gallery). I expect I shall have my hands full, for he will bring the house down!"

This vehement laudation set some of the individious musing, but it was too late to revoke their hasty conclusions, on the poor waif tossed between indigence and affluence.

After that begrudged and insulting rehearsal, as of a funeral *cortège,* Kean went with his inseparable Moses to their lodgings.

The worthy had, by working at his old trade, contrived to keep them from sinking altogether.

Moses was a tailor by trade.

"I have been playing in my turn—in 'Measure for Measure!'" joked he, to cheer up his ward.

They shared a pint of something called port wine, over a cold mutton-pie from the famous baker of meat pasties at the sign of the monstrous gilded York Ham, Russell street corner. The actor made a wedge of it prudently, to fit into a place in the box in which he packed up his meager necessaries for his "making up" at the play.

"Don't forget the Spanish brown," said Moses, thinking of the Moor, and superintending.

"I will get two-pen'orth of the first chemist's," returned the other gloomily. "I could black up more harmoniously with soot!" His eye was lack-luster and his voice "distant," as if he could not get it up early that morning, as his companion had found the difficulty of doing with him, personally.

Unfortunately, while the slight product of the needle and the goose had renovated the inner man, it had done little in its way for the outer cover. To be sure, Moses, intimate with his fraternity and community, could have borrowed a suit from any of the Cohens—his name, Kean, is only another spelling of it—but his *protegé* shrank from anything second hand. "Clothes of mine own, if tatters!" he had said, "until——"

So the poor *débutante* sallied shrinkingly out, in his seedy garments and his well-worn boots.

As Kean would have slunk in after Moses, who served as a screen, shaking off the drops, at the dark stage door, a man opposed his passage with bravado. He was like the figures always standing by such outlets to ogle the ballet girls, or offer a drink to a clown amusing him; but he was under a fine cape-coat, and his beaver hat was uncorded and unclasped, so that the flaps sheltered while concealing his head.

Folding up the front brim, he revealed himself as Jessamy Newell. The actor cowered at such an evil omen, so that the noble must have interpreted this to be the tribute of poverty to wealth, for he hissed with the utmost hatred:

"Master Edmund, myself and my friends are determined not to leave a bench unwrecked in your theatre if you persist in trying to foist yourself on a London audience!"

Kean clinched his fist to deliver another such blow as had made Gideon forever in awe of him; but, instantly, felt that this was a base attempt to entangle him in a vulgar scuffle, which might prevent his appearance. Without delivering the blow he simply brushed Lord Newell contemptuously aside.

"By Heaven!" returned the actor, without looking back, "if you cross the British public, you will be kicked out, noble though you are, and you will not cry for benches to sit upon!"

With this Rabelaisian Parthian shot, he disappeared within the cheerless interior. When the enterer is in Kean's depths of despair, he sees, over the portals, the Dantesque legend.

Moses had stopped and turned, without recognizing the

interceptor; he had divined that it was one of these enemies of the rising geniuses who strive to throw a tripping
rope across the path.

"Nothing—merely that Lord Newell!" said the other,
briefly.

"Oh, good—there has been no fracas! It is noble of
you to master your natural impetuosity!"

It might have been otherwise if the actor had guessed
that his rival had placed himself there, not without mis-
givings, to try to upset his nervous system, because he
believed that Miss Danby would attend that first performance; to see her watch the other triumph would be
wormwood added to the hyssop in his filling cup.

Baffled, he went off to collect some kindred spirits, to
try to make a spoiled evening of the *début*.

Contrary to custom, still another petty wet blanket to
dampen his order and disturb one of the irritable genus!
a separate dressing-room was not provided for the
stranger. "The contestor for starry eminence must come
out, if he can, from the nebulæ!" said the duster of the
greenroom, who, from inhaling the fluff of the play-
wrights' coat imagined that he was a wit of the first
water.

Kean, therefore, had to share a room not too capacious,
with several young and rising comedians. They scoffed,
in a badly-subdued tone, and criticised the limited appurtenances of the new arrival's outfit; and very derisively
summed up the additions to the wardrobe, which Moses
brought from the store by instructions from his fastidious
friend.

Kean would have preferred real armor, if the weight
could be borne, but he had selected an imitation, a corselet
and arm-plates of black steel, inlaid with gold; a sort
of steel-guarded turban cap, which Haroun might have
worn; a flowing riding-cloak of white, setting off the
figure when gracefully sailing out when he walked; and
half-boots of stained and embossed leather, which he
had picked up in the curiosity shops at a rare expense,
so that he starved for the luxury. As for the complexion,
he forbore the African hue of stupid usage, and wore a
delicate tint as became an aristocratic Saracen.

He made his change of countenance without haste, with

the sure hand of the portraitist, having insignificant
means, careless as to refined art, because he did not need
its extremes.

"He may have been a harlequin in a show," observed
Oxberry, the low comedian, yielding at this proof of experience, "but he has a head over the nimble pair of
heels!"

As for a bright actor on Kean's other side, Bannister,
he suddenly pushed over toward the stranger his glass of
brandy and water.

Would they drug him?

Kean looked over to Moses, who nodded. In such a
period of exaltation, no false stimulant can have effect.
Kean drank without knowing it was stronger than spring
water. Returning the glass to Moses, to be handed to the
donor, he spoke this first pleasantry in that repellent re-
ception-hall:

"I little thought that my sole support in this road to
fame should be the Bannister!"

He spurned tradition, donning neither beard nor wig.
His hair was black, rather long—because he could not
afford the crop even at a penny! and his mustache was
marked. But by some necromancy, his lineaments became
those of a warrior at the prime; he was lofty, grave with
consciousness of superior and proven worth, and so dignified that no one would pass him without bowing.

Instead of the annoying chatter, silence reigned.

CHAPTER XII.

SUCCESS.

"It takes a poet to judge a poet."

Meanwhile, Manager Arnold had been spying him through one of those peepholes with which knot-holed scenery abounds; they may be enlarged by hand, however. He shook his head, in spite of the transformation. Such placid retention of natural and forgiveable emotion shocked him. As the attire was donned, piece by piece, he began to alter his opinion.

Shaping the folds to him, adjusting this or conforming that, every move for the better, the actor was like the snake accommodating itself to the new skin. And just as the new skin seems when thus animated to become glossy and lively in hue, so the new, gorgeous habiliments took on a sheen and play of light which fascinated.

In briefly addressing Moses, his husky voice cleared and was attuned. It was the difference between the violin loose in string and off the pitch with damp. Though he spoke commonplaces, the tone was tender and touching; this was a way of showing the indefatigable adherent that his ministrations were fully and cordially valued.

"It's a spirit," thought the not quite convinced watcher. "The weather has made a mummy of him, washed him out, pulped him like wet paper, and made him lack color! It will be vapidity, not even the rapidity of the fire of straw, catching nothing more from the footlights. A pest on such a hopeless waste of a night! Belliston is a plotter without sense, and as for the mysterious backer, who swayed the gentlemen of the committee to give this man of wax a show, I wish I knew who he was, to dissuade him from another such blunder!"

Kean stood alone. Moses had glided away to take the conventional "look at the house!"

"What a bran-stuffed mannikin to appeal to the generosity of the first theatre of Europe!" muttered Arnold.

The outlooker came up, like the sea captain, to study the weather, and returned with all his belief in his idol, under a poor, false smile that was dashing instead of encouraging.

The wide hall was practically deserted. There might be fifty in the pit, which held over a thousand, and not packed either. By their air, many had come just to get in out of the wet; others showed by their grimace of resignation that they had entered "with orders," given or sold cheaply by the tobacconists and small shopkeepers. The few deluded mortals, who, in their sweet simplicity, expected good to come out of Nazareth, submissively awaited a painful ordeal.

As for the critics, a formidable row, they grumbled at the dampness, cited failures, hemmed, snuffed and hawed, and chided the young gentlemen from the schools and universities who, up to town for a "lark," would have been joyous under a water-spout.

These collegians were under the beck of a lately emancipated fellow of theirs, apparently, whose pale face, exquisitely chiseled, dark curly hair, indescribably intelligent eyes, and alert, graceful manners, denoted a rare being. One pictured him with laurel over his high brow rather than a helmet and plume, but he seemed born to lead to glory or to death.

His intimates affectionately called him George, or Gordon; it was the poet Byron.

It was providential that he should be here to see Kean make his trial, for as he versified the emotions he experienced, so would our hero represent those he, too, had undergone. In both of them the gold was hammered out and fashioned in the burning forge, which seared their front and only overheated their brains.

This "cock of the colleges" had in his hand a paper-covered pamphlet of the play, which, rolled up, resembled a baton; but he had no need for it—like Kean, he had his Shakespeare by heart.

"Few," reported Moses, frankly, "but discriminative!"

Kean bit his quivering lip at this diplomatic story. But nothing now was to curb his long-restrained vigor. He was fully aware that while he should enact the loving husband of Desdemona with all his own fervid tempera-

ment, yet, as he conceived him to have been a refined
Moor, temporarily varnished with civilization of the
florid order there in progress, the vivid creation must
show that the strength and quiescence are innate—only
when the tiger is dragged out of its chains must it roar
and rend.

In the opening act, "the lion of St. Mark's" is in repose, in military trammels—Dante's figure: *"A guisa de
leon quando si posa!"*

As a puff of hot air runs before the sirocco, so a thrill
vibrated in the scanty audience, palpitating as the company of Othello proceeded to the Senate hall, where the
Doge and the seigniors awaited their general.   In an
instant, one saw the separated auditors snuggle up to
each other to compact themselves and not to lose that
charming tremor of the consolidated crowd.   Fellow
feeling! The groups were compressed.   The rear benches
were quitted that the front ones should be without a gap.

"Dang 'un! I was told that he were a leetle under-
sized man!" grumbled a country squire, indignant at his
misinformant of the theatre, on being taken aback by this
dark-visaged soldier, with imposing dignity, and such a
martial air that Brabantio was clearly robbed of half his
hatred.

"Order!" For like the Arab at the oasis, not a drop
must be lost of the precious spring, struck out of the rock
by the magic wand of Shakespeare, worthily wielded.
They contemplated and hung upon the finely-cut lips of
this man with the new style, the fatal eye and the Italian
physiognomy.   With the first stride, one stopped to watch
him; with the first syllable, one listened and wished to do
nothing but listen, while that mellifluous voice intoned
such apposite phrases.

"There, there!" said Lord Byron, in a softened voice,
"do you doubt that some men can talk naturally in verse?"

Through the oriental serenity appeared, fitfully, a smile
of haughty unconcern raising the tremulous nostrils.

No longer was there languor among the spectators; the
most listless were the more intent, now; and the stillness
was of the spellbound, like that dreadful conception of
the Arabian story-tellers: the man still living in the
brain, turned to marble from the waist down.

In the relation of the martial courtship, the voice became penetrative and so melodious that one glanced up to see if a nightingale had not alighted on the scenery.

How sublimely proof he was to the last shaft of malice: "Look to her, Moor!" and with what unfaltering trust he left his "moth of peace," this dragon-fly, in charge of Iago's wife, after the hour of love which he was allowed to pass with her.

The charm redoubled while all listened to the dialogue of Iago and his dupe. Nothing abrupt or angular could be carped at, for in both bearing and diction was the unerring inspiration of mind at its superlative degree.

"Shakespeare is turning in his coffin!" said the Boanerges of the pit. "Amazing power! If I had not lost the faculty of weeping, hang me in my own shoestrings but I could blubber now!"

"Never was English verse more explicit!" expatiated the delighted poet to his circle.

On the other side of the bar of light, intuition woke up the actors from their crass reluctance to admit merit. In the very flap of the torn canvas, the squeak of the pulley-blocks and the hanging of the green baize covered wind-doors, a voice kept murmuring:

"The great god, Pan, is living again! Success is here!"

The players gathered around the panting actor as he entered the common dressing-room; but he shrank from their congratulations. In his ears was the thunder of the popular approbation like the sea thundering on the rocks.

Bannister nudged Oxberry, and in a whisper said:

"That Cognac is great stuff! We must get in a gallon —and drink it!"

CHAPTER XIII.

GRIST TO THE MILL.

The auditors were like those honest peasants who, jogging to town as usual with their marketing, found they had arrived on a royal celebration day, when the fountains, commonly doling out water, poured wine.

They "fraternized," as the new word went, touched by the common delight, chatting like old friends, slapping backs and shaking hands like new-met brothers. Then a kind of awe succeeded, due to intense admiration. The fisher who saw the genie float out of the sealed bottle could not be more amazed. They felicitated themselves on being present on what would .be a memorable night.

As for the enthusiastic young poet, who had not a drop of envy in him, he stood up among his cohort, for they expected him to "voice" their unspeakable feelings.

"There has rolled out on the scroll a red-letter day which I no more expected than you!" he said, readily. Then, as if a. plan had appeared to him full-fledged, he added, peremptorily : "Let us be worthy of the prodigy! Young gentlemen of my school, of all the great educational houses of England, it is for us to hail this rising star! Get away, right and left, into the west, and rout you out every man who adores learning and her sweet sister, poesy! Say that Lord Byron invites them to 'sup with Shakespeare!' that a meteor's light illuminates the dark passages and all the beauties leap up without a veil or shadow!"

He concluded in Latin familiar. to them as scholars and divines intended : "The feast is ready! the guests must be brought in from the highway!"

Rubbing his carefully-kept hands, of which he was proud as a lady, he observed, by way of apology, to an old person who frowned at his animation :

"By your leave, sir, do you see? This marvel is to be the delight of the coming brood, for he is young yet, and it is meet that they should not let the chorister of Diana's groves be chilled at the first flight and first song!"

"Hum! Very good, young sir! but wait till the second act! Wait till he is writhing in that scoundrel Iago's coils!"

Whereat he offered the lordling snuff out of a Scotch mull.

While the orchestra was lengthening out an aria of Lulli's, the collectors for the author of "British Bards" went out in the wet to seek their acquaintances and classmates in the pleasure resorts. The pit promised to be half filled by their garnering.

Lord Newell saw, with sharp vexation, the coming in of these springalds, nodding to Byron and clapping their congeners on the shoulder, uttering cries of scholastic recognition to those at a distance, and forming cliques which, be they individually powerless, are as a body courted by the wise since they vote *en masse.*

They did not reck whether the call was a false one or not; they were happy because they had light and life around them, though they would have preferred a farce, and not one caviled at being summoned from revels rude and brutalizing for a feast intellectual. As long as the bait shone, they did not care whether it was metal or minnow. The pit was no longer an ice house; it glowed and fumed. The very lamps cast out a brighter ray and the candle-snuffer, crossing the stage on his duty, was not bantered or pelted by the many-headed.

An unfortunate partisan of the antiquated schools, bolstered by the Newell malcontents, having essayed rebuke, was himself covered with unanimous reproof, and but for being begged off, would have been expelled.

"Quin? Kean! Olympus to a mole hill!" cried Byron. "This is how all those affected to be—and it was affectation, by Jupiter!"

Just before the second act, there began to be a little movement in the boxes; feather-dusters and wiping-cloths were whisked about; attendants brought in extra cushions and footstools; the boxes were here and there about to be occupied.

There came in some of those ladies, with their little courts, who scent opportunities for notice. The indefinable crier of a great city had gone under their windows and shouted:

"Some doings at Drury Lane Theatre which you must not miss!"

So the French viscountess, the Belgian beauty, and the Greek cynosure came in with swishing petticoats and great hats, which they retained because this was not a state function, and nodded to acquaintances with smiles of the princess trained to execute so many a minute.

Then there rose a prolonged shout from the street through the hall and lobby:

"The company for Mr. Danby's box!"

Money is a great tittilater; everybody was on tiptoe to see the millionaire's company.

But the rich man did not appear. His daughter was escorted by as many noted gallants as could crowd into the box. Her chaperon—by courtesy "Lady" Filander—was a portly dame in gray and silver, wearing mourning for her husband, the colonel of a regiment slain in a blundering Flemish expedition.

Lord Newell was minded to go to the box to ask after Mr. Danby's health; but, really, he could not even risk his nose in at the door under pretense to inquiries about Lady Filander's.

So he fretted in the walk behind the first tier, watching Miss Danby and envying the cavaliers who, for that matter, were not comfortable in what was called a "box," but was more like a horse-box.

Miss Danby came late. Kean directly had looked for her, and he had dispatched his acolyte particularly to spy her out.

Love is like that vandal who cast his sword into the scales to bear down against Rome's entire wealth. Love induces the lover to weigh against all creation his individual fancy, and with the little god's quiver dropped in where she sits, up goes the beam-end and the devotee thinks he has full weight for his ardor.

This reappearance of the "plum" on the matrimonial tree, for Danby was the foregoer of the nabob, or rather of the Rothschilds and Goldschmidts, annulled the ridiculous rumor that she had fled her residence and gone off to the Continent to avoid her persecuting *fiancé*.

The vanishing of her maid had led the servants' hall to issue this bulletin.

Kean knew of this auditress before he came on the stage in this act. But his gratitude at being able to show her that he was not below her attention did not reveal itself on his countenance.

But in sympathy with him, the audience understood that the unruffled serenity of the Moor serves as the standard to gauge how the tempest gathers while the sky is still untroubled. Kean did not force his musical voice; his gesticulation was still sober and governed as by disciplinarian. Yet, by the "summer-lightning" in his speaking eyes, all foresaw the part was comprehended perfectly, the right course taken.

Alba saw, and doubted her vision. Was this the youth who had bounded upon her and snatched her away from the forest peril—the chevalier who had similarly leaped to her rescue and thrashed Lord Newell's bandits with the weaver's beam?

She wished she could act like the mob and her enthusiasm be exhibited as theirs as his progress went on like the tide,

Then her glee was calmed by her sorrow and a kind of shame; here, in the center of the world's civilization, a wonder like this was wearing his heart out to fascinate a handful! But what could a lady of the world do to fill this crater of the almost cold volcano?

She thought she knew, and she was silent and absorbed when the curtain was rung down to the deafening acclamation.

The echo shook the greenroom rafters and made the censorious shake, too.

"How the deuce so few can kick up such a devil of a row is a miracle!" said Oxberry.

"So few?" That was what rankled Miss Danby. But she had a remedy to allay her own rising fever.

"The miracle is here!" said Bannister, as Kean walked past their room into another, devoted solely to himself. The acting-manager guided him, with candles in his hand, and begged him to accept of his black boy a tray of Lisbon oranges, "for your tasked throat! You have so thundered with your tongue!"

In the house, the Etonians, Rugbeians, Cartusians, Harrovians, even the supercilious Grecians of the schools, shook hands with Byron, as astronomers congratulate a brother on discovering a comet.

Miss Danby was one blush, with having solved her enigma. She beckoned to Lord Riquets, "fashion's own knight," for the nonce, and said in her most bewitching tone:

"My lord, all know you are art's worshiper and most faithful. We must not let this magnificent godsend play on to such a meager herd of citizens and scholars. You who have so wide a circle of acquaintances that you are as the sun to them, surely you can at the bare request fill those boxes. Let them come and show their approbation if only for the last act!"

All the gentlemen spoke together:

"Madam, we will crowd the playhouse to bursting!"

Out they poured, leaving Miss Danby with her dowager-duenna. The hall rocked with their shouts, and their valets in turn shouted for the coach-runners on the wet pave to bring up the carriages of this and that. They were soon rattling away, as on a steeplechase, to bring friends to their misery or delight—for this flash might be "fool-fire."

During the serenade introducing the third act, the music was drowned by the bustle in Bow street. Footmen bellowed and smote the stones with their bamboos; horses champed and stamped; linkbearers ran into one another and strewed fire like bombshells; ladies and their cavaliers alighted at the rotunda, in their toilets of the supper or the ball, for Riquets and his compeers had used irresistible arguments. And how refuse anything to men who can make or mar a party by their presence or absence? The stairs and box floor looked like the antechamber in St. James' Palace at a drawing-room.

In the short scene where the Moor gives his lieutenant letters of advice before "walking on the works," he could in a glance perceive that the pit was nearly filled and that the grand tier of boxes, blazing with light and exuding perfumes and glitter of precious stones, offered many noted beauties and expectant countenances. He found it hard to believe that she now had comparisons in such number around her. If he had suspected that, like Byron for his part, she had procured this accession by her emissaries, he would have felt professional gratitude as fervent and great as his love.

Whether he acted at her or not, for his fire blinded him, and he was not cool from this time forward, her bosom, and others, melted at the adjuration:

"Excellent wretch, when I love thee not, Chaos is come again!"

Mark, as he says expressly, Othello sees all that is going on. He is not so lovebound as to let himself be hoodwinked. He has absorbed suspicion as the ocean swallows up rocks. But the shock buries his burden in his breast; there ached the raw and tender spot where the Florentine serpent is to inflict his tooth. But Othello denies that he has winced, while the poison is distilled into him, drop by drop. His spirit dashed? "Not a jot!"

One dramatist maintains that the verb is all; another that it is the adjective; Shakespeare has made it plain that an immense passion can expose itself with monosyllables, and be eloquent.

But, doubting, the ferocious Moor only falls into repining, deeper and deeper. The pathos of the farewell was ineffable; no man durst look at his neighbor lest his tears would gush to meet that other's; the ladies buried their faces in their kerchief or behind fans.

Box door-openers who had been toughened by many a theatrical woe, sobbed like boys caught red-handed in the preserve pantry. The dowager beside Miss Danby made the noises of a grampus rolling when storm impends.

There was almost a chorus of "Amen!" when Desdemona, perplexed at the vague terrors hovering over her, prays Heaven to "keep that monster, jealousy, from Othello's mind!"

This time Kean returned to "his" own dressing-room with a guard of honor. Moses was for a wonder not there to swell the applause. Two dressers replaced him.

Do not think that the tireless servant was overcome by his exertions or the joy at their being rewarded. On the contrary, he aimed at making the triumph perfect. Boxes and pit are all very well, but what is acclamation to which the great gallery does not overwhelmingly contribute?

"I don't know how the upper class has been drawn, any more than those schoolboys, but I have a winning card up my sleeve!" he muttered.

He went around and out of the stage door. Always when there is a performance on, boys cling here, to see the players go in, to await the honor of running errands for the known idols, to be kicked aside or to be encouraged by the small change which an actress is too dainty to put in her purse on discharging her hack. As an East End dweller, Moses knew them all, as their fathers before them.

"Ikey, Solly, Benjie," cried he, emptying his pocket of alas! not many coppers, "I want you to spread yourselves out to Leman street and the vicinity. Cry out as if you were selling the war cock-and-bulls: 'Moses, the Schneider's 'prentice, is a-playing "Othello" at the Lane! Be in time and don't let the Gentiles have the glory to themselves of giving him the friendly 'chi-Ike!' "

The gibberish was talismanic if incomprehensible to the uninitiated. The friendly "chi-Ike" is merely a welcome with the wish that one will do well at their new trade.

The boys, like a flight of sparrows, darted off over the mire as if they were shot at.

Moses smiled sweetly, softly and subtly.

"It seems to me that the gallery will be packed to the roof this blessed night! The caste are all very fine, but for greeting a successful actor give me the outcast!"

Before the *entr'acte* was over, a tremendous whirlwind seemed sweeping down over St. Paul's Hill toward the theatre.

"Send I may live!" ejaculated the taker of tickets on the stairs of the galleries, upper and lower; "all Vitechapel is in the uproar! They must have stolen the crown regalia out of the Tower and pawned it to get a sixpence apiece! Anyway, here they are! Vy, s'elp me 'bacca! there ain't no room for a h'eel to scrowge in!"

CHAPTER XIV.

A DIPLOMAT'S WIFE.

In the 'tween-acts, the clubhouses, drinking resorts, gambling houses, casinos and mask ballrooms contributed without cessation to the multitude at Drury Lane.

Men stopped their chairs at a friend's house and called him out to accompany them, just as an epicure begs another to join him at a peculiar delicious regale.

The playhouses had become like that loadstone rock of fable to which all things went of their unavoidable impulse.

Now Newell, like a blockhead, was impelled to imitate Miss Danby and Moses, after his fashion. He saw that already his clique was outnumbered, and that the experimenting stroller was bidding fair to be a favorite.

He remembered certain panics in crowded assemblies, and, with the wickedness of one thoroughly selfish, he wished some such disaster, sooner than witness the triumph of the actor under his ex-bride's sight.

So he called his ready factotum, Gideon, into harness. He gave him his purse and bade him execute a mission of his.

"Giddy," said he, pleasantly, "I believe there is a custom of the theatre management on such villainous nights as this, to let the footmen enter the cheaper priced parts without charge? From their elevated station, they can see when their masters and mistresses wish their carriage called and so run down and around to take their places."

"I dare say it is done that way," said the former gamekeeper. "But there is no chance for it now. It beats me, but the news is going round like a pike in a pond, that this here upstart from the penny booth is making his up'ard ascent into a big success! So they won't be letting nobody climb up into no gallery without paying his noble sixpence for the loft, or his more noble shilling for the

next floor under. If we were in there, we could see that
they are both pretty nigh full!"

"That is why I give you the coin. Pay the way in for
those robust fellows. Who knows? The sea may meet
a hindrance and tear back as rapidly as it rose to carry
this cork imp on the crest. You can insinuate what you
like; only—if there is a reversion—I expect they will
hiss, groan and 'boo' this intriguing fellow off the classic
stage!"

"I understand," said Gideon. "After all, they won't
care what they shout if they have their pay in and a drop
of something to oil their whistles!"

But secretly, he meant to get in himself and take very
few of the footmen with him, not to diminish the sum
too much.

Villains would often do more than they do, if they
could find honest men to help out their devices.

Gideon's recruits, like his master's, saw meet to keep
quiet. In the fourth act, it was palpable prizes without
any blanks, disquietude and anxiety were gone from our
tragedian on the gridiron. He was jubilant, although the
boards were not yet strewn with roses. The house could
not be contained when the slumbering lion fully awoke—
when the veneer fell off the man of the Barbary wilds
and he took the arch-villain by the throat. The claw had
scratched and he saw blood! The audience sank back and
shivered, like the throng before a menagerie in a thunder
storm, congratulating themselves that there are bars between.

"Incredible in a young man!" said Lord Byron. "He
must have led a previous life to understand jealousy so.
He can only have loved, but what a love is his!"

Some women left the house, though urged to remain
for the best to come by all around them. They had
supported the calm of assured affection, the growing sorrow of its loss, and the distress of the doubter. The out-
pouring of the volcanic fury had left them unnerved.
But they could not witness Desdemona's immolation, and
the great heart's foredoomed collapse. What grief would
be that almost pardonable murderer's—what madness
must befall him? He would pass away soon, in suicide.
Mere dramatists have let such a hero live to wail a yard

long of Alexandrines, but Shakespeare knew that an Othello cannot outlive a Desdemona by an ace.

The audience looked tearfully and pitiably one at another; they were partners in misery; they were all on the same immense rack.

If any philosopher had wanted a proof that minds are the same, however different are their human molds, he could have pointed to this congregation all as one; from Miss Danby to the apple girl in the back of the pit, from Gideon, forgetting his task, to the shop-boy away back in the upper gallery—all followed the soul-wringing story.

The excitement overflowing into the street had drawn many a face to Brunswick square windows, where the Countess of Koefeld, the Scandinavian ambassador's wife, yielding to the universal curiosity like a vulgarian, instead of abiding a report from her dressing-woman, opened the curtains and the windows, spite of the wet.

It was their own carriage which entered under the coach archway.

"This is odd," said she. "Is it a bread riot or revolution over that poor prince being allowed his pocket-money? What meanness in this rich nation! How comes my lord home so soon after announcing he would pass the evening with the Prince Regent in a most important conference under the rose?"

When Count Koefeld joined his wife, eager to communicate the news of his disconcertment, they presented a couple who were the talk of London.

The powers of the North were believed serious allies or enemies. It was understood that, leaving out Russia, all the countries jutting on the North Sea and Baltic had formed a family pact. Although Koefeld was accredited from one of the league only, he was widely known as the Scandinavian ambassador. He allowed himself unofficially to be so addressed, merely smiling blandly.

Augustus Koefeld was a very fair giant, pink and snowy, with fine yellow hair like corn silk; his teeth were large, but faultless; his breadth of shoulder was only equaled by his breadth of mind; to all seeming he was without the least captiousness and bore all things like an optimist.

Graceful and light in the dance, charming in chat, he was the desired of all desired.

His wife, Elena, was hailed as altogether delightful. She was one of those exotics who, by their utter contrast with English types, always create a sensation in London *salons* and, if stylish, guarded about forming acquaintances, and circumspect, soon have a drawing-room of their own.

Certainly she acted harmlessly enough; she made more male friends than feminine, but as she was of Italian origin, this was set down to the custom of her birth-country, where the cavaliers are tame cats.

"Anything happened?" queried she, with animation.

"A disaster!"

"A disaster?"

"Amazing! The prince excused himself from seeing me! He was closeted with that coarse Mr. Danby, whom no amount of gilding makes agreeable to me. Pugh! gold made an ass of King Midas—so, I suppose, we must yield to its making a bear of others."

"Oh, if the prince is still worried about money," observed the lady, with fillip of the fingers, to imply such was the lot of the lofty, "he must count these bullionists."

"But Mr. Danby was not talking money! He was going on like David over Absolom. It appears that the lively and accomplished Miss Danby——"

"Yes, an impeccable blonde!" said the dark woman, testily.

"Well, it is an admirable rarity to have the good word of nearly everybody in such a strait. To fly in the face of society, annul a family contract, rebel against her father, renounce her wealth, all because she dislikes a young and noble man!"

"Or likes another not necessarily young or noble!"

"But to my own affair. Mr. Danby was raving like one who would not be comforted; he was begging the prince to exert influence over the Court of Chancery— as if the Prince Regent, under a constitutional monarchy, had any power!"

"If he has no power, why do you so assiduously court him, Augustus?" she retorted, savagely. "But, surely

Miss Danby has not acquired so much importance that her rudely jilting this Lord Newell is what has raised the stones of London! What is the meaning of our houses in the square being depopulated by callers, who carry off the inmates like bandits?"

"Oh, it is mixed up with the Danby episode. Miss Danby has had the intuition of a prophetess; she has set the tone; she collected a bevy of gallants, and, hie! she went off from her pleading sire to the theatre!"

"Good! She is more wise than I rated her. He would not follow her any more than her *fiancé*. They would not make a scene before the scenes of the theatre."

"No; but why should she even show interest in a new and unknown actor?"

"Why does a lady set up a new flower, a new kind of dog, or a new dye? To attract attention on what reflects on her, in time. You men attach yourselves to a race-horse, a prize-fighter, or an admirable Crichton, do you not? It is all vanity!"

"As I left, unable to get a serious word in, for the prince is a boy or an old woman for a novelty, and was talking of rushing off to the play also, if only to elude Mr. Danby's tears, threatening his waistcoat——"

"Oh," said the lady, suddenly grave. "It is not surely this *début* which has turned London upside down?"

"Something like it—Miss Danby has simply set a snowball rolling which has gone on augmenting. As I came along, a dozen friends shouted, as they hurried past, that I must, too, be in the swim! not to miss a 'jolt'!"

"If it were a new actress, I could account for the flocking. But an actor—something intellectual! The English are no longer barbarians!"

Then, knitting her brows out of their superb arches, she added, with a sharp glance:

"I suppose, then, Augustus, that you persisted in resisting the temptation to hurry home and dress for the prince's party."

"What party?"

"Are you not dull? Did you not say that if, only to avoid Mr. Danby, he would go off to the theatre?"

"I did not say that, but it would not surprise me."

"Then, resume your broken interview—haste to the theatre, since you will rejoin the prince there! Besides, no one will suspect that you are cementing a fresh arrangement in his box over a sherry *sorbet!*"

"Well thought of! but I do not care to leave you alone, my dear Elena!" He regarded her fondly.

"One night alone, more or less, what matters? Besides," yawning delicately, "the new light may make me blink. Take me!"

A maid was at the door.

"I am to dress for the play," said her mistress, quickly. "Get all ready, Gilda, *presto!*"

"I do not think the horses are taken out, so I will have them ready. A minute for my own toilet——" At the door he paused, saying:

"Miss Danby had Lord Riquet with her."

"A jackal of the prince, you see! Poor Newell!"

"Then you think the prince will attend?" anxiously.

"I am sure," answered she, laughing, as she hastened out, with irony under the melodious mirth.

Although time pressed, she did not at once put herself under her dresser's hands. On the contrary, she called Gilda to her side and whispered, very lowly:

"Take a hackney coach to Carlton House and see Mr. Bonnell, the prince's confidential gentleman. Tell him to be at the Drury Lane Theatre to-night to set the seal on the new actor. I shall be there."

Gilda was a Genoan, acute and alert. She nodded, winked both eyes to conceal their instant flashes, and ran out of the room.

She found a prowling vehicle and was rattled along toward her destination before the Koefelds set out in their carriage for Drury Lane.

Their equipage was only one of a train.

"See!" said Koefeld, as it had to draw aside and give the pass to a splendid turnout.

"It is the Duke of Norfolk," said he, "and going as a royal household officer! Look at the scarlet and gold! And it is a state carriage! Has the prince given him the hint?"

"I was sure he would be there," was her quiet reply.

Another and another state carriage distanced them,

showing the footmen in an armor of gold braid and shoulder knots like masses of bullion

All at once a beacon flared before them; the torch-bearers had cast their brands in a heap at the end of the march through the wet, for there was fog, although the rain had ceased; this formed a glorious bonfire in the crossroad where the theatre formed a corner. Children and street idlers were capering around it and cheering each arrival.

They came up to the Koefelds' wheels, caroling:

> "A penny, a penny! for granny, for granny!
> It's bonfire night! Halloa, boys!"

The lately poverty-stricken house was illumined; there were crushed spectators in the orchestra; the minstrels being dislodged. Every space had a body in it. "The fifty in the pit," enumerated by Moses, had become thousands! They were still beating to the strokes which the actor had sent upon every chord. From his maestro's *báton* had emanated fire, passion and sentiment as if a port fire-stock.

Foreigner though he was and frigid, the ambassador caught the universal infection and began to believe that there was no delusion. He might felicitate himself that he arrived at the finish. His wife continued to survey the house with her lorgnette. Miss Danby was bright as polished silver—casting her diamonds into the shade. Around her the gentlemen lucky enough to serve her in her design to "make a house," were also radiant, reflecting her happy smiles. Alone, the surly wretch, Jessamy, scowled hideously at the back of the tier, his hand buried in his bosom.

Only one gap in the rows of delight was evident—the royal box.

Moses had taken a long and loving look at the immense pile upon pile of rejoicing and expectant faces, and returned to his friend, where he said:

"All the town will see your fifth act!"

CHAPTER XV.

"As good as comedy," said Belliston, beaming, and corruscating with witticisms against those who had derided him for having "found" the star in the dust holes of the country booths. He was more brilliant than the star himself, with the reflection of his glory, illogical as that is.

He had hastened to notify the "best style of men," the notabilities, his hail fellows, and they were more numerous than the actors, on and off duty that night, to huzza for Kean on his way to recuperate for his last bout with the masterpiece.

The fine lady of the stage, having no jealousy now as she was about to wed an earl, generously pronounced his action vitality's self, and said that he had bounded like a greyhound into public favor.

Manager Arnold had assumed a smile from ear to ear and preceded a liveried messenger, carrying a tray heaped up with puff-cakes and with a brimmer of negus, to greet the lately-neglected "heir presumptive" as "Sir!" as if he were already made a knight.

Kean bore this cringing very well. When we have once tasted the honey, the sting may be forgot.

In his gloomy region, the old stage carpenter listened to the hum of satisfaction enhanced by longing for more to come.

"Ha, you see!" chuckled he, "Garrick imitated a turkey-cock, but this one does the eagle downright!"

There was laughter and a cheer; "the dusting brigade" had entered the blank—the royal box; they were going to put it in order; the Prince of Wales had heard of the to-do and was coming to give the casting vote.

Like all amusement-seeking princes, George was a king at the theatre.

It was at the height of the scuffle between Iago, Cassio and Roderigo, when a flourish of silver trumpets and a ruffle on the kettledrum were heard in the street; the royal party must have arrived, escorted by a troop of horse; the Grenadiers had been mustered to receive their monarch.

Lady Koefeld, who had been restless, resumed her superb serenity, and was the only woman who did not so much as glance at the royal box, where the light suddenly blazed.

Her husband stared; he had hoped for the prince, and still more to be remarked so that he should be called to his place.

The acting-manager, with his servants, was agreeable to usher the party into the box at once, but the prince, who knew all about true politeness, if he did not always practice it, preferred to delay so as to take his seat, with his bedizened *cortège,* during the shifting of the scene, and not divide attention.

Newell could have howled with rage at seeing Sir John Whipstaffe, Hanger and others of his coterie surrounding the sovereign, and the last ready to give the actor his encouragement if only fairly justified,

"What could have induced him to leave his cards and toddy?" muttered Newell, at his patience' end; "if I could imagine that Alba is doubly playing me false—that there is a bit of truth in the tales that the prince prefers to borrow money of Danby so as to hear of his daughter—ah! I see how nobles become regicides!"

Lady Elena still would not gaze toward the temporary point of all gazing, content at the proof that she could draw with a word; and the prince, as if there were a mutual understanding, 'took care in his embracing glance not to let it dwell upon the Koefelds.

The royal suite looked to their master as the curtain descended; they had not a voice among them, of their own.

"Shakespeare, I think, need not grieve for the 'Othello' lost with Barry," remarked he.

Rising to go forth, he said, loudly enough to be heard by the throng in the lobby:

"This is as sure a card as ever won a set!"

This characteristic *mot* went the rounds.

"If the prince said that, then we are good for three

seasons!" said Belliston, perking up as if he had suggested the phrase.

On being hailed by the mob in the street, one hoarse
voice bellowed with that cordial footing of the vulgar
with their ruler, in England:

"Next time, Ge'horge, bring your father!"

With great tact, he took this seriously and observed
sotto voce, to his friends:

"I would if I could, but he could not bear this Kean's
harrowing of the heart."

CHAPTER XVI.

How is it Kean played up to the mark when not above it, that night of nights?

It was because he was in the plenitude of that spirit of sympathy, comprehension and kindred creativeness which true actor-intepreters of the poets feel sometimes.

Miss Danby saw nothing of the prince, whose arrival had diverted attention. She was enthralled and weeping silently. It was the scene which the ancients could not imagine since they were ignorant of melancholia, the muse of Shakespeare and Druer. Into the bedchamber —cloister of purity! stole the dark figure, so sinister now, of the oriental, in his snowy burnoose, soon to be sullied with blood. It was less unearthly than the ghost of Denmark, but more human than the stone guest of "Don Juan."

Turbulent passion was unseemly here; every syllable and act was majestic and exalted—some sublimated so that none had the impulse, known when acting is grossly realistic, of wishing to interfere counter to the crime. Admiration was dragged through ice into the flame like the departed soul in the mediæval hells.

At "Weeps thou for him to my face?" Othello's wrath burst forth in one of those lion-like roars which Kean uniquely sent from an overburdened breast.

The actress with him was really frightened; she who should have met her unjust doom like a martyr, turned also leonine and fought wildly though hopelessly for her life.

The audience was so stunned by this departure from the "business" into nature, that Othello's own death, deserved and inevitable, for it is expiation, fell as a fresh shock after all susceptibility seemed deadened.

Kean's foregoers had struck with the sword or dagger as they considered appropriate. Here again, he offered novelty; he "made *siccar*" by seizing the poniard, which had chastised "the turbaned Turk who traduced Venice," between both nervous hands, so as to drive the blade irresistibly into that harassed heart. Then, staggering more with his disillusion, his blasted love, his sorrow at his own sentence carried out—unable to reach the couch, he fell on the rug, just able to die with his palpitating lips on the cold white hand, dangling off the bedside, like a lily broken at the stem while in full blossom.

A scream resounded over the audience—it was made by several women at the same instant—but to Kean, Alba Danby's was predominant. She had fancied that he had given her a last look, as if he were veritably dying.

As if the very stage machinist felt this woe, the curtain was lowered slowly, as the pall covers in the face of the dear dead at whom one wishes to look to the uttermost.

The lookers-on could not keep their eyes off that direction; all sighed as after an execution. There was the feeling of semi-guilt at letting an outrage be perpetrated.

Then the collegians "chaired" Lord Byron, and all the rows of spectators started to their feet.

"We must have him out!" cried some one in the gallery.

The house shook with the stamping of feet and the slapping of the board partition with open hands.

"Take the time from me, gentlemen," said Byron, looking like a visitor from the shades of Poets' Corner, with his hair crisping up and his white throat bursting the collar away. "Three cheers and a huzza!"

So Kean, bowing stately, but with such pleasure under his swarthy tint, received the ovation given heretofore only to Garrick.

The accepted tragedian withdrew after ineffectual attempts to depart, and as he pushed aside all the scores desirous to offer their arm or hand, he singled out Moses and leaned on his shoulder.

He whispered to him—all the old fun of the player in the penny show bubbling in his joy:

"We have done the trick, Mo'!"

In the vast hall there was not one dissentient voice.

Lord Newell was in torture at the tragedian's triumphant visage, and Miss Danby's as rapturous.

His handful of parasites were hand-clapping or shouting with the mass, and would have regarded him as mad if he had set up their preconcerted cry:

"Out with the ladies and down with the house!"

He demolished Drury Lane because his rival had vanquished!

Meanwhile Manager Raymond trotted on one side of his great player. On the other Manager Arnold—"that traitor, Arnold!" said a veteran of the American war—repeated, "A hit, a palpable hit!" while Belliston, almost capering like Malvolio, paced before to the dressing-room, fluting:

"Way, gentlemen, if you please, way! for Mr. Kean, who has saved us from ruin!"

Kean did not know his room; it was changed again! They gave him the best, a suite in which one could live and receive a host. His two attendants had doubled and the pair of wax candles tripled. In that glow was the transition of his winter to summer.

It was half filled with the privileged, shareholders, the committee and their friends, fulsomely showering applause. He threw off his costume, hurled an article which had offended him into the lustrous open fire, and sternly compelling the official dressers to leave Moses solely to his duty, retook and put on, before all that body of lace and glitter, his old street garments, damp, threadbare and terribly repulsive now, even to the broken boots.

All stared with bewilderment save the one or two who honored the rebuke to the managers, blinded with ignorance, haste and hate. Had this sudden glory driven him mad?

"Blessings on the prince—he came late, but better late than never! He said—" began Belliston, in a pause. "He said——"

"Hang the prince!" cried Kean, preparing to walk out, independently, if not disloyally. "The pit rose at me!"

He quitted the stupefied gathering with only his faithful henchman.

But at the point wherein a dark side door allows communication between the playhouses proper and the public hall and offices, a man stood in the doorway. It was Simmons, the treasurer. As a token of office, he held in his hand, clutching the neck of it, a bag of gold.

"Heaven reward you!" said the old fellow, tearfully; "we are sure now, Mr. Kean, of our salary right on, and the arrears! Bless you a hundred times! You are Niagara to the Versailles waterworks! Bless and excuse me; but—here is a hundred in gold, in advance, on account! It is not office hours and this is not authorized business—but deuce and all! a night like this knocks method all to smithereens! If they won't approve of the act, why I will make it up out of my own pocket!"

No man could offend a treasurer like this! Kean made a sign for Moses to relieve the worthy cashier, who had "discounted" the triumph in ready money.

"Don't thank me, Mr. Kean," continued the other, wiping his eyes; "it is I who am obligated to you, sir! For you relieve me of much worry! I do not refer to the cash, but to mental worry. It has always been a moot question, particularly to me, how much 'the Lane holds. But now, I can firmly answer—I can pose 'em! We have taken six hundred and seventy-three pounds, two shillings and ninepence! But I cannot explainify the ninepence!" continued the cashier, after he was left alone, "unless, in the rush, some one palmed off a ninepenny piece on the collector for a clipped shilling!"

CHAPTER XVII.

SKY ROCKET, OR LAMP?

The benevolent, retired sea captain who had the residence built in the early Georgian style, in Brunswick square, which the Koefelds had taken, would have been surprised to see the transformed drawing-room where he had smoked his pipe with ancient mariners, as the sumptuous reception-room of the foreigners.

Nor had Captain Corane ever seen such a hostess. Elena, with her Italian voluptuousness, round face with aquiline nose, blackest of black hair, and tireless, consuming eyes, was one of those whom no amount of jewelry can cause to resemble a mere show window.

It was sheerly vying in luster.

The sapphires, diamonds and rubies in her hair paled into glowworms.

She was a fine hostess, astonishing the English, still brought up as ladies of the house. She had superintended all the preparatives, the card tables, the making of genuine Roman punch after the family receipt inherited from her ancestors' boon companion, the epicurean, Cardinal Bompresso; the musicians and the cigars which gentlemen from the military becoming acquainted with them in Spain, asked for, etc.

It was going to be a very late ball, since it was less perilous to return home at daybreak than in the small hours.

So the hostess, napping on a deeply-cushioned ottoman, was somewhat surprised at a caller.

The footman had announced:

"The Countess of Gorsewold!"

The earl of that name was one of those men afflicted with ponderosity of mien and person, with which is associated a denseness of mind. Nevertheless, while this prejudice kept him out of government office, his advice and profound acquaintance with diplomatic ruses, made him sought by the chosen. So he was absorbed in study

to maintain this reputation. Marrying a young shoot
of a good but not wealthy family, he almost let her become
the proverbial old man's darling. Amy, of the Gorse-
wolds, therefore advanced. in years without doing so in
gravity. Unfortunately, as she was free of tongue, she
said not only too much but much that was, unintention-
ally, cutting and rankling. It seemed impossible that a
shallow person could speak such penetrating and sensible
phrases. Then, with a round, guileless face, and a mouth
innocence's own, these quips were heard incredulously as
if a pretty Parian statuette spoke like Pasquin.

Elena herself did not lack for those insolent sentences
which in any rank but the highest would compel one to
horsewhip a man and to send a woman into the Arctic
Circle, and she liked this chatterer, who, she believed,
was only pretending unconsciousness of her sayings.

Besides, always learning English, and fond of its humorous expressions, she found in her companion a veritable mine.

She bade the servant show up the countess without
delay.

The lady came in with a pretty, mincing tread, and
opened out her short, dimpled arms amiably. Her lips
pouted and her eyes beamed with childish, cerulean light.
She was dressed for a party, or a ball.

She was inclined to look vulgar, from wearing her hair
cut in an even line across her low brows, a fringe,
adapted from the fashion started by one Anne Catley,
an actress of note.

Lady Elena embraced her heartily before asking her to
sit beside her on the couch.

"What a good dear you are, Amy, to come betimes !"

"Oh, I have not come for your party—pardon me,
Nell, for I was having one of my own, but the men have
fled from me horribly ! And I was setting up such a
fine table for quadrille—they care no more for quadrille
the cards, than quadrille the dance ! hash them !"

Elena had long since suppressed any movement when
the tomboy-lady swore.

"What calls them away ?"

"Oh, the play ! All of a sudden, some one falls 'queer'
at the theatre and that magnet, Quin—no, Kean ! he gen-

erously sacrifices his idle night and appears to relieve his management from a quandary! Unfortunately, as I said, the act relieves my list of the desirable partners, and I shall not see an agreeable countenance all the night unless I go to the play, too! but that lord o' mine, he does not care for it! I believe he is the only man in London having a box at the Lane, and yet lends it to his friends without going once himself. It is true that it is wretchedly placed. It was fine in the days when one wanted to chat with the performers, since it is a stage-box, you know, and when the curtain falls, one is shut in, on the stage! Ah, how that destroys illusion!" sighed the matter-of-fact woman, hypocritically.

The truth is, she would prefer to have been on the audience side, so as to quiz and be quizzed.

"What manners you have come to London to see, my poor friend! Even the Chesterfield 'cub' has not apologized for his turning recreant."

"Then this Mr. Kean is not a flash, but a steady illuminant?" she spoke with apparent listlessness.

"Nay, it is more than ever an Englishman's duty to worship the pride of all nature and of every nation!"

Amy spoke in capitals, as they wrote all nouns at the time.

"Hold! the interpreter of your great Shakespeare may captivate all nature, but to enthrall all nations—that is another matter!"

"I do not see, if you have seen him, how you can disagree?"

"I grant that the actor is unapproachable, from the throng, but irreproachable? Oh, I have had critics of admitted caliber cut him to mince in my parlors! a common-born waif, who read his playbook by a candle-end in a garret!"

"Well," returned the visitor, coolly, material herself, "those who give twenty guineas for a peep at him would not walk around that statue there to see your critics in a row. Some of our friends actually submitted to passing the night in our horrid box rather than lose such an event as his Romeo, Hamlet or Coriolanus! They agreed with that unhappy boy-poet, Chatterton, who calls him our 'all-in-all!'"

"Yes, you insulars are so close that you allow no rivals to your favorites. I suppose we must tolerate this Kean to the end of his natural span!"

"You are like my uncle, Sir Alexis, who will not give in to his eminency, forsooth, because he saw him at the outset of his career under unpropitious aspects."

"Ah?"

"Yes, in the country; his mother or a woman purporting to be such, came to his house, cap in hand—I mean the boy, for Kean was a boy, with enormous black eyes and a precocious absence of bashfulness, which startled even the three-bottle, hard-riding squires. This little Bellower being put afoot on the dining table would run his fingers through his long, crisp locks and 'spout' it out, yards of poetic text, for a collection of shillings and half-crowns in his cap. Now, they would fill it with sovereigns!"

"I should judge he was a remarkable boy; the eyes would not change—they are such as never grow old!"

"He went by the name of Edmunds, and he looked like a lad whom the gypsies had stolen and trained to antic at a fair. We have a sketch, that is, a sticking-plaster picture——"

"Eh? ah, a silhouette?"

"Yes, a silly thing, all black and profile! It shows this imp with one shoulder hunched up, so!" She tried to imitate, but her rounded shoulder only let the dress-band fall off, and they both laughed. He has a sardonic grin on his lips—and a rasping voice!"

"Wonderful sketch to show that his voice grated!"

"Oh! I do not mean that—but they said so. But he was just as enjoyable in comic as serious poetry. He sang all kinds of songs, and danced a hornpipe among the gentlemen's snuffboxes and repeaters and rummers on the board! I should like to have seen that! Do you know my desire has been unconquerable, all my life, to look on when the ladies leave the room for their dish of tea, and the men stay for the curacoa and broiled bones."

"It would not be so interesting as the boy-actor!" sighed the Scandinavian countess. "What a world it is, for genius—he amused a score of rustic barons, then —now, he has a dozen dukes under his spell!"

"And duchesses, do not forget the duchesses!"

"He is fascinating—in a demoniacal way! I have been haunted by his expression when he whets the knife, as the Jew merchant of Venice."

"So you felt the universal rapture?"

"I have quivered when he ground his teeth as 'Othello!' He is vastly followed."

"Because the great exult when a diamond is extracted from the rough casing, as do the common people when one of their own is at a height."

"Hem! they discover—because they are going to knight him, seeing that the regent is his friend and patron—that he is of noble extraction!"

"Do you believe the tale that he is a Howard?"

"Oh, it is the Duke of Norfolk's doing, to have some of his splendor? I have heard him chuckle, like grazier over a bargain in beeves, that Mr. Kean had conquered all Mr. Garrick's business.'"

"He is extraordinary because he more than makes you forget you are at a play—you do not know where you are!"

"What charming oblivion! That's why the men run after him, who, like him, are harassed by creditors!"

"Who says that? I thought that he was munificently recompensed; that he was worth a mine to the theatre proprietors."

"Squanders it! aspires to confederate with his betters! and the abettors, too, of all sorts of waste," continued the fair scandalizer, with her wonted smile of fair-seeming, "a companion of the prince requires Peru."

"Then," said the patrician, sharply, "it might be a proof that he is superlative; he is probably, by part, of foreign origin, of a race which scorned mercantile principles in its revenues!"

"I do not know about that! If he is a gypsy, as some say, they, too, are indifferent about whom they choose; whom they cope with—hem!"

She might have said that the Italian should not flout the storekeeper, as her Genoan forefathers combined trading with brigandage.

"Then," said the Englishwoman, after a pause, "since

you are glutted with the genius, you would not object to
my using your box ?"

"Fie! any time! that is, if my husband should not require it to bestow a diplomatic favor—he will do anything for that!"

"Oh, I only ask a seat or two, and the diplomats never
mind my presence—they go on talking all the same, as
if we women knew nothing of what goes on in the courts,
and on the back stairs, too!"

She looked wise as an owl, and the foreigner shrugged
her lovely shoulders.

"Though it is on the stage, it will bring me nearer this
wayward Kean, and I shall be able, next you, to see
really how enamored you are of him!"

"Enamored—that is a strong word!" Her eyes
warmed and the fair one could hardly support the en-
kindling ray.

"Enthused, then!"

"The man is superior, if not supernatural!"

"Lord Gorsewold refused Mr. Danby's offer."

"Mr. Danby offered his box?"

"He offered it for sale—so like him, when there was
a bad feud between him and his daughter about the pro-
posed wedding, and——"

"It was patched up, since she occupied it, to the full
capacity, too, on Mr. Kean's first night!"

"Yes, I would I had been there—at the last, when the
house filled up so magically. What a miracle—all the
town emptied to cram into that deserted house! I never
can understand how the prince was impressed into the
actor's service."

"No one can understand his caprices—like a woman's!
I dare say," with negligence, "that he was allured by
art!"

"Art? fiddlesticks, in the Hanovers! "Boedry and
bainding!" she grunted, in imitation of George the king
sneering at Hogarth. "If I had been present, I should
have watched to see to whom he sent an attendant or who
was called to his box."

"I watched," returned Lady Koefeld, quietly. "He
sent an equerry, certainly, but to have my husband give
him a look-in!"

"Oh, to confide a diplomatic secret?" dubiously.

"No, to pronounce Kean a marvel!"

"So, that is why your box is always occupied?"

"When my lord does not go, and he cares only for see-ing a character once, I keep up paying the compliment!"

"That is it! the idea of insinuating that you were en-chanted by the mountebank become tragedian!"

"I? as well say that of Miss Danby, who follows his every movement with her porcelain eyes!"

"It takes a brunette to decry a blonde!"

"No, a blonde—they are more likely to be rivals!" was the rejoinder.

"In any case, since the alliance with the Newells is a thing of the past, broken and tossed into the corner, Miss Danby may be allowed to worship the actor!"

"Lor'! she can do more than that! She can have the idol in her own shrine, in her lady-chapel, at home!"

"What morals!"

"Oh, what should I mean but that she can let the min-ister say the orthodox words over her and Mr. Kean, in-stead of over her and the unsaddled Lord Newell!"

"Marry an actor? I forgot, though, that she is of no grade!"

"Money, my dear Elena. This actor is called the money-getter of Drury Lane; who has picked it out of the gutter, so to say, worth a hundred thousand a year, look you! He outbids Lord Newell, who, for all I know, may be in the usurer's toils—I mean, Danby's!"

"Absurd!"

"By your rising color and the twitching of your hand I should fear that for a similar absurdity, you would break your fan over the mouth that said it!"

"Not this fan," but your matrimonial projects are so risible!" She rose and walked up and down the room, stopping at a pier mirror to see if she had betrayed her feelings by her blush.

"Surely, you do not go to that theatre every Kean night, only to play secretary to your lord, when he meets the cabinet ministers and the chief of the state there, and no one suspects—except such sages as my lord, that sub-jects of importance are carried on between them under cover of seeing a play?"

"That is it, my dear! They have all got the Kean fever, and no one but you blames me!"

"Blame! I am rushing into the contagion, am I not? in begging to sit beside you and be inspired by this wonder! What will my lord say? He would smile—for he thinks the drama more enjoyable in the book in the study than on the stage, thrilled forth by a parrot!"

"Kean, a parrot!"

"How impulsive you are! I shall try that test with Miss Danby!"

"No doubt, it would be safer. She has not a spark in her."

"She would not break her fan over my silly pate!"

"Amy, in a word, what do they say?"

"That you adore the theatrical gods—at least, their high priest!"

"I adore Kean!" She uttered the most hearty laugh ever poured out of woman's throat, trained never to be natural.

Her hearer was astounded, for there was no deception here; still, there was something more than the joy of her tormentor being on the wrong track.

"Who says that?"

"Nobody, and, everybody! It fell out of the 'Montgolfier' airship which, by this time, ought to have crossed the Channel and fallen somewhere on Dover Downs!"

"This is said of Miss Danby, of the Countess of Willowslea, of the Duchess——"

"They do not deny it—they are proud, I guess; but your admiration borders on idolatry!"

"Little Amy of my heart, in every age there is a fashion in the temporary toys of ladies. A little while back, each had her West Indian boy; now, we cherish an actor! At least, were there a grain of sense in this popular error, I could be pardoned, for I have chosen the principal!"

"Acknowledged!" and the countess clapped her plump hands. "Alack, my poor Nell! you are just one of the faggots bound for the pyre on which burns the sacred flame! For this Kean is not a man only, a gallant like 'Gentleman' Dick, or Jack! They were actors who could play well; but off the stage, what apes and ungainly pup-

pets! This is a soul, for none but a soul can play Othello
or Hamlet! This sounds above me! I admit, it is Lord
Byron who speaks—he said this in my husband's gallery,
before 'The Brigands,' which—I do not know—was
painted by Salvator Rosa or by the German master,
Goëthe!"

"Lord Byron," returned the Italian, merrily, "has gotten up on the Drury Lane Committee, and, bear in mind,
he has a tragedy up his sleeve, for which he would induce
Kean to create the hero."

"Well, a light heart lives long! I am ready to see the
whole Kean gamut from 'The Gamester' to 'Sir Giles' the
hideous——"

"Blood curdling!"

"Bad! for my blood is milk! But do not fear that I
shall be dragged by my tresses at his chariot-wheels—I
will crop my hair like a jade in Bridewell, first! I prefer comedy, and low, at that; the lower the better! ha, ha!
Ah, poor Dickey Suett! that's the man I could have held
in golden chains, since to adore an actor is the model.
A merry Andrew who would have been Queen Amy's
jester, if I ruled Merrie England!"

And she twisted up her dumpling of a face so comic-
ally that the proud beauty deigned to laugh.

"Well, you know your society! Odd mortals! It is
a vain suppose; but you upbraid one who falls in love
with a great actor! Yet you receive singers and actresses
who marry into the peerage!"

"You have the cold end of the fire-iron; the woman is
received—the mountebank tolerated!"

"Indeed! and this is the state of art in civilized England!"

"As long as they retain their vocation, we stretch a
rope—silken, it is true; but it is a rope, that one could
hang another by. We stretch this rope across the room
so that the goat, however trained and amusing, shall not
mix with the sheep and the lambs, particularly the lambs!
Over there, they squall, bawl, cut their monkey-capers,
and, after having refreshment by themselves, receive a
purse from the butler, and, adieu! Monseer the Arteste!"

"Then you do not receive genius as the peer of a—a
noble?"

"Not talent, for a thousand talents of silver; not in our parlors; still less in our boudoirs; for shame!"

"There is something out, here! My husband has met Mr. Kean in very select houses. The Duke of York——"

"Pooh! the duke knows how to descend! Did he not drop his privileges to fight with Colonel Lenox?"

"And the prince is Mr. Kean's chief adorer!"

"Ha, ha, ha! you diplomatists know so little! The prince is his patron and his—pupil; the great secret is out! You would not guess that the actor is 'coaching' the king's representative to speak his thanks when he gets his relief bill passed and must reply, of course!"

"Well, it is bruited that I adore Mr. Kean more or less in good and elevated company?"

"How persistent you are. You would not be conspicuous among the many, but that you are so conspicuous! I do not allude to your beauty alone—but to your sighing, flourishing your fan, rolling your eyes, hanging out over your box-ledge, throwing bouquets instead of sending them by your footman; in short, you overdo the homage —but you are a foreigner; that would be excusable as it is in its own proportion in Miss Danby; but you—oh, you are a married woman! But be patient, as am I, in thraldom; and, after a while, I may be enlisted in this band of inveterate worshipers!"

"Do they go so far as to say that—that he makes any returns for this adulation?"

"Among so many, if he tosses the handkerchief, it would be torn to fragments not fit to wipe an eye, so that no one can snatch it! His heart is like Romeo, cut into little stars, to make heaven more fine—correct my quotation, dear, since you have the part—and the actor—to heart!"

"You rattlebrain; he will not be my fool unless he be my fate!"

"More likely Miss Danby's *fête!* Then—poor fellow, a married actor, like a married painter—no more masterpieces!"

"Come, come, you would not shut the door on one to whom the arcana is opened widely?"

"No, not to him, but his own shocking reputation."

"His fame——"

"I am talking of his ill-fame! They have promised the white keys till they are sick of it, and point to the black ones; his vices and devices, to mask them. He is more clever at acting to that end than in his written parts. But it is out—made a song of!"

And she began to sing a popular scurrilous ballad about "The Actor and the Alderman."

"You alarm me! Run out of the virtuous track?"

"Does he act now save when under the influence of the god——"

"Very good—Apollo!"

"Not that kind of inspiration; the little brown beer tub of a fellow who rises on a cask and waves a vinestick wreathed with grapes."

"Bacchus! Mr. Kean drinks?"

"Only in Scandinavia is that news! Kean is the renewed Lord of Misrule and Master of the Revels; the prince is reformed beside him. The histrion is trying to efface the memory of Lovelace by the list of his Saccharissas. In luxury he vies with Heliogobblers. Ah, if he would only match guineas with peers, spin the roulette table for countesses, or dance with the eligible parties!— he shows his extraction, which I do not believe of the Howards, now! When he throws off Gloster's scarlet and ermine, it is to don the marketman's or the seaman's dress and finish the night in the cellars of St. Giles!"

Lady Koefeld laughed.

"This is very incompatible with his alluring the belles?"

"Oh, it is because one of them plays with him; it is not fondness for rum and tobacco, but disappointed hopes!"

"You blow hot and cold with the same breath. This man with his contradictions is certainly on all sides interesting, like the chameleon. You are showing up both sides of the medal!"

"I do not understand any vexation of love that would make one prefer Jamaica to the imperial tokay, of which he could fill up, at Carlton House!" smacking her lips playfully.

"He could have it out of his own vault, with a hundred thousand a year!"

"Not a hundred crowns come to him, for he is riddled

with debts.   That is why Mr. Danby could have him lead
his prize lot to the altar any day, be sure!   Who knows
but it is rather his purse than any fond dame's ridicule
out of which he procures release from the sheriff's officers?"

"Oh, do you think that Miss Danby has saved him
from the debtor's prison?"

"More than once, if at all!" positively.

"The count prides himself on his secret information
bureau," observed the countess, with some bitterness,
"but this is severe.   I am ignorant of what you know so
well!"

"Lady Gorsewold settled herself back in the tufted
squabs to discourse at even more ease.   She delighted
in thus roasting her confidants.

"I am going to tell you.   Mr. Kean was at Baron Met-
calf's residence at Hampstead, where the process-servers
entered, as if they were the extra-waiters.   They were
going to serve the guest—in faith, 'collar' him, my dear,
at the end of the recital, with which he paid his scot, so to
put it.   That bears out what I said of our actors being
remunerated guests.   Now the acute jester had recognized the bailiffs.

"So he concluded his revelations by saying:

" 'Gentlemen, I am going to show you that I still retain
the tricks of my early profession, a ground-and-lofty harlequin,' and——

"Therewith, my dear, he leaped out of the French window through their clutching fingers!   But he was not
familiar with the premises, and it was sixteen feet to the
ground.   Another man, without his training, would have
been maimed, if not killed outright.   The beholders were
so delighted that they paid off the jackals; the dears did
not do it that time."

"You harp on that string of his being courted like M.
Baron, the Parisian actor?   Pshaw!   A lady of birth and
breeding, to say nothing of a golden throne, become
fascinated by such a Scaramouche!   But you are not
drawing a portrait!"

"It is not a caricature!"

"I could not dream him thus to have been," said

CHAPTER XVIII.

A TORCH TO THE TAPER.

A gentleman in black entered by a side door as his master by the main double ones; it was a secretary, who gave through his pale-blue spectacles a glance at the ladies and a slight bow. He directed his gaze on the ambassador. The latter had a bunch of writings in his hand, which he turned over to him. He wrote in his carriage, fitted up for the purpose, and dealt with his correspondence on return.

"Have those copied, Stromer, in the official language," he said, in his smooth, yet authoritative voice. "The others in the red tape are to be sent off by special messenger. Let him take the first packet out of Dover, or hire a fishing cutter. No delay, mind!"

The secretary, bowing jerkily, vanished.

"Alas!" said the Countess Gorsewold, shaking her head, "I see that the great furnace of Europe is kept hot for the count of Koefeld to 'fry his own fish!'"

"Pugh! mine are such small fry!"

He embraced his wife in rather English fashion, and not at all French.

"White bait to catch whales!"

"I discharged myself of all the business for the present, since I saw your ladyship's carriage at the door. How is the rose of England who comes here to shed her bloom and perfume on the air?"

Now, as the countess' rouge had flaked off, and she used a particularly irritating patchouli, this might be supposed to prove that the bland and suave count followed his lady in saying sharp things. Luckily, while following the fashion, Amy could dispense with paint and fine flour, so she overlooked the remark.

Besides, she was reckoning up the advantages which the ambassador possessed, and to which he owed his exalted post. Count Koefeld was in the prime. Very fair, he dressed to accentuate the blondeness, but, at the same

"This blanched, prattling fool; she takes care that the half of the world which would not know what the other half did, should learn it! So, I am pictured as dragging behind Mr. Kean's triumphal pasteboard car! Fools, fools—as if I aimed so low as that!"

"Are you telling over a kindly speech to Count Koefeld?" inquired the visitor, hearing indistinctly.

"No, I let my heart speak to my Augustus!"

"Deceiver!" thought Lady Gorsewold. Then aloud: "Oh, when are you coming to one of my chocolate parties, dear?"

"It would be no new dish—I was surfeited, while the count was envoy at Madrid!"

"Oh, not for the thick soupy drink—for the company! I can have the Duchess Exshire there to meet you——"

"The Exshires?" repeated the lady, nonchalantly; "we are known already. As the ambassador of Scandinavia, my husband was invited to her at-homes at Mareshall, before we threw off our traveling wraps."

Amy was not invulnerable; she bit her lip and paused a little. Then she cried out, as there was a sound of somebody approaching:

"Oh, I am going to see our dear Koefeld!" She said to herself, spitefully:

"I wonder how he will bear gibing at his wife's craze for haunting Kean?"

CHAPTER XVIII.

A TORCH TO THE TAPER.

A gentleman in black entered by a side door as his master by the main double ones; it was a secretary, who gave through his pale-blue spectacles a glance at the ladies and a slight bow. He directed his gaze on the ambassador. The latter had a bunch of writings in his hand, which he turned over to him. He wrote in his carriage, fitted up for the purpose, and dealt with his correspondence on return.

"Have those copied, Stromer, in the official language," he said, in his smooth, yet authoritative voice. "The others in the red tape are to be sent off by special messenger. Let him take the first packet out of Dover, or hire a fishing cutter. No delay, mind!"

The secretary, bowing jerkily, vanished.

"Alas!" said the Countess Gorsewold, shaking her head, "I see that the great furnace of Europe is kept hot for the count of Koefeld to 'fry his own fish!'"

"Pugh! mine are such small fry!"

He embraced his wife in rather English fashion, and not at all French.

"White bait to catch whales!"

"I discharged myself of all the business for the present, since I saw your ladyship's carriage at the door. How is the rose of England who comes here to shed her bloom and perfume on the air?"

Now, as the countess' rouge had flaked off, and she used a particularly irritating patchouli, this might be supposed to prove that the bland and suave count followed his lady in saying sharp things. Luckily, while following the fashion, Amy could dispense with paint and fine flour, so she overlooked the remark.

Besides, she was reckoning up the advantages which the ambassador possessed, and to which he owed his exalted post. Count Koefeld was in the prime. Very fair, he dressed to accentuate the blondeness, but, at the same time, his stature and bearing could not render him effeminate, though in almost ladylike refinement and butterfly bedizenment. His shoes, of Spanish leather, had pink heels; his stockings were clocked; his knee-strings were many and of azure silk; his hair was done up like a peruke and bound with blue ribbon. His metal trimmings were silver only; and his diamonds were steel-blue. His muslin cuffs and neckerchief could not be whiter, and yet his hands seemed more so.

"What equanimity!" the Englishwoman said, clasping her hands. "Now, my husband never returned from a consultation with the government officials without being all awry. "You look to have come out of a wig-case!"

"I came out of a Tory cabinet, at least," laughed the Norseman. "Calling on the regent at his residence, I missed him, but I fell into a host of politicians besieging him in his privacy, and I had to run the gauntlet to escape with my portfolio unrifled!"

They all sat and lolled at ease.

"What a pity that in exchange for our bustling, restless, anxious existence, all for trifles, too," said La Gorsewold, "that we women cannot have a diplomatist's life!"

"You see," said the nobleman, nodding to his partner in all senses; "a proof to the contrary; madam is a *diplo·matiste*."

"Oh, no—I was not sent abroad to lie for my country!" returned Elena.

"Nor to flirt for it!" said the English countess, with her air of a maiden at prayer; "not like the Princess Lieven! Lord Gorsewold says that, nevertheless, wherever you go, you set the leaven working—you leave ball and hall in a ferment!"

The countess laughed; but she could swallow flattery without stint of this sort.

Amy had never been so well greeted for her second-hand wit.

"What I like, here, in your circle," continued she, "is that it incloses the well of truth!"

"Which is occupied, when you are here!" said Elena.

"For my part, here, between the harmless fire-dogs, I put off my official armor," subjoined the genteel man, rocking one leg over the other knee, to show off his small foot.

"Yes, but habit is second nature!" objected Amy.

"But, though I am candor itself, I am on my own hearthstone, so I must not speak out freely——"

"You look at me as if you meant to cut me up!"

"Not you, but your attire!"

Amy looked over her person complacently.

"Usually he criticises me," said Elena. "It is your turn, Amy, to stand fire! Faith, my lord, we have riddled everybody else but my companion—so, fire away!"

"Countess, your dress is cut shamefully! You select a shade which subdues your roseate color." Amy wore the red of a peony. "The red, red rose shows up excellently from a bed of primroses, but you set off by that sash of jonquil? fie! A severe, regular, non-exuberant beauty like yours requires a little touch of the startling, the *outré*, the extravagant!"

Amy, severe and classic, and lacking eccentricity!

"Am I not right—by my lady—or the glass?"

"I shall not look! I believe all that—you have not said about me!"

"No, I have shot all that was in my quiver."

"Then you must have left those politicians, collected at Carlton House, looking like pincushions!"

"Yes, Augustus is charming—he is like the bee, this diplomatist consort of mine—he leaves his sting in his foes, so that at home he is so inoffensive!"

"Betrayer!"

"No, no! she is like your secretary, I think," said the visitor. "She deciphers all your secrets, but tells none of them! But I am as afraid of your honey, my lord, as of your sting! I shall regret that I have not with me a fan like my lady's! It would be some way a shield!"

"Fan? indeed, it is a striking object!" said the count, riveting his eyes on the article.

"I never saw the like, and yet I am a collector of oriental curios," remarked Lady Gorsewold, determined to have that fan off her mind.

Elena was so pointedly aimed at that she had to explain.

"The fan," said she, "is the tribute of an Eastern rajah

to the crown. The court jeweler, in Pall Mall, rating it a
marvel of Benares work, borrowed it to have a part of the
intricate design copied. I saw it at the shop and ordered
it to be sent home. Then Mr. Longitharm, the senior
partner, discovered that his shopman ought not to have
sent it. The Prince of Wales, hearing of the blunder, in
the most gentlemanly spirit, insisted on your accepting it,
my lord——"

"The first I heard——"

"Yes, for I was carrying it about with me to show it
to you and ask if I might retain it!"

Amy watched the pair with "all the eyes in her head,"
but she could not discover any traces of unusual feeling.

"Oh, you must not reject a princely gift under such
circumstances! Unfortunately, I did not see the prince
this evening, or no doubt he would have mentioned the
occurrence!"

"I doubt that, since, to him, what is it but a trifle?"

"Let me examine—yes, it is exquisite work!" said the
Englishwoman, delighted at getting the fan, so far as it
kept it out of the count's hands, itching, she believed, to
dash it on the floor.

"You will know it again!" said the ambassador, at
last obtaining possession of it, smiling, and daring to give
it no more than a cursory inspection. "Lord Gorsewold
would like that—and he is a judge from having been
governor in your Indian possessions!"

"He prefers swords to fans! Besides, he is indifferent
to his collections; he is intent on other business——"

"Business?"

"The project to lay out whole streets of fine houses
from the Oxford road to Kilburn."

"Insane! Does he think that London will grow out
there?"

"Mr. Danby says——"

"Oh, is that anaconda encircling Gorsewold in his
coils?"

"Oh, they are friends, and friends do not entangle one
another——"

"The exchange floor is a neutral ground—no friendship!"

"Mr. Danby wants to buy our Lawmead mansionette,

as a present to his daughter, since Lord Newell only leases his town house!"

"Newell and Danby again? I thought that was all in the clouds!"

"It has come down—this little house is the price of Miss Alba Danby being reconciled with her father."

"And with Lord Newell? a prig, as you say! How you steadfast English waver!"

"Oh, he is prudent—he was waiting till this passing furore blew away!"

"What—has Miss Anna——"

"Alba——"

"Oh, Alba! the white name of premeditation!"

"Yes, they foresaw she would grow up into an alabaster figurine!" sneered the dark countess.

"Like to like," remarked the count, lightly. "Hence, the prince estimating her as a representative beauty, which she will be when he is crowned and can really hold a court!"

"Yes, you would know his intentions!"

"More likely that way—surely, courtly than politically; it's a pity."

"Never was there a fair woman since the one of Troy, so tossed about from one battledore to another! Granting that she has bewitched everybody, can one never learn who has bewitched her—lord, prince or actor?"

The Italian was ferocious.

"How animated you are, Elena!" said the count and the countess, under her breath.

"I confess that the marble statue irritates instead of calming, over against me, in her box! with a legion of smirking fops about her!"

"Oh, in the theatre? Now, I did not think to study her —to see if she comes to view the actor or the prince!"

"You would not learn by your study!" returned Amy, knowingly. "We Englishwomen look simple, but we are *sphlynes* when we have a riddle!"

"I am not good at guessing that kind of a riddle," said the count, stroking his flaxen mustache; "but, according to a rule very popular and hence founded on experience, Miss Elba Danby—— Alba, thanks! I am corrected.

Miss Alba will pair off with a dark cavalier, being the Blanchefleur of the troubadours!"

"Then the actor——" began Elena, as if relieved.

"Will carry her off from Newell, who is between colors, and the regent, who is German-fair!"

"I have it!" cried the Englishwoman. "Let us all go and inspect the trio, as if we had them under the microscope!"

"What trio?"

"The actor on the stage, and the prince and Miss Danby under our eyes, in the house."

"It will be a study under pleasant surroundings—to me, between you ladies!" answered the Scandinavian, smiling. "I only hope as a cap to the luxurious evening that Kean will play 'Othello.' "

"You enjoy that the most of his creations?"

"I do not think 'enjoy' is the word; it is as one looks into the Vesuvian crater—sublime, but causing apprehension as to what terror will be sprung upon you! All his conceptions are masterpieces in a square room of one's Louvre! In 'Othello' he performs an autopsy on the old style of acting, lingering in our North. The stilted progress, to a sepulchral march, to the tombs. I am haunted—I whom little clings to—pained and furrowed by the anguish intruding on my pressing labors, by his 'Oh, Desdemona, away! away!' "

Lady Elena stared at him, forgetting herself; was this placid man capable of appreciating the jealousy which Kean so admirably depicted?

"Oh," she exclaimed, to cover her astonishment, "what an actor—of the new school—was lost in you!"

"He is the leading actor already, on his own stage!" said Amy, encouragingly. "Let me see, as you are a Dane—it is 'Hamlet' you would most fairly represent, with his fullness of melancholy!"

"He mope and moralize!" replied the Italian woman, dubiously. "I think these sluggish men are to be dreaded like the glacier! They are fixed, to the eye, but they do move and so irresistibly that whole towns are, in time, overswept! Beware of the glacier, my dear!"

"Glacier?" laughed Koefeld. "It is a question of proportion. I am to a glacier a mere platter of Tortoni ices on a sponge-cake—I give at my worst a delicious chill!"

"And you are after that all through, delightful! But it is agreed; we make up a party to fill your box, count?"

"With pleasure!"

"Then mine is the luckiest star above!" cried the ripened hoyden, slapping the occasional table at her elbow. "Your box is——"

"On the stage—directly opposite the royal one!"

"I saw the old king in that, when I was a child!" said Amy, reflecting. "What a drawback to poor old George! not to see the greatest luminary of his age!"

"With us," continued Lady Elena, "you will be able to lose nothing of Kean's dumb show——"

"In which he is so tremendous!" supplemented the count. "It is a very, very difficult art to evince feeling without uttering a syllable—to throw love into a bosom with a glance, to convey a warning, a caution or advice in gesture!"

In spite of his command, he did not dare to let his wife catch his eyes; it would have betrayed him. Betrayed what? That he was a glacier, like those over Hecla—veiling, and thinly, the volcano.

"Which character is most likely to bring the prince to the theatre?" asked Countess Gorsewold, loyally.

"Oh, the prince?" responded Koefeld, a little nettled. "One of the horrifying—'Shylock' or 'Sir Giles'—a sated Sardanapalus—he must be frightened into emotion, even into pleasure!"

His countess averted her eyes now; they would have darted on his scathing look. The pretty, stupid woman perceived this.

"La!" thought she. "Am I on the wrong tack? Is she enamored of the prince?" Then aloud she cried, as in ecstasy, "to see his effulgency nigh—to have the dust cast up from his robe; to catch at the feather in his cap!"

Her extravagance was too great—it no longer made either of the couple smile.

"I am sorry you are raised to the highest power of enthusiasm," stated Koefeld, with coldness, "for I cannot outdo that. I should have liked, though, to have added to your pleasure of anticipation by a foretaste, immediately! You might see your English Roscius nearer even than from our box on the stage!"

Both looked at him, with growing fear that something boded uncommon to the quiescent gentleman.

"Nearer? Oh, how, when, where?"

"One question at a time! Why, here! soon, and across our dinner table!"

The two stared as if he had gone mad.

"Yes, it is not necromancy," resumed he, smiling easily. "A mutual friend—you can fill in the blank!—G—— P. of W., suggested that, as a Dane, I could help Mr. Kean to perfect his exposition of our mumchance prince! and I wrote to the tragedian, placing my local knowledge at his disposition."

Lady Elena had closed her lips tightly and her look was of incredulity and vague wistfulness. Her companion was simply astounded.

"My lord, have you invited that personage—personage—here, without notifying me?" the hostess sternly demanded.

"Where would be the surprise? Half London would fast for a month for the same 'treat,' as the English say, so drolly. I wrote Mr. Kean what my dinner hour was. I know he can dine with celebrities every day, from the primate, who told a mutual friend that his 'Beverley' was as good as a sermon against the ruling vice; but I expect he will come."

He spoke with complete conviction.

"For the sake of your *chef?*" suggested the Englishwoman, gayly.

"For the sake of the host!" said the countess, politely.

"For the sake of the hostess!" put in Lady Gorsewold, unable to resist the shot.

"If I had known it, I should have put in the *post scriptum* that Lady Gorsewold would attend—and, then, there would not be a vacant chair!" said the foreigner, with even more politeness and venom.

He had managed to put both his hearers on hot coals.

"But, at dinner!" repeated his wife, frowning. "How will he sit at table who is, I suppose, to talk business, and theatrical business at that, with your lordship?"

"Oh it is that we of the North are barbarians. The

etiquette of King Louis XIV. receiving Molière as his gentleman-in-waiting because, as an actor, he could not be in the royal presence, is unknown to us as well as your own regarding those whom you ask in to entertain. I honor art too much to degrade its liegemen. Only once in an age have we Canova, Girodet, Chénier, and it is not derogation to banquet such gifted mortals. Though not born in the purple, they shall wear it and lock arms with those swaddled in it. They should share our wine and company on perfect equality. Otherwise, the future would say we mistrusted them and showed our blindness. Once in a lifetime, I say, and we get our laugh out of the meeting!"

"Laugh at Kean? You are a barbarian!" said Lady Gorsewold. "You deserve to have that fan broken across your head!"

"All this does not explain to me, my lord," persisted Elena, "how you have, without my knowledge, invited even a 'uniquety' to my table!"

"It is a surprise!" said Amy, the peacemaker, in a peacemaker's voice, partial to both sides.

"Nay, it is a ruse!" broke in Count Koefeld, making a palpable sign to his wife that this was an old story between them, if new to their confidant.

"A ruse?" cried the latter.

"Diplomatic! But it is a secret confided to two who are as one. You are similarly monuments of discretion and silence. My lady is aware that it is my especial mission to court the favor of the future ruler of England. He is surrounded by watches—or spies, to use a strong word. So we have our important confabulations at the least expected moments and places. Our carriages cross; we play the same wheel of fortune at Soho House; we go out to sea from Brighton on the same small sailing vessel—in a word, we meet, and no one could have divined that we executed the draft of treaty, and so forth. So I give a dinner to Mr. Kean, the reigning favorite, and I am bound to invite his arch-patron, the arbiter of elegance! The company have ears but for the great tragedian, and the prince and I draw up the pre-liminaries of an international paper! Ladies, you have exposed the whole bag of tricks!" and he made the gesture of the conjurer drawing off the sheet from the globe of goldfish.

"Dear me! you use a Kean as a cover!" sighed Lady Gorsewold.

"Since I cannot discuss problems with the pro-king in the theatre circle, I must do so in my family ditto! Eh, my lady?"

Elena said nothing. Was this quiet plotter placing her between the two guests as if they were touchstones?

"The prince and Mr. Kean!" exclaimed the other lady, overjoyed. "'I am done on both sides!' as my husband said when the new cook served up not only a superb Gascony tunny but a splendid Torbay turbot!"

The Scandinavian smiled on this simile, went over to his wife, and said to her alone:

"Elena, are you not pleased by this double attraction? All will point to it as the dinner of the season!"

"Yes, I admire royalty and the royalty of genius as much as, like all my sex, I detest baseness, cowardice and false play!"

"Oh, Mr. Kean," returned the other, deliberately mistaking her trend; "Mr. Kean is not of base descent! He is no coward, since he, without early education, fears not to sit at the highest part of the table; and he is not a false player!"

A respectful, and yet hurried knock at the door, told that a pressing communication had come for the master. Indeed, the steward entered on being bid, with some haste. A letter had come "post, posthaste!" for his lord. The ladies assented to the interruption, Amy, from gladness at any pretext to prevent the outbreak spoiling her new brilliant prospect of a notable evening, and Elena from simple curiosity to view what events portended.

The letter having passed to the count, he read, after a glance, the whole offhand:

"MY LORD COUNT: I am deeply regretful to reply that I cannot accept your favoring invitation, as I am bound by a promise to read a certain play, and not to do so might affect the future of a promising author. Be so good, my lord, therefore, as to present my sorrowful regards to the Countess of Koefeld for disappointing her guests, if I may be so arrogant as to use the word 'disappointment.' "

Elena breathed in relief.

"He is a coward!" thought the man. "He shrinks from the impudence of defiling my board! the actor not coming, the prince would also excuse himself, or stay only temporarily, if arrived at all."

"What a mishap!" moaned Lady Gorsewold, dabbing her eyes with her handkerchief.

"Vexation!" ejaculated the host, looking at his wife, steadily. "A singular era when the poets' echo refuses foreign ministers' invitations to dinner—while not, you will observe, Lady Gorsewold, with any desire to hear him reiterate his fooleries!"

"I—I think it is only an excuse for the time—not a flat refusal!" stammered Amy.

"Oh, I know what a snub is, though it is not diplomatic, but very plain English. I am used to less blunt tones, however, for three times I have tried to find a wife for—for one who shall be nameless!"

"I should assume from the reply," observed Lady Koefeld, as if debating a subject without any sympathy, "that your invitation was a trifle haughty and not any too diplomatic!"

Amy fidgetted—the stupid and tetchy persons seemed bent on quarreling, and the pin point scratching her was that she could not see what they were wrathful about. She hoped that if they must come to a rupture, they would let her have their box to herself—she would soon fill it with her friends!

In the embarrassing pause, the steward, as if he divined stormy weather was brewing, and sought to throw a diversion—firebrand or handful of snow on the spark, called out:

"His Royal Highness the Prince Regent!"

CHAPTER XIX.

The prince regent, who was eventually to succeed an inane father by his own inane self, with all his defects, never could be blamed for not "dressing his part."

He came in the difficult line of a guest to the "star" feature of the evening. To be Augustus and Mecænas in one is a burden. It was impolite to outshine the tragedian, and yet he was bound to continue, as he thought, to enchant the Countess of Koefeld. So he had been as trying to his master of the wardrobe as a fashionable actor.

All was superfine upon him without being over-expensive. Thanks to his commanding person, not yet given to *embonpoint*, he carried his trappings easily and yet with showiness. In another time, his would have been the theatrical costume, but since the Restoration and after the somber interval of William and Mary, dress was in the front again.

So he wore a coat of mixed silk, that is, with changeable effect; spangled buttonholes worked with gold thread, buttons of cut stones, and arabesque braid widely along the seams. This, parted to disclose a blush rose-colored waistcoat, not only worked with needle but covered with a net, fine drawn, so as to seem raised on the ground. The velvet breeches were tight as wax melted and ironed on, while the silk stockings were pulled into place like a dancer's tights. With an idea of equipoise, he wore two watches, and as each had its quota of charms, amulets, keepsakes, the ornaments rattled almost like the bells on a dray horse. His head was powdered so that he spread fine dust. His feet were no longer shapely and elegant, but his shoe buckles defeated scrutiny by their enormous size.

Thanks to the two repeaters, George was more than punctual. He had tripped with the smile and carriage of

a herald, as if Scandinavia House was to be gladdened
with news.

"Now, by my George!" he exclaimed, in his full voice,
laughing without waiting for the salutations to be cere-
moniously exhausted, "here is a marvelous thing!" He
rapidly ran his eyes over the trio. "Your ladyship will
overlook my running in like a skipjack on St. James'
lake; but I am the bearer of news!"

They were stupefied and began to show some indefinite
eagerness. He always liked his being the center of a
group. He paused with intent to enjoy the inquiring
looks.

"While I speak, there is running about London streets
the funniest venture, without any mask either, that ever
King Lud knew!"

"We certainly overlook the manner of the announcement," replied Lady Koefeld, exchanging a glance with
her husband, "but only on condition, since one may make
conditions with a prince coming as errand-runner, that
your news is worth the suspense!"

"It being news," began Count Koefeld, sincerely puzzled.

"Now what can he have learned that I know not?"
mumbled Amy, distressed as at a rival scandalizer
springing up in her own field.

"So, so, you are not informed!" chuckled the prince,
muttering: "I have outrun even her long tongue! Well,
I am pressed to notify you. It is too rich to preserve!
Like the king in the fable—of the ass' ears—I am fain
to go whisper it to the rushes on the Serpentine rather
than hug it close! You all know Jessamy, Lord Newell?"

"Of tragic memory? Yes; we Danes are not romantic
save in a dreamy way, but I believe we should have made
a drama of that affair; how he came into his brother's fortune and title so oddly!" remarked the man of the North.

"I know what is coming! Mr. Danby has bought our
house—and all being smooth with the young couple,
Newell will marry the heiress!"

"Danby, like a father, would approve of that step, but
I will be expatriated if he would of the actual one! If
there is any marriage, it is not yet! A pity, too," said he,

with a vague touch of real feeling, "since Miss Alba of the Danbies seems sweet as honey laurel——"

"And as dangerous to the silly sheep!" quickly rejoined Elena.

"Dangerous?" repeated her lord, surprised at her tartness.

"To be sure; a mountain sheeted with gold is as dangerous as one clad in ice—is she not cold as one and rich as the other?"

"Ice melts, gold dissolves!" said the messenger. "Egad, both run unstable as water!"

"Run?" repeated all three, from the emphasis he laid on the sinister word.

"And still running!"

"An elopement! What do they want to elope for, when all is repaired?" cried Amy.

"Oh, if an elopement, it is not with her official candidate! What need of that? the families thick as—flies in the sugar-bowl. Newell orders the furniture for the house his father-in-law buys; the paint is mixing and the goldfoil pounded—and he renews his equipages, his household——"

"And his notes—of hand!" insinuated Koefeld, proud as a foreigner to show his acquaintance with the local under-world.

"Yes, Newell renovated all. Not good taste in an ancient stock. The young gentlemen did not do things by half, and he has been 'done' wholly!"

"Would your highness be explicit?" sharply said the Countess·Koefeld.

"Plainly, the wedding *cortège*, metaphorically, comes to the door of Danby House for the bride of the Newell— the doors are open, but out comes the word that the bird has fled—escaped off! The outcome out-staggers the Danby income!" and the relater barely suppressed hearty laughter. "She, this Miss Alba the glaringly white, was not really at Danby at all, but at an aunt's, Mrs. Powis——"

"The Red House at Chelsea Reach?" interpolated the know-all of Gorsewold.

"No doubt; with rooms overhanging the river!"

"Horror! How can you laugh, my lord!" said Amy,

with true feeling. "A death by drowning is so cold, and one looks such a figure. Besides, to drown there, with the soap-boiling works below, at Putney!"

"You mean that the young lady threw herself in, to avoid persecution!" said Koefeld, affected, by his nature, by a watery and doleful catastrophe. "One so young and fair! And yet did not one of your peers, whose river-house was there, complain of the murderous monotony of the river running, running, running like the river of time?"

"She was possessed by her favorite actor!" broke in Elena, with contempt for her husband's German-like re-pining for this kind of submissive death. "She tried to emulate the Ophelia of 'Hamlet'!"

Koefeld turned on her, and in a whisper, in Italian, spite of rudeness, said:

"It is you who are mad! Don't you know the brand on this royal race? Do you speak of madness and suicide to one in whose house the monarch's sword of Damocles has been for three generations suspended?"

No one understood, but they saw by the flush on the countess' cheek that she stood reproved; had the executioner's iron seared her the effect of shame could not be more tangible.

But the representative of the stricken house did not appear to remark the episode; on the contrary, no one could be more unconcerned, for he hummed, more less appropriately, the air in vogue: "Water parted from the sea!"

Countess Amy looked around, with absurd horror, saying:

"To think that a gentleman with a heart like his highness' should draw sport from such a source as that!"

The prince became aware that he had carried his joke too far.

"I am not laughing at the poor singer of the willow song drowning; but at the idea that she was such a ninny! I believe that she may have jumped out of the window toward the running stream, but that she chose her moment well! Was it not an old house like that, on the upper river, Ann Bullen leaped into King Henry Tudor's arms, for which feat a barge was moored under her balcony? Well, imagine a skiff and a man with open arms."

"Ah!" sighed Amy, relieved. "If there were arms to catch——"

"For the running of the river suggests whither it runs," resumed the regent, "which is to the sea and, thinking of the sea, a voyage occurs. Residence in England would not be possible after such an escapade. Now, a sea trip, to those who do not shrink from Neptune's raw breath, is alleviated by a companion in the misery! Hence, she was wise to choose a shipmate. And little as I know of Miss Danby, for her papa is a curmudgeon about his chief treasure! I answer for it that this shipmate will not let her be lost on the briny!"

"Oh, being accompanied," said Countess Gorsewold, as if at ease now. "What did you say his name was?"

"His name is most illustrious in our annals; his title a very strong one to popular acclamation; his 'parts,' as they used to say, sound if theatrical!" and he boisterously laughed again.

"I am on the rack!" said Count Koefeld, watching both prince and his wife, who added:

"And I am on the fire!" as to out-Herod her friend's extravagance.

"But I am not blaming his highness for shielding this black sheep, perhaps belonging to his own fold! he would no longer be his friend, this abductor of the heiress, but he may have been!"

George received this stab with his usual composure.

"All my friends are not worth my shielding!" he replied. "Who is not liable to be deceived by a bosom friend? I am not attacking, because I repeat, I no more attack gallants than I do women, for I should very justly get the worst of it. Ladies, the person accused of taking off the Danby prize and assisting her in her flight to avoid this indefatigable Newell, holds a name—my star and garter! in everybody's mouth! His head is crowned —before mine! which God forbid!"

Everybody loyally bowed; but Elena quickly said:

"Since, happily, your highness is not concerned in this bold scandal, why this pother about it? Such trifles are seen every day, even in England the placid; a woman of

means putting the sea between her and her peppery papa
and her more incensed espoused one—with a gallant preferred. Out with the name! One likes the serpents in
our social snakehouse to be labeled, so that we at least
may know what stung us!"

Her eyes shone too brightly; her attitude was too excited; she was insufferably proud that the prince came,
as if the tie between them were undetachable and irresistible.

"Well all theatre-goers, can you not guess what rose
sunlike in the garden where previously the silly flowers
took the gardener with his lantern for Aurora?"

"Upon my soul, if your royal highness, like the Kem-
ble family, talks blank verse of such everyday matters as
a runaway match, we shall expect him to be numbered
among royal authors!"

"Oh, this is a farce!" returned the prince.

The Northman glanced at his wife and noticed that
she and her confidante were hushed, but not because they
did not more than suspect. He coughed dryly, as one who
has a bitter taste, and said, incisively:

"Since we are appealed to as playgoers, why, here goes!
My shot is at the Rochester of our era—the cedar to
whom the others are shrubs! The levanter with Miss
Danby would be Edmund Kean!"

All repeated the name as if only now they dared
breathe it.

"How shockingly ridiculous!" ejaculated Amy.

"Impossible!" cried her companion.

"I see nothing ridiculous in that, and it is far from
impossible!" observed the nobleman, as if lightened in his
mind. "On the contrary, it explains away his declining
my invitation, for I believe that only a lady in the case
and an affair of this importance would deprive him of
the honor of his highness' company and these others, for
he must for the novelty enjoy being a guest, and not the
merrymaker for the guests!"

Elena shook her head, wrestling unsuccessfully with
the question why her husband should have made Kean
an honorable guest, when he was a stickler in etiquette
and patrician to the backbone.

"Still," continued the Dane, "I am delighted that it

has turned out thus. If Mr. Kean had come, instead of his refusal, and next day the abduction had been noised about, the whole world would have it that we lent ourselves to it as a blind——"

"We?" exclaimed Lady Koefeld, with blazing eyes.

"We; that is you, to amicably aid Miss Danby, who has been presented to you; and I, to aid Mr. Kean, whom, you see, for his talent, I regard as equal of any man living!"

"Which would have combined Scandinavia and scandal," said the visitor, mirthfully, without one being able to tell if he were simple or astute. "Besides, I should be enmeshed in all this, for it would be hinted that the count kindly aided me, too, in the matter!"

"Why should your highness interfere?" asked the countess, forgetting that "royals" ought not to be questioned.

"Mr. Kean is my ward, in a measure! But we have escaped all this imbroglia, which would have involved the representative of a beloved foreign power! So let us rejoice that there will be no difference and that peace will preside at your board."

"You think, with me, that Mr. Kean's excusing himself relieved us of a dilemma?" observed the count.

"I think that this slap in the face to Lord Newell, who is doing nothing more than acting up to a family contract, makes Mr. Kean an enemy of public morality!"

George preaching morality! But no one smiled.

"As for the misguided young minx, she will do well to exile herself, since this shows that, however rich a young woman may be, she cannot be applauded if she jilt a noble and run off with a player! I should not be amazed if, in going howeward, I saw half London—all the houses of the married with marriageable daughters—illuminated, as on my birthday anniversary!"

He took snuff rapturously.

"This Faublas of your stage was formidable?" asked Koefeld.

"Your highness' surmise of the connubial rejoicing seems to imply that this actor had really a following of worshipers, among whom were similarly the blue-blooded and the plebeian!"

"Well, he was at such an altitude that he may have stooped to lift some of them. Oh, I understand what an ennobler art is! when it gives its *accolade,* the artist becomes a knight of an enviable select order. In a thousand years, its veritable member can be counted within a hundred. I shall be favored if, by and by, should I be allowed the fag-end of a reign, it is still illuminated by the sheen of Edmund Kean!"

He said this quite grandly and sincerely. The count was perplexed; for his lady took the eulogy so coolly that it was unfair to imagine any longer that she was infatuated with the tragedian; in that case, was she so with his patron?

"I see!" said the Northerner. "I see the future! All will be forgiven the amusement-monger if, having married the fair fugitive and returning with his fresh American laurels thick upon him, he finds on the throne his first bepraiser! Meanwhile, as Hamlet was, I think, a shade jealous of the First Player, as an actor off the stage himself——"

"Oh, count! But go on—this is funny!"

"Well, did not that prince write up the part for the player as Cibber 'improved' Shakespeare? the part in 'the Mousetrap'?"

"Gracious! do you assert that I suggested his running off with Miss Danby, to secure that competence without which an artist is a Rembrandt hoarding in a garret, instead of a Rubens courting it as an ambassador, and able to give hospitality to a Queen Marie de Medicis?"

"I believe that your highness would favor lovers, as artistes!"

"Upon my royal word, this time, I do not know whether the pair would be crossing the Channel, or the country, to reach a packet at Falmouth or Liverpool!"

"Why America?"

"Because, if there is one thing the sanguine, sallow Americans adore above art itself, it is the English blonde!"

"My lord must not take me there!" interposed Amy, quickly.

"Bravo! I see your highness makes gayety out of all

matters! To the table, where we will drink the fleeing pair *'bon voyage'!*"

But he had not taken one step toward the door, when it was opened and the footman appearing, announced:

"Mr. Edward Kean!"

"Edmund, you sloven!" muttered the prince, with mock horror. "Such is fame—to have your name wrong! when it ought to be 'familiar in household mouths as gospel words'!"

But he was as astonished as the rest.

"A tangled skein! That snow-blooded Northman suspects something. What an odd pair it is—Othello and Desdemona interchanged! But, a fig! it is the Italian who is more likely to use the stiletto!"

CHAPTER XX.

The gentleman, who presented himself with the most befitting ease and in elevated style, was attired in the climax of fashion, to which he contributed his note. He wore, as though accustomed to the weapon-ornament all his life, a dress-sword—Garrick's bequest.

This arrival took the royal hand, held out spontaneously to him, as one gentleman takes another's where both are guests. It was plain that George was, here, ostensibly the privileged guest.

Kean's bow to the ladies was agreeable to see; he gave the rotund English countess a mirthful glance, all to herself, and said to the host:

"My lord, I should not come, but I venture to hope that you would excuse the contradiction between my note of apology and my presence. But an unforeseen circumstance changed my set course."

The prince looked at the others as much as to say: "There was something at the bottom of my budget, after all!" Then to himself he said:

"This pupil of mine is a startler to his tutor! Is he more clever than his master?"

"This happening makes my step a duty—moves it as by a law, and I must bend to it."

"A cool devil!" thought Koefeld. "If he has the young lady on the porch ready to introduce here, then he never could be making eyes at my wife."

Leaving the count to speak confidentially with his wife, the actor turned to the prince and said, whimsically:

" 'Tell me how Wales was made so happy as to inherit such a haven?' "

As this professional quotation entirely threw the others off their guard, the other replied in a low voice:

"Are you pirating, rogue? 'Think you how dangerous it is to jut upon a prince's right!' "

"Right? Ho, ho! Have you gone so far——"

But he could inquire no more as the count had left his wife's side.

"I own, Mr. Kean, that I no longer awaited you. Firstly, on account of the note of declination, and, then, because of news about the circumstance, I suppose—already circulated by irreproachable authority."

"My lord," without following his eye, indicating the talebearer, "it is precisely the calumny set afloat which pushed me hither. Exaggerated, I grant it has some consistency."

"Ah!" exclaimed Countess Amy, with stress.

Evidently, by the knowing look which Kean honored her with, he set down the tattling to her, which caused the others to laugh.

"I am in the position," continued the actor so gravely as to check the laughter, "in order to clear fair fame— of desiring to prove an alibi. Now, an alibi to be credited must be upheld by inexpugnable witnesses. Such are present. Your royal highness, your lordship, and these ladies. The Count of Koefeld can testify that he invited me to dine and that I punctually came, which will stifle the accusation of my quitting the town at no notice."

"We——"

"Allow me, first. Let me avouch for what is awkward, cruelly awkward. Miss Danby has called at my lodgings."

Everybody frowned and looked aghast.

"Miss Danby at your Southampton street lodgings!" repeated Amy, looking aside at her friend.

"I see you know that I enjoy the favor of keeping the suit tenanted by David Garrick. Modestly, Miss Danby came by public chair, found me out, and left a formal note, written while I was at the playhouse on business. A spy who saw her on the Strand watched her enter, but did not have the patience to wait for her speedy coming-forth alone. That is the slender base for a report——"

"Base altogether!" cried George. "When I am ruler in fact, I shall have the laws against *scandalum magnum* strictly enforced."

The ladies smiled at his indignation.

"We must suppress this story," said he, in continuation, with a headlong fire not often his. "Let us do something clearly out of the possibilities——"

"My prince, Miss Danby will never carry out her part of the transaction."

"Thereupon, there being precedents—and you might wed a countess if you were willing, to my knowledge— why not match to the bliss of all? If Mr. Danby is too offish to give his daughter away, I will play the papa with rapture."

"This speaker is fond of him," thought Lady Elena, with that monopolizing jealousy of some women, not allowing the ensnared one to have even a male friend.

"Pardon me," said the visitor, with deep feeling, his gaze eloquent with gratitude to the offerer of great social boon. "As the young lady's reputation must be unblemished as far as I am concerned, and it is· prematrue, to put it midlly, to stop the mouths of scurrilous with a marriage announcement, I` prefer for the time being, while thanking your highness for the lordly compliment, to act no longer as the Spouter——"

"Oh, fie! confound the word!"

"It is a piquant title. But act as your compeer, my lord count. I have hit upon another method of repaying your complimentary placing of me at your board, by letting you back up my confirmation of her impeccable honor and mine own. One honorable act for another."

"By Jupiter!· this is another Edmund the Confessor!" observed the prince, excellent in intention, if not exact.

"Your justification in our hands?" took up Koefeld. "Sir, you must be innocent—or the other thing. If the former, your straightforward denial ought to be ample."

Kean shook his head sadly.

"Your lordship does not know us thoroughly yet, I fear. Do you say that my denial will be enough? As a notable, I am on a pedestal—but, as an actor, on the pillory—everybody feels that he does not sully his hand in throwing mud at me. Ah, what suppositions will be proclaimed. There are leprous managers who would pay richly to fan such a charge against their leading man, so as to have him jammed in a mob between his passage from courtroom to playhouse. My friends will believe when I hurl forth the lie. For I have many—some lofty, some lowly, but all true men alike, bless them! But it will have no weight for them who see in me just a polished Jack Pudding—Mr. Punch, with Gloster's royal hunch and his voice modulated not to squeak! Therefore the repudiation must come out of a mouth none dare deny, from a person whose high position over all Europe and his own stainless character will communicate trust, respect and credence."

The prince and the count looked at each other—thinking that the other was meant. Countess Gorsewold fixed her eyes on her friend, on seeing that the tragedian finished his survey with letting his gaze rest on her searchingly.

"For my part," said the gushing Englishwoman, "down goes my name to the subscription—the alibi which his highness can offer——"

"My dear lady," interposed the prince, "down goes my name to any subscription, too, as I would it could be for gold. It is still dilly-dally in the Lords and shilly-shally in the Commons about my settlement—to which I prefer a settlement in some far-off colony—more substantial footing, my friends. I owe Mr. Kean very, much distraction.

"The other day he found me on perdition's verge: dying of spite for having lost too heavily at Lady Caerbodyn's rooms. My dear Edmund dropped in and revived me with the funniest recitation out of jail! a song told in gesture! ha, ha, ha! I passed an hour which would have been misery in enchanting mirth. I forgot the cool thousand wasted in that hades!"

"I should say that, in Hades, it would not be a cool thousand," Kean said, unable to resist the quip.

"You see," whispered the royal guest to the hostess, "he is not guilty. Punning on the precipice!"

"We are forgetting that poor Miss Danby on the rack!" she uttered loudly, seeing that her husband slightly resented this familiarity of the prince in using a low tone.

"Not I!" replied Kean, who had extracted a folded half sheet of writing paper from the fancy shagreen wallet in which gentlemen carried bank notes to meet the apparition of cards. "I beg to select as my redressor," he said, with dignity and some tenderness of appeal, "the Countess of Koefeld—she may readily be so, after having cast her eyes on this hurried scrawl."

"What is this artful Lothario aiming at?" marveled George.

The countess looked her indefinable surprise.

"Read it out for the general enlightenment," said her mate, with slight sarcasm; "it will gain by your rendition."

Kean did not seem disturbed by this fling. Turning courteously to the reprover, he suavely but firmly rejoined:

"Your lordship will pardon me, but only to women can be confided a secret on which depends the happiness, the future and the existence, possibly, of another woman. Men's hearts do not comprehend some delicate mysteries. Allow me to divulge this solely to her ladyship as Miss Danby's confidence. Were it my secret, my lord and my prince, I should necessarily unfold it in the day-glare, letting it shine in the sun and enlighten all eyes. All I beseech is that the lady shall not reveal it. It will suffice, if ever slander raises its head and hisses in her hearing, she should cry out:

"'Mr. Kean had nothing to do with Miss Danby's disappearance!' All will believe you!"

He bowed, presenting the paper, while his voice was imposing with the certainty of being gratified.

Elena was embarrassed; she wished to be the arbitress in all social matters, but it was magnificent to have at her decision the fate of a rich heiress like the Danby girl.

"How now?" interrupted the chief guest, only half playfully. "Am I not what was, in old parlance, chief justicer of the realm? Does not my rank give me some claim to share this confidence?"

"My lord, the confessional does not open to the king—still less a lady's jewel casket, in which are her private letters! Before a lady's secret all men are equal. Count, I renew my entreaty to let your lady be supreme arbitress!"

"I see no objection, Mr. Kean," was the calm reply. "As long as the lady is not too engaged to undertake such business, and if you really attach so much importance to it as appears."

Clearly, a millionaire's daughter and an actor, however celebrated, very slightly appealed to the man from the snowy North when their characters were at stake.

"Does the lady ratify the count's favor?"

Elena quivered under his searching eye.

Hesitatingly, they heard her broken voice: "If the young lady had asked me——"

"She? That kind of woman does not ask favors of any one! A stricken deer runs not to the surgeon, but into the thicket! Innocence is her sole buckler; but, for my part——"

"Oh, since it is to protect the great actor——"

"Their greatest, Elena," said Koefeld, in a pretendedly confidential voice.

"Count, let me whisper!" said Amy, to give time for this hitch to be the disentangled, and taking the Scandinavian by the arm in her free way, "let your wife learn the secret. She is no woman and you no inveigler of state, if you will not soon know it!"

The prince took the count's other arm and said:

"And then, count, as a good fellow, let me in, too, unless the communication of marital confidence is counter to your cabinet's private instructions!"

Left without supporters, the perplexed countess said, guardedly:

"You may show me the note she penned in your absence, since merely my reading it may justify you."

Kean gave her the paper; it was in a lady's hand, large, sprawling, covering all the side.

Mr Kean—
  Dear Sir: I lose the pleasure of finding you at home. As my entire fortune may depend on this interview I seek, I beg to hope that I shall be more fortunate on another trial. Ever remembering that I owe my life to you, I trust to be your debtor still more
      Your very respectful and already obliged servant,
                                      Alba Danby

"It is nothing—or much!" said the doubting reader. "How does she owe you anything?"

"Oh, that was printed in the news-sheets. I had the

luck to aid her materially. A—a rocket was let off prematurely at the Newell's *fête*——"

"Prevaricator!" said the lady, showing she knew of the first ocurrence, and to show she also knew the second, she went on quietly: "The Newells are ill-fated. This present holder of the title fell out of his chair, in the street, in his eagerness to thank you for the service you indirectly did him."

"I do Newell a service!" raising his brows.

"Had you drawn his brother from the fire instead of Miss Danby——"

"There was no time to draw a line!"

"Well, Miss Danby pursued by Lord Newell's hate, as you are by the same, seeks you to defend her from him?"

"She does not say so, there!"

"Has she or has she not disappeared between your door and her father's?"

"It I thought that, I should not be at your ladyship's party."

"Then she is at freedom to keep her next appointment."

"I hope so, only she cannot make an appointment, while I can, under narrow limits, with your help, lady!"

"Help of mine? Well, what reply did you leave her in case of her coming again while you are out?"

Kean looked around furtively. Between the prince and the garrulous countess the poor Scandinavian was being talked into a dumb show. The pair could not have served the actor more faithfully had this been preconcerted.

"Answer! In a vital matter one must foresee and prepare for all, eh?"

She did not even nod; this sudden taking her into his confidence was surprising, but to claim her assistance so unblushingly was consternation.

"Note for note, I left a line—of which you have the rough draft on the back of hers, there! Turn it and you can read. Pray do so."

She thought this Englishman eccentric, very.

She looked on the other side of the paper. Her surprise grew.

"As my dwelling is besieged," he continued, "and Miss Danby cannot discuss with me there, I have but the theatre as neutral ground to confer at. As she can go to her box without comment, and to yours, if you will kindly invite her, nothing prevents her from honoring me with her presence in my suite, to which a ready usher will show her, and your ladyship, if you will be her chaperon! Forefeeling that this meeting is of the utmost importance to her welfare, her happiness and her future life, I beg your ladyship to aid me in this unique step."

There was a long pause.

"Does silence give the usual?" demanded he, with an insinuating smile.

"He's in love, and deeply, with that young *blondetta!*" she mused. "It will be a task to play him off against the prince, and rouse that sated voluptuary's jealousy!"

It was time; she returned him the paper, saying coldly:

"There is your—that is, the lady's note!"

He took the paper and tucked it away as if it had filled its mission and was no longer of value. He spoke aloud: "A thousand thanks!"

He bowed to the others, and, as if it was all over, forgetting the past, he made as if to go out. But the count threw himself in the way with hurt pride and wonder, and said to his wife:

"Your verdict, Elena?"

Lady Gorsewold and the prince looked hard at the other three, and the man muttered:

"Oh, that Kean! if he has hoodwinked my lady, he is very clever—deuced!"

"I declare," slowly said the countess, as if on her oath, "that it must be wrongfully that Mr. Kean was accused of abducting Miss Danby!"

Kean bowed lowly to her and smiled triumphantly.

"Stop, stop!" interrupted the count; "you need not run away to spread that disclaimer! We will relate it to the full table, and not a nook or corner of London will be ignorant of it to-morrow!"

"For Mr. Kean, I will leave early and disseminate it!" said the obliging Amy.

"And I!" added the royal guest, "if permitted!"

"Nothing of the kind!" declared Koefeld. "We must keep you together as long as possible in order to repay

Mr. Kean for the little charade of which only the countess knows the key."

"Oh, you could not enjoy your regale if under mystification!" the countess hastened to say. She smilingly questioned the actor, who bowed. He considered that he had won her to complicity, and had confidence in her tact.

"It is a stage secret!" said she, with admirable feigned mystery; "Miss Danby, as I take it, is stage-struck!"

"The Kean epidemic!" said the prince.

"We all have a stroke!" said Amy, leering at the tragedian.

"Oh, generally," went on Lady Koefeld, quickly. "She wishes to go on the stage!"

"It is pardonable," said her friend, "for I have been itching to do the same since I saw 'Lady Constance' and 'The Mourning Bride!'" sighing and rolling her eyes as if she were a blighted being.

"And I approve," added George; "for a prince is a comedian from his pap to his night-posset."

"In plain words, outlawed by her father, discarding Lord Newell, Miss Danby, being naturally fitted to shine, intends going on the stage."

Kean drew a long breath, but thought that the speaker would make the greatest mark on that field for duplicity.

"This Lady Elena is a marvel! the man whom she deludes will go down into the family vault unknowing he was led by the nose!"

"Probably because she has no birth!" continued the count. "I no not see any other outlet for a handsome, accomplished young woman in this country. Meanwhile, awaiting your advice and your lessons, Mr. Kean, since your charade is given away—let us to the table!"

"To the table!"

"I promise you," continued the ambassador, "to remove the last scruple about our ways being outlandish, and that as soon as we come to the cordials and the cigars, we shall not push back our chairs to the wall to make room for 'Mr. Kean to astonish the guest of the evening and the honorable company!'"

"Spite of that," resumed the prince, "as the guest who has by etiquette ousted the true hero of the night, or true knight among heroes, from his due place, I shall present him with the honorary snuffbox, according to our custom!"

So, with delicacy, Kean happened to "make play" for a countenance with his snuffbox, the speaker exchanged with him, so that he was the better by a work of Indian art in filigree, microscopically fine, like that Indian fan.

"But you will lose nothing, count! No one overdoes me in commendation of the player's excellence in his art; but I only do him justice in rating him without a peer as table companion!"

The prince waived any privilege and let Kean take in Lady Koefeld, he contenting himself with Countess Gorsewold, radiant with pride. The Scandinavian sage followed, thinking to himself:

"I do not understand these English in their love-making, but I do not far err if I dread the amateur genteel comedian more than the scowling tragedian as a lady-killer. Deuce fly away with all flirts! but which is she trying to captivate—the prince or the player!" Then, slapping his brow, he added, still silently: "Fool that I ever am with her—she is wishful to enchain both!"

CHAPTER XXI.

"No care, no stop! so senseless of expense,
That he will neither know how to maintain it,
Nor cease his flow of riot!"
—*Timon, of Athens.*

Kean was truly speaking when he told Lady Koefeld that he was besieged in his apartments by officers of the law.

He had ended one of his memorable nights of orgie after the commencement of the Convivial Club of which he was chief ornament; and Moses, still opening his wings to cover him, had conveyed him to his own rooms in Clare Market, for fear that he might be transferred to a sponging house, the annex of the sheriff's prison, while incapable of the resistance so good a boxer and fives-court player would, soberly, have offered.

It had been impossible to separate him from the last followers of his battle-flag; there they lay about the room or under the table, from which Moses had prudently removed the ink and clean copying paper. They were low fellows, playing inferior parts at his theatre. They accompanied him to the last in order to pick his pockets in the morning if first awake. This time, the faithful guardian was before them. He had closeted "the equal come to take Garrick's chair" in his own bedroom. The host perforce stepped in and opened the blinds on the haggard and senseless revelers, bestowing on them all as contemptuous a survey as on the remnants of their feast; bottles with their necks wrung, lobster claws, rib-bones mingling their charred odor with that of old cheese in crumbs. A shawl, dragged off some drab in the street, was draping a Mercury; an "upper-Benjamin" coat crushed a flower-stand. Battered hats and a broken cane lay under a sleeper in the mud and cigar ends.

"What dregs!" muttered the host. "I did well to keep from their contamination the famous Kean! the pride of

Drury Lane, the coveted by Covent Garden, the glory of
the English-speaking stage, the very sun of the drama!
the warranted mouthpiece of the Swan!"

He went to listen at his bedroom door.

"A snore!" said he, sarcastically. "The actor who
makes all women glad and all men mad snores like a mere
mortal! But I lay that to the coarse drink! He who
might swim in choice vintages stoops to a stoup of raw
rum for the novelty's sake, as the satiated epicure lets
ice dashed over with cayenne melt in his mouth! It was
a blessing that I found him and steered him between his
own lodgings, which the bum-bailiffs beset, and his favorite tavern. I have given him some hours of repose,
cleanliness and calm. They are rare now! He sleeps
like a child now that he snores no more! Look at the
riff-raff, with whom genius should scorn to associate!"

He spurned the man on the floor with his foot.

"Yes, grunt, you pig! Miserable strollers, no better
than Richardson, who pass passably through such parts
as 'Moonlight' and 'The Wall in Pyramus!' I should be
sorry to have his eyes encounter such dirty fringe of the
stage when he gets out."

He stopped, and to the fellow on the floor he whispered:

"Tom! Tommy, my dear!"

The man woke somewhat, and asked:

"Is it an eye-opener?"

"You are right. I am Moses, come to open your eyes!
Hush! That is Davey, there!"

"I know him—do you think I am blind drunk still!"

"No, only he was—and out of his pocket he dropped
a slip of paper! He is courting 'the tall Dally,' is he
not?"

"I hope not—she is engaged to me! we are to make a
'go' of it before the parson when she gets into the first
row of the ballet!"

"Well, it is no go, then! she appoints the corner of Oxford road by the circus at eleven A. M.! and it is going
on——"

Tom sprang up at a bound; he would have rushed at
his rival and knocked him down in his fury, but the Jew
restrained him.

"I do not like the blood shed here!" said he, firmly. "I will detain him that you shall have a fair start! besides, you will have to go into the barber's and have a scrape and brush-up before you meet your intended, eh!"

"If I had tuppence for that!" feeling his pockets.

"There is sixpence, which you can owe me till next time! Go, Tom, my piper's son—I have always had sneaking admiration for you, and I want you to cut that bull-head out!"

"This is not my hat!" said Tom, the cavalier, ruefully regarding a beaver out of shape.

"Oh, take that one off the hook! it is a three-cocked one, but they may be coming into fashion again! You look commanding in it! Get you gone, my bravo!"

"One off the list!" chuckled the host, after closing the door and hearing the man blundering down the stairs.

The man, with his head pillowed on his folded arms on the table edge, was emitting a smothered sound between the bellow of a bull and the growl of a bear. It was the roar of the player of the lion, whom Mr. Bottom the Weaver envied.

"Well roared!" said Moses, facetiously, "but let him not roar again, David!"

The drunkard lifted his head and stared with yellow and leaden eyes.

"Are they 'plauding me? Am I called on?"

"Not the public, my dear!"

"It's promt," mo', by gollops!"

"Yes, and you will get no collops here! Larder empty!"

"This is not my five-pair-back?"

"No, it's mine three front! Let me see, you live in Chandos street?"

"If I ain't locked out!"

"You are not locked out, my poor friend! Only burned out."

Instead of starting into activity, David sat up statuesque.

"Then I am quit o' my rent! I don't lose a blessed *mag!*"

Moses was intimately acquainted with the wardrobe of these familiar friends of drunken men.

"I dare say, to have your abode perish in a blue flame

like snap-dragon does not ruin you, sir, or the Duke of Bedford, either, who is your ground landlord——"

"Grinder of a landlord, you ought to say!"

"But the fire did not stop in your rooms or your house —it leaped over and set ablaze No. 1, at the corner!"

This address galvanized the toper, sobered instantaneously.

"The pawnbroker's!"

"Precisely!"

"Then, I lose my best coat, and best hat, and best shoes."

"If you would save your bacon, you had best hurry! You know what the mob are! They will plunder the ruins, though redhot!"

"This is not my coat!" for the upper Benjamin was so voluminous that he disappeared from head to foot in it, this personator of the kings of the animals.

"Oh, it will conceal the fact that your apparel is not your first best. Hasten! or you will not even see your duplicate ticket burn."

He assisted David to the doorway, since he tried on the skirt of the topcoat, and slamming the door on him, said joyfully:

"Two off!"

He found the third carouser sitting up, caused by David's exclamation over his loss indirect.

"Why, it's our dear Bardolph!" cried Moses, effusively, calling the actor by his principal part. "Do you want to shake hands that you put yours out to me!"

"Bah!" retorted the surly man, evidently one of the quarrelsome when in his cups. "I held out my hand for a drink—a refresher, a stir-up cup, ha, ha!"

"Oh, since Mr. Kean came to my room for shelter last night with the string of you merry dogs, something has happened!" He gave the man a glass of limpid fluid. In his thirst, he tossed off half of it, but stayed the rest, making the most horrible face.

"What kind of poison is that? Ugh!"

"New River water of the first tap, my dear!" replied Moses, tranquilly.

"Never did I taste such rot with my friend Kean in

company. Where is he? I shall complain of your prank!"

"You will not see Mr. Kean again as he was—he is converted! Like Barton Booth, he swore off strong waters, and he will keep his word, too! Henceforth, water is our only drink here, as well as in his own home!"

"The devil! I must have drink of the real brand! not wash!" He tottered about the room. "Where is my hat—my cloak—my cane?"

"Your stick is snapped in two! your hat and cloak have been taken—do you not know with whom you came into my rooms last night?"

"With my old partner, Kean, of course! and with——"

"Tom and Davey, naturally—are you not inseparable when Mr. Kean is the connecting link?"

"Tom and Dave—you are right, king of promoters! But no such corrective lynx for yours truly! Kean! a good actor as actors go! but no head for lush! But he carried the purse—he must make good my hat and togs lost in his company—that is tipplers' law!"

"My poor Bardolph," said the Jew, with commiserating expression, proving that a fine mimic was lost in him to the stage, "when a man forswears liquor in favor of water, things have come to a pretty pass, or, rather, there is no pass. If Mr. Kean comes to me for a night's lodging, it is because, as you, with your acute penetration, will guess—because the grabs are occupying his own, waiting for his return to nab him. That is why we drink water!" He drank a little of the scorned beverage, which caused the illustrious Bardolph to renew the wry face.

The latter made another tour, spying all the articles of discarded wearing attire.

"Seeing how cold and hard was the outlook," continued he, "I do not blame your companions who, feeling 'hot coppers' like you do, not only capped and coated themselves legitimately, but took what they reckoned to bring a shilling or two at Uncle's, and decamped while my back was turned."

"You let Tom and Dave scamper off with my hat and my cloak?" thundered Bardolph. "The laws ha' mercy on you! A pretty host who lets a guest, confident in his watchfulness over the sleeping, abscond with headgear and backwear! Moses, I meant to have 'divvied' with you what Mr. Kean would reimburse, but now—Moses, you shall not touch a stiver of the promised land!"

And donning the first hat that he kicked in his stride and plucking the shawl off the statue, he draped himself and stalked forth.

The nobility of this step was tempered by his stumbling down one flight of stairs, but only a Moses would have laughed, as he did, at the reproach.

"Three and all gone!" joyfully cried the inconsiderate host. "If I had not induced them to depart, they would cling on to my poor Edmund again, and he would be in for another of those debauches for which we cannot forever find a screen for the public. Will he ever sicken and break off, or is he like another Clarence, to be 'washed to death by fulsome malmsey?' "

CHAPTER XXII.

He opened the sleeping-room door. Even there the bottles were milestones on the road to intoxication. It was not a fair combat, since the defeated warrior had naked hands, while Bacchus had shot at least three bottles at him. The "Old Trusty" of the illustrious tragedian, friend of the Prince of Wales, of the wits and beaux, who ought to hold a unique sceptre, and did hold an empty flask, lay there, silent now, flaccid, red, far from sublime.

Yet to that epoch, it seemed correct that a man of extreme gifts should travel like a pendulum as far one way as the other; that, to compensate for rising to the altitude of Pegasus in his flights, he might descend into the ignoble gulf of dissipation and disorderliness.

In trying to take the drained bottle from the supine hand, the act, though soft, awoke the sleeper. He looked up with a dazed expression, but when their eyes fairly met he could not but recognize Moses, though the surroundings were not familiar.

"What are you about, Mo'?" with aerial gayety. "Robbing me of the slumber which I cannot of late gain, save from this nepenthe of cockney distilleries? "Let me the canakin clink, for——"

"No, you are as much attached to a flask——"

"As to a cask!"

"You held it so tight that you might have smashed it and cut yourself——"

"There is no harm in 'crushing' a cup under a friend's roof, for this is, I do believe, your room, eh, Old Joe?"

"In your condition even the watchhouse would shrink from letting you in!" said the other, disgusted.

"I must have missed my own house as the row spun round!"

"No, you had too much sense for that—the enemy occupy it."

"So, so, the bailiffs? you are right. You see, if I promised to be a good boy and go home, I could not do it!"

"You should have prudence in your festivities!"

Kean got up, and adjusted his clothes, freely putting
on a coat which fitted him, from off some clothes-hooks.

"If you could but say: 'Not one drop more—I have
taken as much as my doctor allows!'"

"I could not tell that lie! The doctor allows me none
at all. It would insult my host. I drink to counterbalance the flood of incense, which palls on me!"

Moses watched him becoming, with the traces of de-
bauchery removed, so handsome, smooth and seductive.

"Praise and fortune fail to deprave you as drink does!"

He shied the bottle into the grate.

"Moses, do not blame a benefactor to the revenue tax!
I remember now! 'Moonshine' did want to put his pipe
out, but 'the Wall' stood against it very like a Wall! As
for the Lion, you know that the lion, not the ass, is the
most obstinate of beasts, when drunk!"

"Do you believe that such noisy nights will repair you
after the exhaustion of playing the other nights?"

"Cato, a few glasses——"

"Ah, but it is no longer wines, but rum! Master, you
will burn your great heart into a cinder!"

"Done—transpierced by Cupid's arrow and set before
a fire which spirits-of-wine could not cope with; it is done
to a crust! Nothing will restore it but a few tears of
happiness from that lovely woman's eyes, but, at present,
the tears which fall on it are mine own, desperate!"

"You have made yourself ashamed, and soon you will
make her ashamed of you!"

Kean did not like this turn in censure. He tied his
cravat with a nervous hand and abruptly returned:

"My sober apology from Philip Drunk is in my walk in
the drama. I must know life from the prince to the
pauper to represent them to the quick as occasion demands. Pitch into that Shakespeare fellow with his confounded inventiveness, who has let no class escape him!
To know their moods by heart, I study them in the life!"

The prompter might have continued his lecture, taking advantage of having his pupil at his mercy, when a
timid knock came at the door; it differed from most

knocks, being high up and much more as if made by a hand in a thick glove studded with nails, than otherwise. On the host opening, they saw a young man upside down, who had, with the greatest ease, thrown himself on his hands to drum on the door upper panels with his toes.

"Halloa!" said Kean. "What's up?"

"It's Little Bob!" explained Moses, the posturer!"

The man fell on his feet without haste, and stood at the door.

"Do you think I forget my old playfellows?" said Kean, reproachfully. "You come in erect, Bob."

"To so great a digging-Tory, on my hands or my feet?"

"The right way up, for you will want all your hands to shake with your old pal!"

"Are you going to waste time on him? he only came to get a shilling off me!" rebuked Moses.

"The eagle suffers little birds to sing!" returned Kean, kindly.

Bob shook hands with a grin, showing that he had heard of the actor's fame since leaving his theatrical cradle, and held this friendly clasp as an honor.

He was a compact little man, with his eyes, nose and ears distorted from having met with innumerable hurts in his professional career as tumbler and balancer.

Kean examined his costume, after his features and mien.

"The show is not in high water?" said he, sadly.

"It's under the water! wrecked, master!"

And he executed the difficult feat to common mortals of wiping a tear out of his right eye with his left elbow.

"Richardson has had bad times," said Moses, curtly, knowing that a man recovering from a drinking-bout is apt to be maudlin and overgenerous in succor. "There is dearth in the country, and the laborers are not looking at shows——"

"Saving your presence," interposed Bob, touching his forelock with his toe, "the farm hands are marching to town with their mattocks 'craped' in straw, singing: 'We have no work to do!' So Master Richardson says to them which stuck to him: 'Boys and ladies, all the chicken, though raised in the country, goes to town to be eaten! If you want to eat once more before you kick the bucket, we must get to London!"

"Ah, and you advance, then, because your legs are stronger?"

"No, because my appetite is stronger. I do so like to eat, once in a while!"

"And you have not fed an old comrade?" said Kean, warmly, to his host.

"I fed him so well that I have not a crumb left for my own breakfast."

"Ah, well! what are you going to do now, Bobby?"

"Advertising the Wauxhall Gardens on the balloon ascension days—they put me in a blowed-out canwas-frame like a balloon and the boys follow me to see me go up!"

"So, can you do anything but tumble?"

"Law, yes! I succeeded to your line when you shook us!"

"My line? Rich. Let you attempt high tragedy?"

"No, only the low harlequinade! I quit the stage, and stick to the ground!"

"Ay, but I did all the leaps and took all the traps!" said Kean, sentimentally, recalling, when triumph in that branch surfeited him with glory! "Do you come to me for a lesson in the lofty acts?"

"No, no; but I should like finishing in the egg-dance! At present, I break some of them!

Kean went up to the line of clothes-pegs and uncere-moniously took off such garments as he judged would suit Mr. Bob. He threw them to him and pantomimed that he was to exchange for them.

"Oh!" said Bobby, obeying.

"Eh?" said Moses, who saw his extra habits going.

"Yes, he does not wear the proper garb as Mr. Kean's envoy."

"Envoy to whom? the king of the Cannibal Islands?"

"Don't send me there, Mr. K-K-Kean! anywhere but where they eat—I want to eat, not be eaten."

"No, you are to return to our companions and bring them to town!"

"I am off—that is, I should be off, but it will take a long time to step it!"

"That is why you should take the carrier's van——"

"Well, the carriers do give fellows coming up to town a lift, but, going back, they expect a man has made his fore-money! now, I——"

"Feel in your pockets, boy! Do you want to be beholden to another while you have a penny in your pocket?"

To his stupefaction, Bob felt a coin and drew out, disbelieving the sight after the touch of a gold piece. The donor must have slipped it in there, since Moses' surprise denoted that he had not so lined the garment.

"I thank you, for the show! I shall have enough change to bring them up finely!" He bowed so that his chin brushed his toes.

"And not to break the yellow-boy for drink on the road, pray Moses, give him a drink—there must surely be a heel in one or the other of all those bottles."

Bob saw with growing interest Mose raise a half-full bottle to his lips and drain it.

Then, setting down the vessel with reverence, he said:

"I forget what that's called, but a fellow ought to have a gullet as long as the fire monument is tall to do justice to it! Good-by, and God bless you, Mr. Kean, for the troupe!"

And, making "the Catherine wheel," he rolled out of the room and down to the stairs without altering this model of quitting a house, so that the landlady, coming up with a tray of breakfast things to Mr. Moses, dropped all and fell against the wall horrified.

Her lodger ran out at the chatter.

"The whirligig of fortune!" remarked the tragedian. I am wasting here, and Richardson and his crew are trapping!" He glowed with sympathy. "Patriarchal family! how many a time I have pleaded that I had had my supper 'out!' I was 'out' a supper, ha, ha! in order that they should have my share!" He sighed and looked around at the fragments of the early morning debauch. "Have I gained in happiness by leaving that rude nest of the drama? A Triton among the minnows, they then looked up to me, and I am proud of my petty royalty! I was hailed by the men to whom these grandees are no nobler and kinder, and as for dear Mrs. Carey, the semblance of another—who, with her cold and

supercilious patronage, can be set up on her level——"
He paused. "It is true that I was not of the age to love
—or I might have wedded some more than usually intelligent milkmaid! And now—ah, Alba Danby, why this
accursed silence? Has your father sequestered you, or
Lord Newell this time succeeded in his oft-renewed plots?
Am I never to——"

A knock came at the door; odd, as Moses stood not
upon order in his coming into his own apartments.

"Oh, come in!" said he, testily at the interruption.

It was the landlady, with smiles on her face, enframed
in long ringlets under a not too snowy cap.

"If you pleases, Mr. Kean!" said she, speaking the
name in capitals and smirking at the honor of having
such renown under her roof, "It is a young lady who
found that she could not find you at your chambers, and
——"

In the passage, behind the stout figure, Moses made
a series of signs. The two men well understood each
other.

"Heavens! Miss Danby has sought me here! Oh,
show her in, but beg her to wait!"

He hurried into the bedroom, for the toilet in which one
may not indecorously receive a harlequin and contortion-
ist, is hardly fit for receiving a millionaire's daughter.

CHAPTER XXIII.

A TRAGIC PICTURE.

"You must be her master, and she'll your scholar be."

Had Moses a glimpse of the possibility that a strong and pure love would be his dramatic ward's salvation? It was he who had given the clew by which Miss Danby tracked him to his humble quarters.

This place offered a glaring contrast with his rooms where Miss Danby had fruitlessly called. No antiques, heirlooms of the theatric worthies, curios, armor, weapons, paintings, statues, furniture of historic wood, etc. Instead were play-books and tailor's fittings to betray Moses' dual occupation.

On the other hand, Miss Danby was inclined to overlook such surroundings; indeed, she was under such disguise as was afforded by discarded apparel which the defaulting maid had, with her nose in the air, repudiated in her perquisites. Moreover, she was in love, and while that passion sheds a glamour on some things, it veils others. It is needless to add, therefore, that in her mood she would have met this man in a robber's cave.

Hence, she hardly would know again the landlady or Moses, who escorted her to the odd waiting-room. The woman had barely hidden away the evidences of the revelry and retired.

Moses stood on guard without.

Meanwhile it took all the actor's long deftness to repair his attire; he did not scruple to call again upon Moses' stock, not stopping to consider whether the articles were his property or in keeping for remodeling or renovating.

So he was able to present himself thus transformed, and with a respectful countenance and bearing opposed to that he had shown when aroused by his friend. He even refrained from any curiosity about his being traced to this retirement.

"Madam," began he, for she could not open the conversation, "you did me the honor to call upon me—elsewhere—and leave a note for me?"

His speaking to her, face to face, chilled her, and then warmly thrilled her; this was the same voice so potent on the stage—familiar now, and not awe-inspiring, but she was abashed. It was like that statue of the Egyptians discoursing when the sun fell upon its lips. Yet she was offended with herself; still, she had never paid him for his repeated services; again, she was requiring a favor! It was a poor excuse that she deemed them all priceless.

"May I be so happy as to learn how I can be of utility to you?" he asked. He wanted to be formal and courteous, but felt that his voice betrayed his inner emotion. "Now that I am blessed by the powers, I may be so!"

"Will you excuse my confusion, Mr. Kean, for it is natural? However modest you are, sir, you understand that this is a great stride from when I first saw you, for your fame, your recognized abilities, your acknowledged talent!"

"Oh, hold!" with a wave of the well-kept hands in the flowing cuffs—of another age, but he could not, with borrowed linen, be precise to an epoch.

"I must, with others, put it at genius! Since then you are surrounded by those trophies and testimonials to your eminence in art, you must be truly 'at home!' "

She had found her tongue at last. With feminine tact she perceived that it was he who was afraid of her—a little or much—he was afraid! And, woman-like, she was going to reap all the advantage out of that.

"Your kind reception"—he had not said a word on her being welcome—"emboldens me; for your declining to see me the other time came as a warranted rebuff for my ungrateful conduct."

"If any one is an ingrate, is it not Mr. Danby? but without knowing it for fact, as perhaps you do, I believe that he smoothed my way into the theatre!"

"I could not tell. He is so secretive a man."

"I doubt Mr. Belliston did it all, simply because Mr. Belliston claims all the credit. He, then, had not the influence to move the theatre committee. Let it pass. If

"He spoke so gravely and feelingly that her eyes became dim."

(See page 175)

I owe Mr. Danby, I shall pay him. Meantime, I will do anything for his daughter!"

"This is painful to me, sir! for I know what I owe you, and yet I cannot, cannot ever repay it!"

"Let us pile up the debts, then, on both sides!" said he, lightly, with a twinkle in the eyes. "Some of these days we will offset and strike the balance!"

"I hear that you are, in the burst of sunshine, as good as ever, kind, while cheered as great and dignified! Don't protest, for you must be greatly good to allow me this piece of your time!"

"Oh, this is my off day; no performance to-night!"

To emphasize his words he placed a chair for her in the twilight from the dingy window which *passé* women adore and fair young ones do not dislike if of that blonde brilliancy having an aureole of its own. He went to the door and was not surprised to see Moses in the passage. He thanked him with a nod, and said, in an audible voice:

"My friend, do not let us be interrupted!"

Then, returning with a chair caught up in his steps, he placed it at just that right distance which reveals the lover whose respect is complimentary.

"Your persistent calling indicates that I can be of service to you. My desire is so pressing that it needs no spurring. Luckily, when one has ample means, a service is soon done!"

"That kind of service is soon forgot! Now, I have to be inconsiderate to you, for this is a selfish visit. The question turns on my happiness, my future, my very life, maybe!"

"Your happiness?" repeated the hearer, struck by her earnestness. "No, no! for you wear on your serene front none of the furrows from unhappiness. Your future? I should plunge to drowning in her own caldron Dame Hecate, if she dared forbode to you anything less than eternal felicity. Your life? Ah, you are one of those, charming and touching as a girl, truly companionable as a woman, and comforting and revered as a matron!"

He spoke so gravely and feelingly that her eyes became dim.

"You are so kindly toward our sex that—that you must have had a good mother!" she faltered.

The moment she spoke this last word, she could have wished it were her last. The handsome, bright face darkened as if a cloud swept over it of tempest; he sprang up as though his heart were split by an arrow; impulsively he paced the little room, turning so swiftly that it made her giddy, and it was only thus that he subdued a spasm of anguish and a kind of resentment.

"I suppose," said he, finally, in a low voice, "I must have had parents! But I no more remember anything of them than I do of having friends!"

"No mother—no friends, in your youth!" muttered she, who had been the one worshiped child.

"Soon after I reached the age of reason," went on he, grimly, "I did encounter friends. You saw one in that hook-nosed man at the door! Sharp, hard as steel to those whom he does not like, he was affectionate and patient with me, I who am a trial for the patient! There was also an old actress who imitated him in playing the parent and instructress! Bless them! But for them—well, at last, when the trial of life came, I ran away from them. Only, my friend Moses, he would not be run away from! He is my censor, my Thersites, my—in a word, he is indispensable to me! Never mind my life's star's source. Yours has golden rays! flowers spring up before and beside your path as under the sunbeam!"

"All kinds, yes, and nightshade among them!" returned she, with a waning smile. With sadness dimming her eyes, she proceeded: "Maybe the years lying before me will be more happy, for, Mr. Kean, not so long ago I wondered whether my bridal dress should not be used for the lining of the coffin!"

"You are exaggerating!"

"You cannot imagine how nearly impossible it was for me to make a second attempt to obtain your counsel!"

He shuddered; it seemed doubly wicked in one so young to press on to heaven. She alarmed him, for firmness accompanied by placidity daunts any one. When the pellucid pool becomes suddenly royled, and in the turbidity movement is seen, one suspects that it is caused by terrible monsters.

"All are banded against me, sir! To force me to wed a man to whom they assign transferred rights from the dead! I won't be held and given away by the dead hand!" she cried, abruptly rising and making the gesture of tearing aside a grip of her wrist.

He was amazed at her showing such a burst of temper.

"Now, I despise that man, Newell! I scorn and loathe him who makes parade because the newsmongers hawk his big-boyish fooleries. No, they are not even amusing—they are infamous! A Nero inspires some awe with repugnance, but this ape of the depraved makes one dash out a hand for a broom to sweep him into the gutter and hold him down there in the mud like a rat!"

"Bravo!" said Kean; "you are a magnif—that is, Newell is a bla'guard!"

"You know better than others—what my father will not believe from me of him! how he engaged bravos and persons of his stamp—brand, I should say—to have me carried away for a clandestine marriage. Oh, he intended a marriage—that is all the justice I can do him—as if I would stand by his side at the altar!—I, who would prefer the stocks! I have rejected him as a bridegroom! Think, instead of fleeing to hide his shame, he brazens it out, pretends I would have run away with him! and my father, my own father, intimates that I more than half winked at the sham abduction. Oh, it is driving me mad, to doubt my word! I hold to my word as if I were a Plantagenet!"

"Glorious!" said Kean, but this time under his breath.

"Beyond a doubt, he hired a pen—for he cannot write good English—because he cannot think good English—to launch on the town an account of the 'Farcical Elopement Frustrated; or, Miss Moneybags Is Out for Hiring a Coach and Four!' He is elevated in this pamphlet, and I debased!"

She hid her face, one coat of blushes, in her quivering hands.

He tried to speak, but she put out her hand to stay him.

"Let me have it out, once begun!" said she, mastering her voice. "I could not fail to have words with my too-doubting father! I went into shelter, when my lord spread the news that I had left that abode by the window—perhaps falling into the river or being received in a skiff! Nay——"

"I heard that a person in a boat did receive you under the window, an innovation of Romeo in the balcony, recommended to the Twickenham regattas! I doubt all this, because it is averred that the wherryman who received that heaven-sent fare, conveyed it prosaically down the Thames to a ship sailing for America, and yet his name was Edmund Kean!"

"Then you know, and yet you have not avenged your name taken in malicious sport?"

Kean ground his heel down angrily. To be precise, he had been out carousing, when he ought to have punished the lampooner first and sought his employer for the same end, elusive as that peer was. In his indignant start, he knocked down a plaster statue, which flew to flinders without either noticing it.

"I ought not to have said that, sir! and I beg your pardon. I am distracted—believe me, you have given me too many proofs of your courage for me to doubt that!"

"You shall have proof of anything in my power! Lord Newell shall not escape—I am no more a physiognomist than the next man, but that rogue dies by violence, believe me! His time is written there!" he pointed upward, "and here!" he tapped his forehead, and his face wore a gloomy aspect. "In what way can I be your counselor after being your champion?"

He sat down as calmly as possible.

"Well, let the counselor have the first say," observed Kean, with the gravity of the chief justice, though she had clapped the torch to a near-dry pitch pine tree. "It is very bad to run counter to a rich father and a fiancé both rich and of rank. As far as money goes," continued the tragedian-in-vogue, complacently, "rest easy. I know Mr. Erskine, the advocate really of value, and if anybody can plead successfully against parental and premarital bonds to a British jury, being married men and paters, it is Erskine. He will induce the Court of Chancery to appoint a guardian for you!"

"Oh, dear, no, Mr. Kean! I want to be out of the leading rope—out of all tethers altogether—not to shift into another! I shall be under the spectacles of an old soul more or less in sympathy with my father! The old hold together just as the young ought to do! I never thought of applying to the law!"

"Oh, you can do without law and justice, can you?"

He searched around. On the almost naked wall was a penny print of a duel, and with some aptness it was framed in two pair of foils, crossed at each angle of a square.

But his look of relief died away.

"That cock would not fight last time!" he said, lowly, with regret, "not even if I taunted him before the prince and his cronies, or in Mr. Danby's presence!"

"Do you see another defense?" she asked, surprised at his gravity.

"I see another attack, but whether it can attract is another matter!"

"But you must not imperil your life——"

"Against him? pooh!"

"But you would be imprisoned for duelling!"

"That's the rub—I should be imprisoned. He—if he 'scaped me—would be simply fined! Then, you would be without your counselor!"

He caught his chin between finger and thumb, like an old judge.

"Yet by playing upon his vanity! yes, Parolles was made into a hero by his vanity!" He began to laugh heartily, but did not unveil his design save by the words: "After all, I ought to devise something as telling as that Newell spring-gun!"

She trembled a little, but at that instant a bell tinkled.

"Never mind that—it concerns the lodger whose rooms I make use of! To recapitulate——"

"Rather that than capitulate!" said she, smiling again.

"Good! You are not without means?"

"Next to none."

"And you propose——"

"I thought of seeking subsistence on the stage!"

"Whew! You are so candid, and, excuse me, such a perfect simpleton, that it would be wicked of me not to speak out my thoughts. As you seek my counsel, I am your counselor; as you seek instruction, I am your preceptor."

"I beseech you to be all that!"

"Supposing I accept—as counselor and instructor, you become a pupil and client, and not a beautiful young lady! You are under my charge and my honor. I should speak to you as a teacher to his pupil.

"You are goodness itself!" she said, very effusively.

No man dislikes approval, but when it comes from a young person impelled by instinct he feels its full power.

"Seeing only the finished side of our web binds you!"

"You are forgetting that I come of prosaic, practical stock," interposed she, trying to be frigid and clear, as if her resolve were long distilled. "I wish to embrace a profession which seems to me to demand more nature and application than such as have purchasable short cuts!"

"Oh, money will work wonders on the stage, too!" said he. "You have yet to peep at the seamy side, where the work shows, with its frayed and broken ends—so many snapped hopes, wrenched conceits, and tedious and yet abortive attempts. On the right side are the roses, on this the torn fibres and the unteazled shreds. There are matters as well, hard to state, but useless, if blunted and smoothed down!" He looked solemn. "My experience has trebled my age! You must not be hurt if my tone is bitter and the expression mars the thoughts, chaste and lofty in themselves."

Her smile was lofty, as if no man whom she allowed to address her frankly would speak what no others should hear.

"Mr. Kean would say nothing to Miss Alba which the young man destined to figure in society should not know," he went on, "yet Edmund Kean must speak wholly to the recruit wishful to enlist under the banner he is proud to bear for his campaign. In return for her trust and the honor of her consulting him, what would be indecorous in the first instance becomes duty in the second. Now, one of those olden poets has said that to draw tears one must first have wept!"

"I have not wished to cause anybody tears, but I cannot boast that I have never wept. I have suffered, anyway. Brine poisons and does not slake—yes, tears or none, I have suffered."

"You are fine looking—oh, everybody says so and has

said so for some time, I am sure, even those who slander.
That is much in the pursuit you aspire to. But far from
all. It's not half the battle so much as it brings on a battle which keeps the brain and blood active. For as
women can be anything—the coat or the petticoat making
the sole difference betwixt duchess and dairymaid—for
a woman can imitate beauty as she can conceal age, especially on a stage so badly lit as ours. Nature having done
her part, how about art?"

"With you my tutor, I should progress!"

"That's artful, not artistic! Grant the art, you might
in five or six years command trial in town. But, no more
on stage than in the courts of law, a trial does not entail
correct judgment or a final consequence. Mrs. Siddons
failed here. My own manager, Belliston, albeit a consummate comedian, had to return to the provinces. I—
but—nothing can be done without time and study. Like
other English ladies, I suppose you were not cloistered
and not too much hedged round by old tabbies and
prudes; but yet you can hardly have studied the habits
of any but two classes, the well-behaved and your servants. For the stage authors have ransacked creation
for diversity of sorts and conditions.

"Granted that some endowed persons are born with
genius, the statue must be in the block before it sloughs
off the surrounding crust; still, there must be the hand
to let in light and exhibit the Venus or the Moses. You
may be one such. I suppose so. But if you are reduced
to the one property, health, and you undermine that by
burning the candle at both ends; if you learn under priva-
tions, your body will fail you when the tireless, insatiate
mind calls upon it to respond! You will shatter to atoms
like those glass flasks which the maker inflated to undue
fragility. On the stage we see the earthen crock outlast
the china vase! At the least, can you devote half a year
to incessant study?"

Alba reflected deeply. This was not at all the interview she had imagined.

"My father was not always a well-established merchant," she said. "My mother was domestic and set me
to work among her maids. I am expert in all the petty
arts which produce what the dames of state desire; I mend

lace, ornament dresses, embroider, 'take up' stockings, furbish old jewelry, bleach pearls and revive rubies—in a word, I can earn a livelihood!"

"Madam, our young actresses, what our jargon calls 'walking ladies,' earn some fifteen shillings a week; this may rise to twenty; after your half year in the harness, grant the essay promising, a manager may offer you a hundred pounds a year!"

"With my tastes plain and governed, it would be a fortune."

"Wait! that is but a tithe of what you must lay out on your costumes, finery, jewelry! . Time was when a placard saved paint, for the audience accepted as gospel that it stood in a palace yard or a woodland grove! Time was when we paced in our patron's cast-off frippery—as the hangman frisks on Sunday in the highwayman's coat and feathers. Now, we must be the life—the gold must resist the acid, the diamonds cut the glass, and I have to bribe the royal tailor to cut the grass from under the prince paramount with the novel suit! This is why Cæsar's wife, on the stage, cannot wear silk velvet without suspicion! All the patrician guards could not stifle insinuations of where the leading actress found her Golconda. Never in your case could your family or friends, proud and gratified by your victory, find the means to soothe your cravings. Still, by that means, you would happily avoid the foremost danger, the dragon which crouches on the mud-sill of the stage.

"You are so fair that you must have perceived the envy excited by charms when set up as a standard. You do not know what the critics of a great city are? Madam, most of them comprehend the honorable side of their mission, and art partisans of the divinely noble, the beauteous and the grand. These, the glory of the press, are national recording angels.

"But there are others, whom the inability to produce anything original has turned to criticism. Jealous of everything not having their dull or bilious tints, they bespatter all that is white with their gall-made ink. Hating everything wholesome, they stab with the stylus and smother with their blotting-powder. One such mar-all will discover that above being virtuous, studious, high-reaching and lovely, you are lovable! He is of the sort which tears a masterpiece in a gallery with his cane ferrule, shatters a vase, drops the dust off his hat into the font, sullies anything that is admired! He will begin by aspersing your talent—attributing your looks to the paint-pot and dealer in false hair, but, in time, he will assail your honor. Then you will demand of a mutual friend—for such reptiles have bosom friends, good lack! How come you to be maligned by a man whom you do not know!

"Mr. Mutual Friend will answer that it is the very reason; if Backbite had the pleasure of your acquaintance, never would he have mistaken you! B. never reviles an acquaintance! So you perforce smile on him, even if he were a Newell, and he has made you a hypocrite who never will cease to locate yourself!"

"I cannot be brought to that!" cried she.

Filled with her own indignation, he uttered stirringly and scorchingly:

> " 'Cats! that can judge as fitly of his worth
> As I can of the mysteries which Heaven
> Will not have earth to know!' "

CHAPTER XXIV.

"Go on, go on," pleaded the girl, although the picture tormented her.

"Supposing you escape those two tests; the meeting of the milliners' bills and the charge of the lapidating regiment—a third host menaces you. Your rivals—for in the playhouse there are no fellows, no mates, no comrades —all are rivals—they will do to you what they have done to me. Each coterie will shoot out its hundred tentacles to prevent you rising any step higher; its hundred mouths will spit black venom at you; and its hundred voices will alternate praise of its idol and damnation to the public's— you! To ruin you means will be employed which only your Lord Newell would employ. But they will ruin you! They will expend more than your father's treasure to buy censure and insults upon you, and it would require more than the war debt to buy and hush up this deluge of diatribes.

"Careless about their puppets, otherwise busy, ignorant of matters behind the stage curtain, credulous when a pedant avers, having no idea how these libels are spun out, the public will accept them as founded. At length, you will perceive that baseness, ignorance and mediocrity are all allied with intrigue. And study, talent and genius itself will be strangled like the hierophant by Apollo's serpent.

"You will not yield and believe, but you cannot for long keep doubting. Then, with the flood of tears, your heart heavy with disgust, and your soul wrung with despair. you will curse the day when the fatal idea urged you to pursue the rainbow glory, costing so much in the chase and worth so little in the mart. Well, look up, Miss Danby; I have finished pointing out the mud on Thalia's skirts."

She saw his despondency; that downcast mood which, it was said, he could lull only with riot.

"Then you have gone through this, Kean? But you—what did you do to battle with it?"

"Yes, I bore my share of the stings, stabs and refuse that they pelt their unrecognized idols with! But a straw for all that! I was alone!"

"You had no one to sympathize with, none to console, no sister, no mother?"

"Mother?" exclaimed the actor, again with profound sorrow and an indefinable yearning. "My mother? Some say that ravens foster forlorn children the whilst their own birds famish in their nests! My mother may have been over good to others—but never to me!"

She wept in silence, for she detested herself for reopening this wound.

"As a man, I could defend myself against men. My acquirements belong to the critics; they may pull them to pieces, hack them, twist them askew, and show them upside down or the wrong side out! Such are the censor's prey, and he plays havoc by license. Without being mightier than Ajax, I scorn to buffet Thersites. But when," he went on with alarming and concentrated fury, "some one, high or low, meddles with my own life, the scene changes! I have threatened even a Lord Newell, and it was not I who quaked. But, unhappily, I see that while doing his utmost to injure me, he directs his worst spite against you. He will assign your evasion to cowardice."

"He ought to know me better! But he will see that instead of fleeing from London, I remain and conspicuously—on the stage, if I can set my foot there!"

Kean shook his head.

"Like you," she cried, "I believe that all the ills you have arrayed against me will melt at the multitude's breath, crying: "Behold the queen!"

She was delighted, for her own latent spirit, or one he infused, permeated her. Her color was high—her eyes sparkling.

"The queen? three or four times a week, with a gilt scepter and 'Bristol diamonds' in a copper circlet! I rule a realm thirty-five feet square, and a court which runs to cover when the callboy yells 'To the greenroom.'"

"But when all applaud and revere?"

"When I am most envied, I most envy the teamster sleeping on market-cart shafts, the porter sweltering under his tower of fruit baskets, or the seaman pressed to the bulwarks by the biting gale!"

She thought that she saw his hope.

"Until there shall come along a fair and rich woman, to fall in love really with the ideal lover and appeal to him, saying:

"'Genius! my love and my riches are for you, if you will spurn this consuming hell of falsity—throw off the costume burning you! Oh, quit the stage! and you will quit it all!'"

He looked at her as if she came from another country and could not comprehend his own ways. His frankness went on for nothing.

"I, I, Edmund Kean, quit the stage? Oh, you know nothing of this yoke! When one grows up under it, it cannot be detached without the bone and flesh coming with it—ay, it would draw out the vitals! Kean quit the stage! Like Samson, I should pull down the temple with me! Turn my back?—I, who never had a home, on Old Drury!" he uttered the affectionate epithet with the same tone as one speaks of the paternal nest, "where the air is full of such emotions, such delights and such enjoyable dolors? Am I to give up my conquered foe to a newcomer who will make me forget in a year—in some months, nay, in the time it takes to substitute one name in type for another! on the playbill! Bear in mind that the actor is Friar Bacon's Brazen Head—he re-creates the author, but does not re-create! he brings nothing and leaves nothing! He lives out his life and his memory dies with his generation! He falls like that star, never to rise again! It is from noonday to midnight—from the throne to the dust of nothingness!"

Beside this woe, her private griefs and prospects seemed so small!

"Quit the stage!" he pursued, as if glad to have at last a confidante to whom he could exhale his gathered bitterness. "No, no, woman! Once the foot is set forth in this fatal course, it is a Marathon race, to be run to the death! Those who perished on the field were perchance happier! As he set out, his sun began setting! Few even die like an actor with whom I played. In 'Jane Shore' I heard him softly breathe:

"'Mercy befall me at my latest hour!' Then he fell into my arms, dying. The audience, seeing but earnest acting, drowned his last groan with frenetic applause."

"Dreadful!" murmured she, clasping her hands as if she saw the speaker thus finishing his life on the stage.

"Better than death, or else Molière's, expiring amid hisses, than in dumb show to pass in solitude the remnant of hateful days!"

His hearer dared not raise her voice. She never had surmised that an actor can have serious or even tragic thoughts not written by the poets.

He was wringing his hands, when, returning from his rhapsody, he exclaimed:

"Yet are you here?" He looked around. "Oh, this is not my home! No place for you! Let me see! You are on the threshold—you can return. You need not enter! Believe me, oh, believe me! on my honor, best not intrude!"

"Your advice is an order, Mr. Kean," said she, reluctantly, but submitting. "Yet, if I bow, you will believe that I was not inspired. What am I to do, the stage door shut in my face?"

"Is it the only one? No, no, child! Go home with your maid. Without knowing that fathers are, save 'the Roman one,' he forced a smile incompatible with his brooding face. "Stay with him—it is your place."

She shook her head and her lips met closely.

"As long as Lord Newell is cherished there, it is not my place."

"You must have relatives."

"They are so serious, sir!"

"Gad! is there not one frivolous in the Danby home set?" laughed he.

"Well, there is one, whose husband is related to us and under monetary obligations to my father. He has offered me his kind offices, but I believe that his wife rules him, spite of her levity and zigzag flights. I believe she would champion, just to be pillowed with me in the lampoons sure to be showered on us both! I can hardly see myself in those plump arms, under her roguish eye, but here goes—I will beg Lady Gorsewold to take me under the battlements of Gorsewold House!"

She tried to be merry.

"Amy, Lady Gorsewold!" said Kean, amused more than surprised. "Zoons! after all, her laughter would defy and beat off ridicule! Lady Gorsewold, indeed! She comes of a heroic stock! I do believe that she would, once accepting you as ward, break the last dish in her toilet service in repelling a storming-party!"

They laughed together at the picture.

"The silly head may have a sound heart! I believe Lord Gorsewold votes against Newell."

"He is influential!"

"But if your father lends the ousted lord and the other money——"

"All Pactolus would not make the Countess Amy fluctuate!"

"Well, we will send you to Gorsewold House in style. keep my carriage, by the way. Moses!" He went to the door, which opened. "If those claws are not on my livery, get my carriage around to this door for the lady!"

Moses beckoned him out into the passage. In a whisper, he said:

"Who do you think is below and long waiting?"

"The dev——"

"No, sir, or a subordinate one: Mr. Bonnell!"

"The prince's gentleman-in-waiting?"

"With his own carriage! his carriage! a valet with a carriage-and-pair!"

"The prince has come in for his money, then! Huzza! but what did you say?"

"That you had come to my lodgings to get peace for study! You had been up all night over the book and was now rehearsing with some of the company!"

"You had better have said that I was out with the owls! George would sooner believe it! Get Bonnell into a room below, where he cannot see the street! I am going to send my visitor away in his carriage!"

"Oh, Ned!"

" 'Sh! it will teach him to stick to a one-horse chaise."

Shortly after, Miss Danby, who had come in a hackney coach, departed to make her call on Lady Gorsewold in the unexceptionable equipage of the regent's confidential man.

"Well," said the latter, mollified, as he knew that Kean was a privileged hoaxer of his lord's intimacy. "If you took my whisky on a state affair?"

"Stage affair! You are not the man I believed you, Bonny, if your whisky is not at your friends' call any time!"

Bonnell regretted there was not a crowd by to hear the great Kean call him, familiarly, a friend.

The actor mounted the rickety stairs again, and pondered over the complicated situation.

"That man's intervention has saved me from a piece of folly which would have canceled my previous wisdom. To have sent away from an obscure lodging a young lady of her condition, and faith! all but accompanying her—which is a hundred times more damning— were disastrous! All her father's coin could not be welded into a chain to drag any man to the altar beside her! As it is, the lamb arrives at the new fold without a fleecy lock singed. Strange, but I feel that I am her bounded protector! That is a terribly attractive woman! I think I could play Brabantio well, since I learned what a burr to the guardian is charming woman! That girl would make a fine Juliet, her hair under a black wig and her eyebrows traced with a burned stick end. Yet she has not her innocent audacity! That Elena must have been the type! Only, that woman is too much art—such act all the time off the stage, so that they are useless on it. Hoity-toity! I am playing false to my own divinity! I am saving that dove from the Moloch—of the stage! All for—for—Juno, I suppose, since my friend Byron, who is on the committee just to get some tragedy a mile long to an act, upon my hands! declares her to be the queen of marriage. The honey, as usual, is for others!"

Then, rousing himself like his pet lion, he almost shouted:

"No, Alba shall be mine own!"

CHAPTER XXV.

At this period, the river Thames being without an embankment, the water came up in the bend at Charing Cross so as to enable coal and other barges to discharge on the foreshore at Hungerford. To soothe the throats of these navigators, roughened with carbon, the cellars of the houses on the slopes waterward were converted into caves of refreshment.

The tunnels, alleys built over, and vaulted ways, led from these houses up on the Strand and out on Whitehall Place.

The whole tract was a monster rats' burrow.

Like the black rats, the colliers lumbered up, drank to a stupor, were rolled down to their craft and left the field to rats of all hues, who bored this dark lurking place with a hundred secret outlets.

There lodged here as in a sanctuary professional beggars, thieves who professed nothing, but robbed with as much variety as persistency, mock-wounded victims of the wars, land and naval, and seekers after things lost by a little help. But they had not the prowling-ground to themselves; it was the fashion in the set to which Lord Newell was proud to belong, to descend into this black-country to make the finishing of night's revelry.

While the colliers, thieves, drunkards and smugglers held each clan as neutrals, they all considered "the bloods" as interlopers. Luckily, those who regarded the enterprise as a crowning luxury, fortified themselves with experience, strong liquors or an understanding with the watchmen.

But the glory was to have combats with "the rough scurf," and many a noble lord and future bishop was king for a day after beating a Newcastle "Georgie" or a blackleg, or a 'longshoreman of notoriety in a fair stand-up fight.

Besides the watch, lounging along the Strand, with

a roundhouse at St. Martin's Bars, there was a military
recruiting-office in Whitehall, having a secret communication with one or more of the low-ground taverns; and
the King's Arms, public house, was connected similarly,
it was said, with the Fox-under-the-Hill, facetiously
known as "the Coalhole," for tricks concerning the business of crimping—that is, providing candidates for the
lord high admiralship of England—by way of foremast
hands to begin with.

Each man carried the law of this region in his hand,
not his head; the weapon of expression was a life-
preserver made according to personal whim; leaden ball,
netted and slung with a cord, short club, thick pistol
clubbed, but usually the fist, as the magistrates at Bow
street had a prejudice, truly national, against the prisoner using so foreign an instrument as the sheath-knife.

So the denizens relied on themselves against the press
gang or the soldierly trepanners. If one yielded to the
drugged liquors of the Fox or the King's Arms, and
woke up at sea on a gunbrig or in a military barrack
black-hole, he blamed his own weakness in taking the
drop too much.

Into this forbidding, if not forbidden, ground, always
ominous, and when night came on, with a fog off the
river to meet and blend with it, a man nonchalantly
rolled from the thoroughfare as if pure chance guided
his steps.

Congreve could have described his tar for all weathers
from him, without going down to Wapping, and Dibdin
would have sung of him. His black, crisped hair was
plastered back thickly to fend a blow on the pate, and tied
hard in a pigtail, stiff as a unicorn's horn; over that was
apparently glued on a small, hard, round hat with bullet
grazes and cutlass clips. It was set a little provokingly.
The shoes were of South American horse-hide, defying
weather and climate, and, no doubt, from the neatness,
worked at leisure in the forecabin on the tropic seas.
His coarse canvas trousers flowed widely around them,
flapping against gray woolen stockings, the present of a
lass who loved the sailor. At the trim waist, the slack
was drawn in by a broad belt of glazed leather, to which
was appended, or through which was thrust, the *de-*

siderata of a seaman who carries his arsenal with him and to the front—knife, short boarding-pistol, powder-horn, bullet-pouch, a purse, but no cutlass. The pistol was probably unloaded. His fists were not immense, but they were tough, as if rosined, and seemed moved by muscles of steel. His dark-blue jacket covered a woolen jersey, in which Boreas might be jeered at, and he bore the outer garment as jauntily as the hussar his extra pelisse.

Since he had laid aside his hanger, he supplied the omission with a fat bottle worked over with manila spun-yarn, containing liquor emitting a pleasant swashing sound and an odor as pleasant to the passersby, of genuine Nantz. To counterbalance this was attached to the belt a box, which contained chewing tobacco, since he now and then replaced an exhausted cud with a new one from its depths.

Sergeant Hawk and the crimping lieutenant had not failed to remark Master Jack; but both confined to themselves the resolution:

"It is too early to annoy the homeward-bound citizens on the Strand, but the cut-out and bring-in will take place when Jack has his hold-full!"

Having drained his pocket pistol in his idle roamings, the seaman finally smashed it against a dead wall. A rat had incurred his spite, but the libations had muddled his sight, for it was the bottle which came to its end.

Perhaps, he had thought that the explosion would arouse the bashful dwellers, for he shouted in a voice to overcome a sixty-mile gale:

"Come' ye out and come ye on, one and all, and the niggers to boot, hang ye! for I were thrown out, bare as a babby, last time I came ashore to enj'y my liberty, and I've come ag'in to play evens with you bearded pirates!"

But it was full early for the purlieus to begin that night! and, besides, the active inhabitants were confined in the main room of the Fox, where an interesting argument was being settled under their delighted eyes. Its room was crowded, and out of the window came the noises indicative of a much applauded hand-to-hand encounter of at least a couple of men. There was noise enough for a combat of twenty pair.

The sailor accordingly surged over that way. The

heavy and dismal portals were fastened up as if to pro-
hibit interference with the affair. On the window sill,
from which the sash had long ago been carried by a delinquent customer, thus evading his bill, sat a figure so
burly that it blocked up almost all the aperture. Only
a rare student of human nature from all sides could have
identified this novel shutter.

"Why, I know this 'back' as if he were of my own
football crew!" said the seaman, surprised, his voice ex-
periencing a "land," not a sea, change. "It is that constable of Freefolk! Master Dobbin Prettiman! How
comes he here? Oh, could it be he who sent me the
warning that Lord Newell made this house, the Fox,
his rendezvous? and could be met with here? Prettiman!
If he were friendly to me, why the mischief did he not
come to me, for I promised my good offices, did I not?
to get him to keep the door of Drury Lane? If he kept out
the unasked public at the door as effectually as he does
at a window, he would be invaluable! And I cannot be
a stranger to all, even here! and yet I doubt that he
would recognize me, even if I act Ben, in 'Love for
Love,' less well than I flatter myself I am doing."

Upon which Kean, for it was our actor indulging in
one of his eccentricities, but with more than usual founda-
tion, smartly stepped up to the casement. Applying his
shoulder to the bulky impediment so ruddy ensconced,
he uttered a boisterous "Heave together, my hearties!"
and exerted himself so handily that the occupant of the
sill was pitched forward into the interior, like Falstaff
of the three-man trap-ball plank.

A confusion of clamor resounded within: "Not fair!
the referee had no business to pitch in! Put the umpire out of the ring!"

Kean coolly thrust his batted head in at the orifice
which he had cleared.

The view was worthy obtaining, to a student of men
given up to the vilest passions.

The capacious but low drinking room, had the tables
and settles removed to the sides; on these and the
bar-counter sat or stood a number of men of all sorts—
coal heavers, colliers, barges, freshwater fishermen,

beach-combers, "mudlarks," odd-job men, closely packed.

All surrounded what was clear space before Mr. Prettiman had been "catapulted" into it, and floored, sprawling like a man going to be quartered by wild horses. Two other men,·interrupted by his apparition, stood quivering with passion, staring at him as if he had dropped from Mars.

One was a roughly-clad man, whose clothes were partly replaced with second-hand wearing apparel, retaining leather gaiters, fur waistcoat and velveteen breeches. His other things were hung on a chair.

His antagonist was in his shirt sleeves, as was his uniform in business, but as he had to do something in deference to the etiquette of the prize ring, he had cast aside his apron of office: he was Peter Pott, the landlord of the Fox, servant to Captain Figg, pugilistic professor; he held a great fame among devotees of the manly art of self-defense.

Prettiman sat up, rallying after his projection.

"I award the decision to Mr. Pott!" and he got up, rubbing his shoulder. Excellent in temper, he did not look around for the thrower of men, as if that incident were a pleasantry known to umpires.

"'Tain't tair!" grumbled the contestant, "for it were him what knocked me out!"

"Then, to another round!" said the indefatigable Pott.

"Nay! I am not up to your Lon'on ways," continued the vanquished, in whom, as he presented his battered visage, Kean recognized with some difficulty his own opponent in the New Forest. "But you might give a fellow consolation-stakes in a pot of ale! Whoy, I would not have knuckled up to you if I had the price of a mug!"

This frank confession of where he found his spirit to meet the redoubtable "Figg's Novice" endeared him to the crowd, out of a fellow feeling.

At this avowal of destitution on the part of Lord Newell's evil executant, Kean started.

"It is not Prettiman, but this renounced traitor, who has sent me warning; he wants to be revenged on his master! I must wear the disguise more for him than for Prettiman!"

Meanwhile, the landlord had generously drawn "a beer" for the sufferer, slowly infiltrating it when the ex-constable interrupted:

"And pack yourself off, Master Gideon, from London ways! for I am bound for to notify you that I am constable of the Hundred of St. Martin's, and that I am empowered to clap into the watchhouse any vagrant who avows that he be without penny or a lorfle occkypation!"

Kean doubted that Gideon, in his spite, would not turn on him if he met him at the door, and so, letting him pass out there, gibed at for his defeat by those incautiously betting on his prowess, he bounded in at the window, with the warning: " 'Ware scaldings!"

He landed on his feet with a seaman's precision, or a harlequin's.

The dregs adore strength and agility. When allied, they who admired one capable of hurling the stout constable into the arena and playing the human football, received him with a cheer.

Prettiman glared at the man who had displaced him from his judge's box. But the other met his furious gaze with unalterable good humor.

"Another time," said he, "do not block up the gangway!" You shall drink with me, Mr. Rufferee, because you gave it ag'in that yokel! You were right; the Bunnyface had the more science and the more bottom!"

"But if you had knocked all the breath out of my body I could not have given any award!" still grumbled the constable.

Kean saw that his mask was impenetrable.

All were drinking, for the victor was bound to serve his congratulators a "round" without charge.

"So you pummeled the farmer?" asked the newcomer of the man behind the bar.

"Yes, he did not get a crack even at this Pott!" laughed the publican. "He will chew on one side of his jaw till his new teeth shoot! That is, all he gets to chew! The Fox got his back up, for he don't connive at hollow vessels sneaking in here and ordering 'lush' without the coppers to back the said order!"

"Never mind one here and there!" He slapped his

purse. "There is there what can make up the shortage, host!"

Landlords have the weakness of all great men: they wish to be thought infallible in recalling faces. So he let a gleam of welcome illumine his darkening eyes and said joyfully:

"Cor-reck you are, Jack of di'mun's! my hearty! I minds you, my boy! The last time you paternizes the Fox, you left the change out of a Portugee yaller boy and I am not taking any coin out of your poke this trip! And as I walloped the chaw-bacon, I stands 'Sam' on this horse-spice-ous occasion!"

"That is the rule!" was the chorus.

This recognition dissipated any doubts about the sailor being a spy on the smugglers. There was a general jolting as again all massed around the bar. Pott had to call his tapster into requisition.

"I am looking toward you, guardian of the peace!" said Kean, over a frothing tankard to Prettiman, armed similarly; "no harm done ye that a stitch of yarn won't a-mend, eh? I comes ashore, hereabouts and at large, to see 'rum' sights and visions that are queer, but smash my headlights! I did not look for'ard to seeing an officer of the peace ruffereeing a prize fight!"

Prettiman set down the pewter pot and, without a blush, replied:

"It's parfeckly nateral! I come up out of the country-side where the lads spend their spare time pounding each other's spare ribs! I am as reg'lar called the umpire as the parson to a funeral. I will back the New Forest again' all Middlesex for boxing. By the way, we are no sluggards at wrestling, and I want to compliment you on the hold and the sling—I am a man of fair weight for my inches!"

"I broke no bones, then?"

"I am getting fat, instead of bone, in town."

"I had no idea that the town gave a police officer so easy a berth?"

"What, them Mohocks? Well, they cannot, those whipper-snappers, stand me on my head! They would want a derrick! Ha! Ha! Besides, this is between us—I am known to the king-pin of them uproarious rakes, and he would not have his crew roast me—we are clanny in the New Forest!"

"Oh, these devils who alarm London at night have found a leader in some Robin Hood of your New Forest?"

"It is in the *Courant* and the *Intelligencer;* it is my Lord Newell."

"And so you would not play any cross-purposes with your own lord?"

"Me and him, as a New Forestrian, I am bound to wink at my liege lord's cutting-ups, but as a constable in another borough, I—well, we," concluded Prettiman, loftily, and tapping the badge on his sleeve, "we act like those great powers which, when a third G. P. grabs at a fourth lesser G. P., stands nootral!"

It was clear that the warning note was not dictated by this functionary.

"Love for art gets me into that wolunteer office," resumed the officer, as if pricked by conscience.

"You love art—art of boxing, I know!"

"I came into this house simply to procure lodgings for some downfallen, which I used to know 'em in their haulscion days, the songsheets calls them. They had fallen flat by the way, as the Good Book puts it."

"Wretches that rouse a beadle's compassion must be low down!"

"My fishy mariner, a beadle has a heart. I ran in the street out there, up against these strolling players, whom I last saw perform gayly—oh! in their own sumptuous show, called Richardson's Penny Poppy Show!"

This was the remnant whom Little Bob had heralded.

"Richardson!" repeated the sham sailor. "See here! I have not been always on the green, the blue and the other seas. I have trudged across England, and I ran across the wake of this here Richardson. His troop in London while I am present? I will go see them perform. He had a pretty lass in his company, once—a white lily who was backward with her rent, and I offered her the end of my prize money and to her landlord the end of my cudgel!"

"The same!" broke in Prettiman. "Only it is rarely behind hand with the rent and all else just at present!

So, remembering that they gave me a pleasant night when they were in cheer, and that they were likely to have a night on the London mud, with the fog for a coverlet, why—looke ye, lad, I had my month's pay in my pocket! So I brought them in here—leastwise by the other door, and consigned them to Mrs. Pott, who is making them at home. They can recruit for a week—hang the expense!"

Kean rubbed his forehead, where the hard hat left a red wealt, to hide his emotion. Then, grabbing the constable's hand, he squeezed it, saying:

"You are a fine fellow, and I shall never let out at a constable in the to-come, without begging of his pardon if I hits too hard! Landlord, take this ten-pun' note! It's to give those guests introduced by the constable a roaring supper and another week's lodging! You must drink till all is blue, true blue, like your noble self, Mr. —Mr.——"

"Dobbin Prettiman, at your service!"

"Call me Jack! It's a purser's name, but I am the purser for the night, see?"

CHAPTER XXVI.

THE FOX ATTRACTS CUSTOMERS.

Foreseeing that the host had come to the end of his treating, the wise patrons departed, and Kean and the good-hearted police officer were left still by themselves. On finding that the tap-room was comparatively vacated, a man in a cloak to the heels and his flop-hat let down about his ears, ventured in.

He was not of the usual stamp.

His walk, what of his lineaments, could be discerned, and his boots and wig betrayed the man of good position. He stopped on the sill and scrutinized all within. Kean could not but view him in return; but the constable only regarded him, as was professional, as a fish out of water.

"It is Lord Newell!" mused the tragedian. "He does come here—my informant was right in that respect. He redoubled his attention, but was apparently unconcerned in what followed.

Newell finally beckoned to Pott. Now, the victor in the encounter, though so far pretending he had been unaffected by the blows, was beginning to feel aches and pains, lameness and twinges, and his eyes blinked despite himself.

He felt more like calling his man to take his place and going to, couch a while upstairs.

But this was a gentleman, and he obeyed the sign. He walked lamely and he spoke surlily.

"Who do you want?"

"I am seeking the master of this hotel!" was the reply.

"Hotel!" The irritated host was mollified. He bowed to intimate that he was the functionary and at the other's service.

"Has a man, country-looking, been here and engaged a room—for a young lady?" whispered the lord; but Kean heard him with that wonderful art of reading the words on the lips, which enables an old but deaf actor to follow a play and not miss his cue.

"By japes!" blurted out the landlord, slapping his thigh, though the blow made it ache. "What an oaf I am!"

The other frowned as he divined a hindrance.

"I thought the ninny was hoaxing! To talk about engaging my best room, when he had not the price of a pint in his pocket—and for a young lady! A ragged rustic not fit to hold out his hand to lift a lady into the stirrup! He sauced me, and as one word leads to—a blow, we got to punching each other!"

"Oh!" said Lord Newell, biting his lip.

"He has only just stepped out down the hill with some of his hose-teeth loose, and I have my eyes turning all the colors of the Irish. You know it is mousey gray about now—it will be woilet to-morrow, and then yaller, till it recovers its original complexion."

The master of the unhappy Gideon looked more perplexed than angered.

"To be well sarved, you must do things yourself!" observed the landlord, philosophically. He had received blow for blow and he felt that he ought not to be blamed.

"Yes, it appears that I have chosen my agent badly!" admitted the employer. He seemed unable to obey his own impulse freely. "He is a rogue, who would have 'shaved' his requital in the transfer, while, with me, you will receive the ten-pound note intact!"

Pott's eyes were closing, but the amount mentioned opened them.

"Listen to me, and bear in mind what is said!"—he spoke peremptorily like one accustomed to issuing commands.

"Well, a young woman—that is, a superior young woman—that is, ladylike, will come here at any time, soon, and inquire for accommodation for the night." He looked around, unimpressed agreeably. "It seems hardly where females would apply——"

"Bless your heart, noble sir!" said Pott, warmly. "This here ain't the front face of the Fox! No one knows the capacity of the Fox! We have a perfeck Whitehall Pallis above-stairs, with two ways out—one to the river and one to the Strand!'"

"What foresight!" As if he did not know this.

"Well, you can prove to her that first impressions are deceptive, where the Fox burrows, which is logical! Give her the best in all ways! It will be lavishly paid for! Show her the utmost civility and the greatest care, and do not let her be molested!"

"Molested?" repeated the outraged landlord-pugilist. "Molested in the public house or private apartments of Peter Pott, Captain Figg's right-hand man and possessor of his unekalled countercut and crossbuttock? Molested! Oh, I will keep my eye open!" Then, as Gideon's blows still threatened to put him in an eclipse, he prudently added:

"If I cannot, there is Mrs. Pott, who rules the house, and I should like to see any three roisterers try to come up the stairs abreast, to annoy a lady lodger, with her at the landing, a little fire-fender in her hands!"

Apparently convinced at this second dragon being insured, the employer put the bank note on the tanned palm, and to impress the action held it down with a gold coin under his thumb.

"The canary for Mrs. Pott," said he, gallantly.

Pott thanked for all concerned. Then awaited gayly for the explicit instructions.

The other darted an inquiring glance at the two lingerers, Kean and the constable. They had set their heads together and, at a corner of the bar, were engrossed in spinning a kind of die on a spindle, a teetotum, by which fate decides who shall call and pay for a round of drinks. The assistant looked on intently, as if it were to him a novel operation.

Other patrons had crept out. It was about time they were at their "work."

Satisfied, but in a circumspect voice, Lord Newell proceeded:

"Mr. Fox——"

"Ho! ho! not a bad 'un! Mr. Pott, please your worship!"

"Pott, be it! as I see that boats come up nigh to your doors."

"No lie! they have to do it, with the tide high and the wind steady east."

"You must be the porthouse of this quarter!"

"Port it is, and rum! I get more nor my share of the dipsey sailors!"

"I understand by the odor of the *eau-de-vie* that you get the right stuff here! Oh, I am no denouncer! I would even send my butler to negotiate for a few cases of the true brand! Enough now that you would know of a fleet little seagoer, whose skipper could be hired with it for a short trip!"

Pott laid two fingers on his swollen nose, tenderly.

"By the bridge lies just the thing—light, steady, fast— a little sloop with a misleading 'jigger' to step which, then, she looks like a two-master. She is called here the *Rotherhithe Rose.* 'Tween ourselves and the post, there has been a change of masters; him that was cap and brung her over from Cadiz; is now muddy-tating in Newgate, and the new skipper, which he was the supercargo to him, is just burning to get away as soon as possible! You can reach out as far as you say, and stay off sound-ings as long as you like!"

"By London Bridge——"

"In the shadow. But her gig is due here about this blessed instant." He looked at a black-oak clock over his bar.

"I have a way of whistling to his coxswain, which will fetch him here from the boat if it has arrived."

"Naturally, I should like to inspect her!"

"Just so—I, too, want to test the plank that keeps me from being drowned. I have a pert boy somewhere in the cellar who can take your lordship down to the Ramp, where he will point you out the cutter of 'the *Rose.* Now, the coxswain will take you to his ship, and if you strike a bargain, why he will bring you back in the long boat with six or eight oars, seeing that it will be risky, later on, to ship you and your baggage. Ha! ha!"

"Good! Let me have the guide. Quick! this atmo-sphere is pestilential!"

Pott sniffed like him.

"You are right, my lord! What with the reek of the foreshore, the cellar whiffs and the coal, it is a peni-tentiary air!"

He went in, leaving my lord impatiently shifting his feet on the doorstep. The latter, in the gap, darted a still suspicious glance at Kean and the constable, whom he vaguely thought not entirely strange, but who kept their backs toward him.

"Scamper down," said the host carefully to the boy, "go along with that fluttering to the *Rose's* skiff. Let Captain Hurley treat him mild, for he is a right nobleman—I am fixed on that. After he gets him out to sea, with or without a companion, he can find out, by making him look into a 'barker' what his quality is, and we may stand a round sum, of which you shall have your 'lay,' to ransom him, or sell him to Barbary if his next in succession wants to step right in."

The potboy, really a man of nearly thirty, nodded, snuggled into a pea-jacket never made for him, and doned a tarry cap which he pulled down over his projecting ears to induce them to be less conspicuous.

He sent before him a peculiar whistle and, quite unchallenged, he and the odd customer proceeded down to the muddy edge.

"Did you ever notice," remarked that sage Prettiman, "that things come in a streak like a string of fish? Meeting of them strolling folk, I seem to see old faces everywhere! You give me a touch up now and then that I have seen you afore, and that 'ere rake in the muffles, he 'favors' a nobleman of my parts—one Lord Newell!"

Kean repeated the title as though a subsidiary one of the Great Cham, and was impenetrable.

"We don't git a chance to drop a pulley-block on to a nob.'s epaulet," regretfully said he, "for all the tiptoppers goes into the army or the clergy! They get soft bread and sweet water ashore, while at sea, times come round when the officers have to chaw weevils in stonehard biskit and drink the rinsings of the water breaker, do you see!"

Pott stamped in, grumbling, as it was a pang in many places all over him to which a bank note was no plaster. "That's a cold-blooded riptile, him!" he jerked his thumb outward. "That fop! do you know it was his own man that I gave the drubbing to, and yet he never asked if he were in the 'ospital or no!"

"Most like, he knew your reppytation," said Pretti-man, flatteringly. "And so did not expect to hear of him only by the undertaker's bill! Like master, like man! Hullo! why, as sure as that nan-tagonist of your'n was the gamekeeper of the Newells, whom I knowed, that jackadandy was his lordship—the head of the Newells!"

"Oh, it's that Lord Newell, is it? My insight was not out by a sight!" said the host of the Fox.

Kean had established himself at a table which occupied a sort of privileged and cosy corner, and called for the landlord, very rudely. But Pott deigned to come to his side.

"Your needs?" said he, rubbing his cheek, which the change of the air set tingling.

"I want some wine, and genuine! And don't you make a botch of that supper to this gentleman's guests up aloft there!"

"That's my wife's business. They will fare like field-mice in a corn rick!"

"Wine—red or white!" repeated Kean, noisily. "None of your logwood sap! I see your cellarman come up from the vaults, so none of your doctored runs. One need not make two or more v'y'ges to Rio to know that con-coc-tion!"

"You shall have a sealed bottle just as it come!" said the landlord, going for it. "These Englishmen who fall in with the furrin tastes, they are the ruin of the trade! I can keep the pump going in the brandy now, when it used to be sucking dry in the ale, porter and beer casks!"

He chatted with his man, who saw that his eyes were closing and his hands trembled, and suggested his taking a rest.

"You are a worthy good fellow to treat those poor players right," remarked Kean to the constable. "That is why I mean to drink your health in good wine!"

Pott had returned, with a labeled bottle of champagne, which his fastidious customer eyed contemptuously. This added to the host's feverish state. A new idea seized him.

"This shark takes uncommon soon to the p'lice officer! What if they are in tow together?—some trick of the excise to catch me tripping! I don't approve of a watchman refereeing fist fights, though he gave me the decision, or a sailor who prefers white wash to rum. If there's any underboard, one-sided cut-ups going on, I will——"

He opened the bottle, but, by some chance, there was not a bubble in it.

"That French white wine, all sparkle and fuss!" sneered the pretended sailor. "I'd as lieve swallow the cork!"

Pott was in a fret; it was becoming fury.

"What's the matter with your eye that you don't see the label? "Chattoh Coat' d'or! It's a favorite brand with the prince regent! And what's the matter with your nose that you cannot identify the bo-kay?"

"If it comes to that, what is the matter with your eye, and your nose, for they are going off together!"

"Never mind me——"

"Oh, if you had another such an eye, it would make a pair!"

"It took a man to give me that!" said Pott, putting down the bottle, not to yield to an impulse to bull it at the taunter's head.

"I recommend a sheet of brown paper and some of that winegar on it!" resumed the mariner. "It is not a nice eye for a host to exhibit; it gives me a slew up'ard, so that I don't want any of your swizzle now!"

"There are one or two other drinking houses in London," remarked the Fox, rather wolfishly, "Tim!" to his man, for some customers dropped in, and it was time to light the lamps and candles and revive the fire, at which meat, bought at the butcher's and brought, could be cooked if the beever bought beer.

"I wager," retorted Kean, still provoking, "that not one of 'em has the ekal of this pug's wash!"

"Now now!" said Prettiman, as peacemaker. "The wine is still, but it is sweet as milk!" for he had tasted it.

"Don't stand that, master!" said one of the bystanders, who had heard of the late encounter and longed for a repetition to give zest to his supper beer.

"In s-s-sober earnest," hiccoughed the sailor, solemnly,

with a half-admiration, pointing to the innkeeper, "none of the proprietors of the beer houses which do sell Simon-pure white wine, have a poached egg for an eye like that!" And lunging forward, he almost touched the landlord's now "retired" eye.

"There are others where that came from!" retorted Pott, conveying his meaning, though the phrase was not clear.

Kean came around from the table.

"Why, it mought be," said he, supporting himself by the table edge, "that you think you are dealing black eyes, as per sample!" and he nearly touched the eye playfully again with a flip of his tarry fingers. "Do you keep open at that trade all night, which your peeper don't do?"

"I hand them out here, in my store!"

Whereupon the sailor struggled out of his jacket, which he laid across his new friend's shoulder as though he were a clotheshorse.

Jack took in his belt one hole and hitched up his trousers.

"What are you doing, friend?" asked the constable, becoming participant in a fight once more, also willynilly.

"Spilling the deck load!" was the answer. "Clearing for action." He rid himself of the tobacco and dextrously flung it over the bar, where, the bartender, eluding it, it spread on a placard offering "Thrale's Entire."

"Now, then, Fox, are you for coming on? Fox, who made that wine of those sour grapes we read about?"

"Matey, you don't know again whom you are pitting yourself!" whispered a sympathetic bystander with well-meaning.

"Figg's pruttyjay!" came another whisper.

"The gamekeeper whom he defeated was the terror of our parish!" added Prettiman.

"Mind your business!" roared the host, stripping in his turn.

"My business," replied the person adjured, "is to arrest you both!"

"No, no, let the constable referee the fight!" was the general cry.

Making a cushion of Kean's jacket, they put it on the

bar ledge, and on it seated Prettiman, before forming a ring around the two men.

"You see me give a drink to the hammered man," said Pott, slyly; "well, I give you nothing! I shall pour out only blood, thou saucy sailor of the seas!"

So saying, he made a rush, fearing that he would go half blind before he could exhibit his prowess. But just as he had beaten Gideon, this unknown, who had also defeated that worthy, defeated the master of the Fox. With a well-directed blow on the sound eye, Pott sank into the arms of his seconder. They bore him insensible behind the bar, and placed him under the drip of the spilt liquor and water. As the assistant was slow, or puzzled what remedy to apply, they tested several spirituous medicaments before giving a dose out of one bottle.

The beholders clapped the conqueror on the back.

"Brief, but beau-tiful!" was the comment.

"If it were not to spoil my credit with Mr. Pott," said a black-faced collier-man, "I would stand beers around!"

"I will do that," said Prettiman, excited. "That was an artistic knock-'em-downer! I can give my judgment with relish!"

"You rate me too high, mates!" modestly said the victor. "That was a poor little caulker's punch. If I had launched out for to hurt the block—but my motto is to 'Save the Publican!' I should have let her slide down the greased ways, and Pott would have had his pot head cracked! And he would not have been brought up till he reached the barges below there."

Laughter mingled with the "three cheers and one little one more to send them along!"

It was the first time the Fox had been so jolly at having its own head knocked off!

Kean slowly put on his jacket, thinking:

"I do not know what unholy machination that nobleman and this ignoble one plotted, but I am sure that the latter will not be in the condition to receive the lady lodger announced!"

Prettiman was settling with the barman for the general refreshment afforded by the victor.

"I wish," said he, "that you will excuse me, and enter-

tain those strolling players, while I go and report that
my first watch is over, at the constabulary office!"

"You may report that the last watch will be over without you till the end, as I know not much of players, but I
do believe that they will not let you, their host, leave while
there is a pannikin full!"

CHAPTER XXVII.

Having rendered Mr. Pott incapable of doing the honors to Lord Newell's introduction, Kean did not wish the girl to fall into the hands of Mrs. Pott. So, having the field to himself, he was eagerly awaiting, when a shadow slipped down the lane and very cautiously investigated the inn.

As this man was without disguise, the actor almost shouted with joy, though not knowing if Moses, for it was he, brought news bad, good, or between them.

He ran out and seized him as he hesitated.

"It is I!" he said, in his own voice.

"Oh, I was looking for a seaman. 'Chips,' at the theatre, tells me that, overhearing Lord Newell and another of his kidney speaking of alluring a young person to the Fox-under-the-Hill, he took the liberty of sending you an anomalous letter, so he calls it! warning you to be on the alert, and to frustrate the game!"

"Oh, that is the source? Then you think, with me, that the person——"

"Miss D., for a hundred!—in revenge more than desire, such villains are tenacious and stick to one aim."

"It is so. My lord has been here, and is gone to see a vessel in the river, to aid him in his plot."

"Then I was right—I thought I saw Miss Danby on the Strand as if seeking a rendezvous; only I believed——"

"That the appointment was with me? Thank you, Old Trusty!"

"I meant no offense!"

"I'll let it go down the wind, for you do not understand how true love purifies—well, I wish you would hasten to the street and urge her to come here—not go in at the other entrance of this precious den of worse than thieves!"

"Very well!"

"Hold! On seeing her under cover here, in my hands, return to the theatre and tell Mr. Belliston that, on the usual terms, I require an off-night for a benefit."

"To raise the wedding fees?" said Moses, facetiously.

"To succor poor old Richardson and what is left of his show. They are stranded, Mo! And that constable fellow of Freefolk took the opportunity, and has defrauded me—they are beholden to him for the shelter in there, and——"

"Richardson come to grief? He was a little hard and close, but I will prompt the performance free!"

"Hasten and guide the lady here! Quick, for that lord may be back with some pirates in no time."

Shortly after, Miss Danby, with a riding-cloak having the hood completely covering her face, entered the inn.

The obsequious substitute for Pott ushered her into an inner room. She stopped short, for the only occupant, seen fairly by a smoking oil lamp, was in nautical dress.

"You here, Miss Danby?" cried he, so frankly that she knew him at once. "I ask your pardon, but your trust gives me rights over you, at least to be enlightened. In Heaven's name, how came you here?"

"I came to hear your explanation for requiring me!"

"Oh, enticed? Voice or letter?"

"A letter! As I do not know your hand, I see that I am a fool to——"

"Youth mounts where folly guides!" She held out a folded paper to him. He scanned it quickly and laughed bitterly.

"They spell my name Keen! Such is fame! But let us retain that as a hint. Madam, Lord Newell or a hireling wrote that! It is so congenial that he should have lured you into the Fox's burrow."

"That Newell, perpetually!"

"Oh, he will run up against something that will bring him to a stop!"

In his anger, he did not dwell upon the woman's hasty acceptance of the gross decoy, but that plainness was what deceived her—revealed the state of her deep-seated affection.

"This is a struggle with an unscrupulous foe. He

would degrade you rather than see you happy in your own estate. But he has been anticipated. I am on guard. I am going to defend you, and chance—well, I will, for your sake, call the power Heaven!—is on our side. A number of my friends, old companions of the stage, were brought indoors here, by a constable whom they treated well in their heyday. So you can be among friends in two seconds."

"As for you——"

"Oh, who will meet my lord?" He smiled scornfully. "I come of the people whose garb I resume now and then—for more or less good purposes. This enemy of yours, driven to the extremity——"

"My father finds that he loses every penny he borrows, at the gaming-table, and he has repulsed him. Now, he turns on him with that old contract revoked. I can wed where he approves, but he will not again advocate a Newell!"

"That is why he would ship you afar!—where you would be at his mercy."

"Mr. Kean, my father would not redeem me from the corsairs unless they threw Lord Newell's head into the bargain—for he hates him."

"To tell the truth, I did not think he loved any one, but I have discovered that it was his means that lifted me into the place I occupy at the first theatre. Thus he expunged the debt of saving your life."

"Alba Danby's was that debt, and she will pay her own!" said she, proudly.

"I am not pressing, as time is!"

"Place me with your friends—this hovel stifles me!" said she, suddenly. There were noises alarming to her in the barroom.

"If my friends are too lowly, there is one here to whom your own father would confine you!"

"Ah! not the—the prince—here!"

She had heard that Prince George, like Kean, executed diversions in disguise worthy to be reckoned with the like of earlier monarchs with a humorous turn.

Spite of the serious situation, he indulged in sincere merriment.

"No, no," he said, "not the prince."

"Your valet, then?"

"Yes, he is by, my Moses. But I mean better than that. Even your family will not jibe at a representative of the active arm of the law! I doubt Lord Newell and his band would cross rapiers with his staff, seeing that the staff is tipped with the crown of sovereignty!"

"A constable here?" looking around.

Kean had gone to the door, where he called:

"This way, Mr. Prettiman, if you are back to the front! Ha! ha!"

The police guardian had returned; the prospect of the fleshpots of the Egyptians—the strollers, at Kean's expense, had attracted him. He hurried to this summons.

"Mr. Constable," began Kean, forgetting he was still the sailor to him, and astonishing him very much by the address, as he had been by seeing that young lady there— "In this esteemed lady you see one plagued by your Lord Newell. I call you to intrust her to you, to be conducted to her home. High and weighty charge, Mr. Prettiman —and—a word in your ear!—rich as Crœsus! Get her away from this pit of Acheron!"

"Eh, certainly. But who——"

"Oh, it is Edmund Kean who claims the law's buckler for innocence assailed!"

The official, fond of art in all phases, bowed to the floor.

"The great Mr. K——" and the name stuck in his throat.

"Do your duty and make Kean your friend!"

"To think I have been docked a day's pay for going to see you play! and not to know you in the pea-coat and ducks! And as I supped with you down at Freefolk, what a blind gull I am! Miss Danby, I am your servant to command. I will get a hack, and my club is at your orders to break any head for your sake, and in the king's name!"

"You will lose the supper!" said the actor, maliciously.

"Pooh! For that lady I would do the long fasts of your friend Moses!"

"I will reconnoiter." He went out. "Dash it all! that

girl has bewitched this watch! To charm a bulldog as easily as a Newell, the hound! It's a dubious gift! Poor Alba! An ugly little plot! A base scoundrel, that! to attack a nonpareil like that—one who ought to be worshiped and he horsewhiped!"

CHAPTER XXVIII.

EQUAL FOOTING.

When Kean stood out on the sill once more, all was very blank and black.

Fog veiling the river; the coal barges looming up like a mound of asphalt; the gutter water oozing along like liquid bitumen; the overhanging houses bidding to embrace. Shadows, a shade lighter than the background, flitting noiselessly. Smothered shouts faintly resounding in the bottom; the navigators calling from the shore to their ships.

"That stage carpenter shall be pensioned off for life, for being Miss Danby's providence!" thought the tragedian. "That false note found, the spiriting away would be warrantably credited as performed under my name! This time he would have realized that scandal which cheated George the Prince. Will I remove the grounds for scandal now, after chastising this wretch? What a foul pool for the vindication of a lady, too! This time an alibi could only be proved by Prettiman, my old play-fellows, and Mr. Pott!"

Two of the shadows, coming up closely, amalgamated as they halted to consult about this sentinel at the door, their goal.

Customers fearful, or Newell and his sea captain?

It was Newell, waylaid and addressed by Gideon. That scamp was in sore straits; penniless, beaten so as to be disfigured, he skulked here, and was overjoyed to see his master. Even at the likelihood of being rebuked for his blunder, he had no other resource. He was prepared to do anything with his hand, provided it could be dipped into the Newell purse again.

He reassured the noble as to the quality of the stranger, for he did not care to avow that he guessed Kean's identity. He wished to bring about a collision, not doubting that his lord, by his superor position, would soon dispose, in this quarter, of the mock sailor.

"It's not the landlord," said he; "only a drunken tar. Go at it, my lord!"

He hung behind. But feeling that he was backed, and that two cowards may be a match for a brave man, Newell advanced, and as Kean palpably threw himself across the doorway, he said, offhand:

"Oh, it's the sailor! You will make passage, my lad, for I am going in!"

"No, you will not, you cursed and silly animal!" returned the intervener, believing that the gamekeeper penetrated his disguise and would inform his principal. "Not for the filthy business you and your hangdog are engaged in."

This was plain, and though the language suited the assumption, the voice was the actor's in its extreme of scorn and loathing.

"What an address!" muttered the noble, set a-shiver by this revelation of opposition, and who was the opposer. He put his hand on the sword under his covering.

"You will hear worse! Your family may have come down from the era when they plucked goldsmiths' wives out of their dwellings, but that is a long date from Jane Shore and her persecutors. Still, there is Shoreditch, which, by my star! yonder river resembles! Only mark this, pride of the peerage! This time, instead of the traditional victim, it is the criminal who is likely to be smothered in the befitting mire!"

"Man, I——"

"Your sword? I wager it's a harlequin's lath, glued to the case! You have already declined to make a stand against me!"

"Master, it's that actor-man!" whispered Gideon, keeping in the rear.

"Will you back me or must I dispatch you to bring those pirates?"

"Depend on it, he knows your purpose!"

"Then I am betrayed! A saucy cur to yelp before a door not his own!"

"I bet she be here, or he would not stick so in the way," observed Gideon, who did not like to leave, and yet wished reinforcements would arrive.

"A coward who seeks still to shift though his oft-beaten bully is at his heels!" He squared himself in the doorway.

Newell noticed the window without a frame.

"Get in at that window," said he, "and take him in the rear."

"Leaving you alone?"

"You waver—you flinch?—it is you who have betrayed me. Ha, sir, you are unworthy gentlemanly treatment; you have purchased my man—the landlord within doors; intercepted my letters, I doubt not! Ah, rob the British mail, do you! You dog me!"

"A watchdog, then! You get not past me, without feeling my tooth or nail!"

"The wench is in there," goaded on Gideon, "for he is but sparring for time!"

But the noble could not be made to advance further.

"You are right," said the actor, with pretended commendation. "There should be no riot over this deed. As far as that person is concerned, silence, for reasons which you are not yet, perchance, too brutalized to appreciate. As to us, it is another row of pins! Let us leave the curtain down, but play our parts where we stand!"

"A fracas in the gutter? excuse me!"

"I am not going to excuse you calling names! I demand reparation!"

He took a forward step, confident that Gideon would not dare to try to slip around by him.

"I am not going to make reparation to an actor, who acts on the street, also! I am the noble anywhere, and I cannot contest with you!"

"Wait—hear my last words! I grant there is a vast space between my stage and your dais in the Lords' Chamber. You are degraded; for you compete, with your inferiors, in your substitutes for the jousts, feats of arms and tourneys of your ancestors—on the race course, at cockpit and in the gaming halls. Your cap of state is soiled with the lees of the wine cup, held unsteadily in your insecure hand and the pitch of your ill-doings clings to your moral condition. Ceasing to stand well, the Newells fall.

"Well, I was found among the lowly, if not the low;

better no name than a tarnished one! But I have made
the name of Kean famous as all the others of price!
Signed to an order on the treasury, it will procure as large
sum of gold as Newell, at all events. Still I grant that
the field of honor is debarred from me, as it ought to be
from you. Yet the player must meet the patrician——"

"You were sensible till you concluded with that!"
sneered the other, breathing anew.

"Let Jessamy, Lord Newell, defame his glory, stain
his title, scatter the coin obtained shamelessly; in short,
wreck himself! I care not, and would not lift a finger
to stay him on the gulf. But when he worries an innocent lamb, whose fleece is what this ermine never was for
purity; whose sole defender he shrinks from facing—and
when his despised and rejected addresses are dead, decides rather than let her enjoy her free will, to have her
carried out to sea, among smugglers to whom pirate is too
good a word; then he must meet her defender, player, or
if beggar, thief even; all are fitter than you!"

Newell shuddered at this passionate defiance, delivered
in a governed voice. He was petrified, like a man under
Mount Hecla, who sees the lava gush out white-hot and
send the snow up in columns of steam.

"You have turned her own father and family against
her; you induced Mrs. Powis to connive at her leaving
that refuge; you will try to cajole Lady Gorsewold into
refusing her hospitality! You see I have gauged you!
That is why the actor, Kean, is your mortal enemy now!
I can be but that, since, if I had been lashed with the
tongue as you are done, and before one of my minions—
oh, I would rush down there and bury myself in the
mud!"

The hearer had long since lost color; he was green as a
cadaver. Yet he listened, as one to an accumulation of
insults, which he wished to repay, but only in his own
way.

"You take advantage of my forbearance," stammered
he; "but, as a gentleman——"

"My lord, I will give you your last chance! Gentleman or sans-noblesse, we are equal; as men, deadly
inimical, on one ground; on the theatrical stage all are
alike! For your family's reputation, for honor and brav-

ery, meet me there! Ah, this course ought to appeal to you, if you have any vain-glory! We have pieces in which combats may be simulated to the verge of the death blow! How happy for you, punctilious dastards! Then will you be punished, not in this kennel, but in the luster of a hundred lights, before three thousand persons, still under the eye of the supernal Justice, as in the olden time when men appealed to Heaven!"

"You are a—never mind, but I accept!"

"Then you are spared the thrashing which—spite of your sword and this hind, whom already the weight of my arm fell upon—would have been yours within these ten minutes. Now, go! The lady is on her way, diametrically opposite; so you will never meet!"

He spun around and walked into the inn, as if confident that he would not be followed.

"Now may the dev——" began the noble, but Gideon caught his upraised arm and said:

"My lord, not before those seamen! As for the devil, he has stopped business since the angels no longer fly to the good man's call. The play-actor is right; how fine to kill him before his friends and huzzaers—on the scene of his triumphs, and no one to hold you to answer— since the sticking him with the file will be just an accident! I would I were in your boots that night!"

CHAPTER XXIX.

"Disorder that has spoilt us now, friend, as ever!"

Like Palmer, a dissolute actor, Kean had been compelled to take up his residence in the rumbling theatre.

He could have had room to keep a guards' barracks, for the reigning favorite is the autocrat behind the scenes.

So to Belliston, who knew what such an asylum was worth, was due this harbor. Few places are impregnable to the king's writ, but the most insinuating of sheriff's janissaries never got past a stage doorkeeper.

If the belief in transmigration is not erroneous, then these porters have Cerberus to animate them during their office. So Moses, as chief guard, was constant at the door of the suite in Drury Lane.

He was preparing beef broth for his master, changing his diet with change of residence, under the large, staring eyes of La Rogueon, Mr. Richardson's comic man and pantomimist. Attending the harvest from the benefit for his old companions, this one made himself useful; as grateful as a homeless dog finding a bone and kennel.

"I don't want to poke my nose"—it was a blunt, flat nose, not constructed for poking, by the way—"into things, and I don't want to poke it into that mess, Father Mo', but what under the son and father, the Georges, is that wet whistle?"

Moses still kept the spoon stirring.

"It is a drink of barley and beef, to moisten the throat with. Mr. Kean does a power of speaking to-night."

"I see! Old Richie uses whisky, and our barley-water up to the North is barley-beer?"

"It is not that I wish to deny Mr. Kean any little luxuries, but the actor in high feather must make the most of his time. Now, to drink heavily takes its pay out in heavy sleeping. Heavy sleeping loses time. We must make all the hay while the sun shines!"

"While 'the star' shines! I 'tumble,' which is my line!"

"I am his bodyguard! I have to strike Hollands and Jamaica off the list. Would you like to taste?"

La Rogueon did so, out of courtesy, but courtesy could not prevent his outrageous wry grimace.

"It may be a fort-o'-fire, but it is cold and tame to me. I own that you are right, Mr. Mo'; for I have known professionals who could keep their heads above water, but when the luck brought a deluge of strong drink, they went under! Like Daddy Noah, when he squeezed the grapes too long and tight!"

He rolled his eyes and let them become fixed with admiration on the contents of a large wardrobe closet, its doors open to air it.

"Is it your rag shop?" asked he.

"Rags? costumes which no money can buy; collection of days, and with deep lore and much cash! You will not see there the cartwheel, hat and hearse-plumes in which Lady Macbeth comes to read her letter, or the Highland bonnet in which her general arrives to pay his respects! No, nor the tinpot helmet and packboots of the guard's ensign, in which Signor Romeo used to fight Tybalt! Drop in to-night—it's for your own 'benny,' and see how accurately we dress our characters! It's Kean reformed the stage! Tybalt wore a Grecian casque before!"

"I know—copper-washed!"

"While we have real gold now. That in the corner, wrapped in tissue paper, is cloth of gold, for King Henry V.'s coronation robe; two thousand pounds would not pay for the material, let alone the work on it."

"Why, when the prince comes to his own, he will not go wrong to beg the loan of that!" He tore a hole in the silk-paper and ogled the flashing goldcloth. "Say, Old 'Un, have you got the crown diamonds here, too, for the new style of producing a show up to Dick? Daddy Mo', look at that!" he pointed to a door. "Now, that is a real door, not a stage one, leading to nowhere—that leads to the street, eh?"

He ran his hands up and down the seam of the doorway.

"Locked!" said he; "you are so distrustful, you cockneys! I bet Mr. Kean so relies on that patent lock that he has no idea that all a 'cross-cove' has to do is whisper, 'Open, Sea-sam!' and—my eye, that door is open!"

Indeed, he had cleverly manipulated the lock with a toothpick or other trifle, and made a fool of the fastenings.

"You viper in the bosom!" cried Moses; "how did you do that?"

"Sleight of hand and slight of conscience!" said La Rogueon, unctiously. "To think that the point of a pen-trimmer and a little elbow-grease lets the cat out!"

"If Mr. Kean knew you were an expert crack-lock, he——"

"Would not give me the benefit of clergy, when I come to the Old Bailey gallows? Well, don't you tell him! Just let it go that I never saw your wardrobe—that it had no door, and that was locked tight. Who pointed out boastfully that there was a suit of cloth-of-gold here? not me! you! you are a tempter, Moses!"

"Is your benefit going to be a draw, think you, my comic boy?"

"That bill, with Mr. Kean's name in two places, draws like a poor man's plaster! At three *pea-hen* the crowd began to collect just as for the first night of a pantomime! I walked up and down, from the fat fellow on a jointstool and eating a bag of doughnuts, to the tail—it took me a quarter of an hour to get around the line!"

"What did you waste time like that for?"

"To reckon up how much cash was in their pockets!"

"Are you a pickpocket, too?"

"My friend, one gets so tired of fumbling in one's own pockets without ever running the nail back against a sixpence, that the itch is tremendous to try a neighbor's!"

"Well, Mr. Kean is coming—you had better sling your hook!"

"Moses, my dear," said the comic actor, in a wheedling tone. "You could not lend me that gold suit, just for two hours? I know a little maid in a milliner's, in New Church passage, whom I should just paraphase if she saw me dressed up like that! I promise to send you the pawnticket for it after——"

"He comes—flit!"

He made a burlesque kick at the droll, who, as if impelled by a seven-league boot, bounded out by a side-issue. It was time, for the tragedian walked in by the inner door.

Moses saw that his brow was wrinkled, and he could have envied the other being out of the tempest's course.

"Moses," said the newcomer, suddenly, with a hoarseness in his voice, "have you a square of carpet—a rug—a wild beast's hide——"

"Sir?" cried the amazed man.

"Anything to tumble on! To tumble? Yes! I am going back to the old trade! Get some bills printed that Edmund Kean, ex-Tragedian, is going to execute feats of ground-and-lofty tumbling in the squares, and in the back-parlors of the nobility and gentry, for five guineas a head! In that way, I may pile up enough for a competency—that is, a little hovel with two standard cabbage-roses in front of it, where I can die, down in Devon, with a hunk of corned beef, a platter of cabbage and a pot of home-brewed to the last!"

"We have had Larogueon here," said Moses, "but he was not half as funny as you! Shakespeare had you in his prophetic soul, sir, when he said that 'if not fellow with the best king, thou shalt find him the best king of good fellows!'"

"Ah, this time I am not joking! Do you pelt me with glory? Art! art! lean specter! starved vampire! on whom we fling a golden robe and worship as a god! I am still your victim, but no longer your dupe!"

"What is the ail, master?"

"As if you did not know—who know my affairs better than I do myself!"

"Oh, have order!"

"The devil take order now! My chambers carried by bailiffs! I must pass the day in a carriage, and my night in some tavern! All of which restlessness makes me an admirable candidate for a hissing, a groaning, or a pelting with apple-cores at night! And all this because I owe some four or five hundred miserable 'shiners'! And you tell me I am the leading light in England, and that

you would not change for the king! You are a vile
flatterer, Moses!"

"It is your own undoing, sir! You ought to have order! Order!"

"What becomes of genius while order rules? Newton
is to go and cook his apple instead of calculating how
it fell! Watt is to make his tea with the kettle, instead
of devising the steam-pump! Montgolfier is to burn his
gas in Regent street to show a light to the pickpocket,
whom the new pockets baffle in the dark—instead of rising into the ether! Sordid minds, what would you with
genius? With a life multiplied and crammed like mine,
have I time to calculate the employment of each minute
and of each shilling? Are my days mine own, or my
coin, either? If I had had order, I should be a draper
in Islington High street, or a ladler-out of soup in
Leadenhall, and not ladler-out of verses in Drury Lane!"

"As for the revenue, you may be easy! As for the
five hundred you need at the pinch, why, let Simmons advance it you out of the proceeds of this benefit to the
Richardsonians!"

"Moses, you offend! Moses, you enrage! Moses, you
will next invite me to go on the highway with that pistol
there! For the takings for this benefit belong to those
strollers! Mr. Danby could not reason more faultily
than you!"

"Pooh! In two or three days——"

"What!" thundered Kean, "am I to borrow of mounte-
banks now? I am to rob old Richardson, thrown on my
bounty when I am in the golden way! I do not hold up
Richardson as a miracle of generosity! But had he been
a tyrant, I should see in him now only a fallen man! I
make him a present, and do not spare the coin I give
away!"

Moses abjectly begged pardon of his excited friend,
whom he would always adore, sinning or sainted.

"Very good! Oh, I want you to hear me rehearse. I
have my 'Romeo' rather rusty, to tell the truth!"

"You are going to give them 'Measter's Yorkshire,'
too! And you cannot have played that farce for a matter of——"

"Are you holding up my gray hairs to me now? Oh,

I have my dialect pat! It is the language of Shakespeare that requires eternal repetition—it is at the same time natural so that the lout understands it, and yet so individual that at times I doubt the Elizabethans spoke like that!"

"Drink of that sedative, made to calm you," said Moses. "I will bring the book."

CHAPTER XXX.

THE FULL-BLOWN ROSE.

Left alone, Kean made the parody of stabbing himself.
"He darted me a reproachful shaft! He holds me an
ingrate!" He drank a little of the insipid brew. "But
he is bringing me around after my fever from that
bout with Newell and saving poor Alba. Dr. Moses! I,
ingrate—like I deemed the Danbys! Rome reputed in-
gratitude a heinous sin, and"—drinking—"long life to
you, Lady Roma!"

His eyes became damp, and the fire was quenched; that
good and excellent 'squire of his was his faithful friend of
all times and weathers. To him he had no secrets—not
even his overwhelming love, and he was the mirror to
him in vanity and sorrow. Lately, when he had drawn
near for kindly words, he had received him with rough
and hasty phrases!

"If Lord Byron had had a friend like that, he would
not set up a monument to his dog!" mused he.

It was a very "mixed bill" for that night. On hearing
that Richardson, of the Penny Show, was in town,
wrecked, disconsolate, wanting money, bread, and a pil-
low, it is but justice to those who had tramped under
his colors, to say that they all wanted to contribute their
meed.

The middle of the entertainment was to be filled by
Kean, who not only was to appear in an act of "Romeo,"
but also in a farcical character in which he would emulate a famous dialect-actor of the day. The strollers
themselves would end the long *menu* with an act out of
their repertoire, with an epilogue conveying thanks for
their salvation.

It is needless to say that the fashionable patrons would
not come early, and would depart after seeing Kean, since
the rest was horseplay and popular antics.

"This is delightfully falling in with my hope!" muttered he. "Miss Danby will have ample time to run in

here under the wing of Lady Koefeld, as arranged, and let me know if the lord has ceased to trouble. As for him, he will, I am under the impression, cease to trouble after this night! Misguided ass! Unless revenge guides him to his chastisement block—the whipping-block! He has acted on my hint!"

He laughed so ferociously that a distant growl responded; it was his pet lion, Ibraham, which, removed from the Southampton street lodgings for fear that he would devour a sheriff's adherent or two, bewailed the ill accommodations of his new quarters.

This interview ought to be important to her welfare and to his happiness, only he did not admit to himself that it so possessed him. He looked at a new bill on the wall; it announced in a line, which to him was glaring, that "a gentleman of this city, for the first time, had volunteered his services in the endeavor to portray Tybalt."

This gentleman of a good will—toward the strollers—was Lord Newell.

Kean had shown him where he could vent his spite; Gideon had seconded this move. Then the moment he whispered to his friends that he should like to go on the stage and show Miss Danby, with her inclination that way, that she was losing as fine an actor as Kean, they cheered him on.

It was the age when the favorite sport was to deceive a hot-head and vain upstart into believing that he was fitted for the stage above the uneducated and dragged-up.

So, emulous of "Pea-green Haynes," it was thought, Lord Newell came to rehearsals and patiently heeded the instructions of his tutor. In the usual course of stage events, he ought to have been presented to Kean, and, at least, gone through one rehearsal with him. Both had reasons to avoid this; but Kean used his privilege as a star who had the piece letter-perfect. As the fencing-bout between the furious Tybalt and Romeo, exasperated by facing one who killed his friend, Mercutio, is but a prearranged school-at-arms lesson, Newell was relieved by not meeting his antagonist prematurely.

What he had to say were words so fitting with his vein

that he could believe them fore-inspired to invigorate him and feed his hatred.

"She must burn to come and see me!" thought the tragedian, eying the promise of contending with his rival carelessly and absently. "I wish she had not to do it under the protection of that Italian-Norwegian countess! What a fool she makes of everybody, her husband and the prince! But that is her world-wide repute!"

Hearing skirts in the lobby, he hastened to the door, with an eagerness revealing his love, but shrank back disappointed. It was not complimentary, for it was Lady Elena who appeared, enframed in the door-square.

She recognized him with a nod, and turned her head; Kean thought it was to address another; that she had conducted Miss Danby according to their agreement, but in Italian she bade her woman, "Gilda, wait for her; she would not be long!"

She came in, and gave the place but a short inspection.

"You have come—alone?" said he, with evident rebuke.

"Oh, you really believe that that young woman loves you?" she said, with her rare but well-timed abruptness, as if she could not find careful language.

"Well, I really believe it!"

"Oh, you men are all unjust and exacting! It is not enough that the poor thing intrusts her honor to your safe keeping, but she must risk the loss of it to provide you a short pleasure!"

"But you have come, and you risk as much!"

"Not at all! The count is not yet arrived. He is, I believe, questioning the worthy but double-dealing Mr. Bonnell about the prince's disposition of his time, hour by hour, this night."

"Take care! Don't trust too much to your running no risk! Beware the Othello which Shakespeare did not draw—the Northern one! the Gothic-French one, who made his faithless wife eat her lover's heart!"

"He is jealous as your Othello! so be it!" said she, carelessly.

"Then, the more reason that, instead of having your maid as shield, you should have prevailed on Miss Danby."

"Miss Danby can be no shield to me, since she is pronounced your idol; why, you are no longer a rival."

"I a rival? Oh, Lord Newell's—well, we fight that out to-night!"

"I came to see him as Tybalt! The *costumier* has said that he has a charming appearance!"

"And the echo behind the scenes tells me that he is going to be distinguished, or extinguished, in the place where we cross swords! He so far honors the actor—on the stage!"

"No; in my husband's eyes, you are the rival of the Prince of Wales!"

Kean forgot all, and burst out into a peal of laughter, such as would never let Moses know that the dispossess from his own rooms was on his heart.

"Well, that can be settled so easily! Bring Miss Danby here. I will propose to her, whatever the outcome of the encounter, and you two can return each to your box. If the prince comes, he will be in his own, the king's, and your husband will no longer be jealous."

"No; he has called my lord here, but never has he yet suggested I should accompany him! It is perfectly well known that the prince honors Scandinavia House purely to confer with my husband!"

"Certainly! Politics—which deceive no one."

"And love deceives no one! That is why I suggest that, as my husband might come into our box, and, missing me, but seeing the prince in his——"

"If he comes on this occasion?"

"He will logically suppose that I have gone behind the scenes——"

"To see me, in my rooms?"

"It is so, is it not?"

"It is so, but——"

"Hence, you will be well out of it, if you slip past my maid there, who is deaf, dumb and blind, when I bid her, and, no doubt, chat with Miss Danby in some nook or other! As they led me here I saw that it was as full of pitfalls and traps as the Castle of Otranto!"

"I go to meet Miss Danby! while you——"

"Oh, I have my maid! I am curious—I will just look

around at these oddities theatrical—this is a new event to me!"

"But——" Still, he made toward the door.

When he had most touched the knob, a knock came at it.

"Your maid——"

"Or Miss Danby! Open!"

But it was Gilda who opened, and with her face pale and her tongue not loose, she gasped:

"The prince!"

"The prince!" said Elena, triumphantly.

"The prince!" repeated Kean, confounded. "Well, I——"

To be stalking-horse for this cosmopolitan flirt to bring down her royal stag—how humiliating. It was a part he blushed to play—even to save a reckless friend.

CHAPTER XXXI.

A CONVINCING BILL.

But Gilda, recovering, hastened to explain her terror, while standing courageously between the pair and the door:

"But my lord is there, too!"

"The count! Koefeld!" cried the actor and his caller together.

"I am lost!" exclaimed the latter, appalled.

There is always this dread moment in a coquette's life, when she feels that her often-successful wiles will fail her wholly.

"Not on mine own ground!" said Kean, with quickness. "Silence, and don't you blubber, you girl!" to the frightened servant. He opened the door by which La Rogueon had been furthered in imperceptibly departing "Go, and regain your box! Make haste!"

The maid dragged her mistress into the black passage, smelling of water-color paint and stale orange peel. Kean let the door swing into place, and, crossing the room with rapid step, held the regular door firmly.

"One moment, prince, with my apologies! but I am 'sporting the oak'—barring all out because of the harpies!"

"Eh! Hunted by the Philistines?" I am not inimitable!" returned a voice on the other side of the panel.

"They have run me out of my rooms, and have, I feared, run me down here for a paltry four or five thous."

"Yes, I guessed as much! But you are keeping us at the door."

"Hum! They are such good actors, those runners for the sponging-houses," said Kean, deliberately. "Of course, I ought to recognize your voice; but, in my extremity, caution is prescribed to me! If your highness would verify who came a-knocking at my door by showing his hand——"

"Open the door for that, dunce!"

"Nay, your august handwriting——"

"What will you give for that?"

"This key!"

At the same time a small roll of fine paper was projected in by the keyhole. Kean took it out tenderly, and beheld a bank note for five hundred pounds. To be sure, it was not signed by the king or his deputy, but the governor's scribble was good enough for the indebted actor.

"It's an indubitable royal token!" muttered he.

He undid the door, and let in not only the prince, but the Count of Koefeld. All the native coldness and all the learned imperturbability of the latter could not ally to preserve his equanimity. He looked around with more curiosity than his wife had shown in the artistical "den."

"Ha! ha!" laughed George, as if lightened of a burden by seeing none but the tragedian. "I verily believe that the count hoped to find you rehearsing with your Juliet!"

"He is not so far out! It was with Juliet's cousin!"

"Eh?"

"In the play! with Tybalt, otherwise 'Lord Newell!' We, as you may have heard, have to get the duel right between us for the short time hence."

Koefeld ceased to examine the scene; but he continued to examine the actor.

"I had no idea that Newell was timid as a woman!" said the royal visitor.

"As an actor making his *début!* Great actors have been very bashful on going on the boards! It is like the scaffold—one must get used to it! 'Oft fitted the halter —oft traversed the cart'!"

"It is like the coronation dais in the Abbey," appended the heir-apparent, recurring to his haunting thought; "but, mind, Edmund, I expect you to show me how to carry the scepter and wear the mantle, as your French brother, Talma, attained the Corcisan usurper!"

Kean had directed his face toward the still-inquisitive count, saying:

"Much obliged to your excellency for paying the actor a visit in his den!"

"A lion's den!" replied Koefeld, with a smile to show his teeth.

"Oh, don't be blarneyed over with his diplomatic glozing!" broke in the prince, who stood on shifting ground, with affected gayety. "It is not your merit, but curiosity brings him hither! Though he has been behind the scenes, politically, all his life, Koefeld has never before paid his footing to the imps who work the machinery of Old Drury."

"My lord," continued Kean, graciously, but with some restlessness showing, "an actor changing his costume is not so remarkable as a bather at Ramsgate! But I must notify the explorer that behind the curtain, there reigns a law of punctuality, worthy of the court royal! We have to be ready betimes on the penalty of being raked over by the stage manager and hooted by the public! I think I am belated, and so————"

"My dear sir, go right on, as if we were not by—unless we really disturb you!"

Kean shook his head, slightingly, and pouted a little.

Moses came in with some requisites; he gave his master one of those subtle pantomimic gestures which let him know that Lady Koefeld had been guided by him through the labyrinth to her box.

"Oh, my prince, the note having served to verify your highness, pray, take it back!"

George repulsed the proffer.

"It's the price of my offering to the benefit!" said he, loftily.

Kean handed the bill to his man, saying:

"I accept it, for the beneficiaries!"

"Oh, then, you would be no richer for it! That alters the matter. My friend," resumed he to Moses, "you need not run to that nip-cheese, for our jeweler, Longitharm, has bought his claims up, and Mr. Kean owes nothing for the trinkets! It is added to my account, which, bless Longitharm's hopefulness! is still in the balance at St. Stephen's."

Kean and his *attaché* conferred on this removal of the legal bonds. The count drew his companion aside, to earnestly say:

"You do not appear to believe that he had Lord Newell with him. Yet they might be rehearsing!"

"I am sure there was a woman!" and the prince sniffed, as if inhaling a known perfume.

"Hum! Would it be that Miss Danby, still harping on the string which would lead her upon the stage?"

"I really cannot say! Miss Danby was to be here, this night!"

Koefeld had let his eyes wander; suddenly they were fastened on an object, on the rug, near a chair heaped with dresses. George followed this concentrated gleam, and was perplexed at seeing his friend seize and pocket an article as though it were a diplomatic paper, which others must not dream of. He had no time to put a query since the actor called out from behind a screen covering the dressing table: "What news is in the air?"

"Nothing—yes, the rumor that Lord Newell ran against a masquerader, at the notorious Fox-under-the-Hill, and got his ears boxed or his nose pulled!"

"No, no—for, judging by his well-sustained *rôle* of the fire-eating Tybalt, he must have killed his man before this!"

"Oh, we do not fight duels any more! It is not that we have cowards in our gentry, my lord count, but prudence governs the seconds! The insult did not sting them, and so they take care they shall not be brought before the jury! They ram home cork bullets and call hands off at the first scratch of the blades, singing out, with wonderful unison—which your chorus in 'Julius Cæsar' might copy, Mr. Kean, that honor is satisfied!"

"I do not fully understand what change has come over your once pugnacious nation, my prince," said the foreigner, "but, still, in my country, when we believe we are insulted, we fight with any one——" He looked fairly and squarely at Kean, whose head showed above the screen; "except such rogues as cannot roll up their sleeves without showing that they were branded by the hangman!"

The tragedian came forth, part Romeo, part Kean, and wholly transfigured by this kind of challenge.

"And a good thing, too! You are noble-hearted. I promise you that if I am called out, and have the choice of ground, it shall be in the land of the fiords and geysers!"

"I shall be happy to welcome you there! Meanwhile, I

have merely now to thank the prince for ushering me into Art's sanctuary, and you for doing the honors!"

"My lord, though you are a novice, note that I have greeted you as an initiate!"

"Are we not to leave Mr. Kean to complete his dressing?" asked the Dane, as if satisfied.

But the host had made the prince a sign that he wished a word with him, unheard.

So he bowed the envoy out, while his companion lingered.

"Now, you must not thank me for that acquittance at the jeweler's!" began the latter. "They are all wolves alike, and it is the duty of gentlemen, like the Russ peasant, to throw them sops!"

"No, my lord, what I have to beg is quite another favor! Your outward tokens of favor, sufficient for my vanity, leave me still a doubt that I can command you—which is a strong word!"

It was, to a royal personage.

"My Horatio, my affection is stronger than my words!" whereupon George, with a somewhat un-English expression, put his arm on the other's shoulder.

"Then I long to ask of your highness, not a favor such as a prince accords to his subject, but a sacrifice between equals—the protector's kindness rising to the level of a friend's devotedness!"

The hearer beat his breast, as much as to say, "prove me!"

"My lord, artistes have passions, limitless, but within the limits of the footlight range. Among the ladies who adorn the auditorium, sometimes, it befalls us that we single out one pre-eminently. She is the living talisman; the luck-bringer, the fetish! As she smiles, we augur that the play is good; as she becomes listless, that it is faulty and charmless. She becomes the inspiritress of our genius. We find that we gain by this concentration —we play 'at her,' according to our cant. Then, the two or three thousand spectators disappear or are amalgamated into a shapeless, foggy mass, but she stands out from among them as a pearl on the heap of shells. Beside the applause of the many, her praise, if only expressed in a flutter of her lips, outweighs it all. Let her cast a flower off her wreath, it is to be cherished more than the duchess' ring or the nobleman's watch-gem. It is communion with her soul that our voice seeks among all the listeners. We play not for fame, celebrity or the gold-paved future, but for her look, her sigh of delight and her tear at Lear breaking his heart over Cordelia dead!"

"Yes, man is so constituted—he is gregarious, and yet draws himself in for a very narrow field—it is, God wot! the preparation for the narrower space which must content him—the grave!"

It was Kean's turn to stare; no one had heard the prince regent speak so seriously.

"He is a man, after all!" thought he, fortified. "I was wrong to test him!" Then, aloud: "Well, highness, if one imagines that the worship is returned; that Galatea responds to Pygmalion's rapturous prayers! if the fancy gives pleasure, however unsubstantial; if the imaginary jealousy gives pangs like reality—ought not the man who causes them, pity the one he tortures?"

"Upon my soul!" almost laughed the prince, "do you rate me as your rival, Kean, my dear fellow?"

"That supposes equality—but I am so far placed from——"

" 'Gloster,' you are a hypocrite! Miss Danby an object of my desire—because her father carries my purse *pro tem.!* You fat-witted 'Falstaff!' I care for no woman, at the present, but the unattainable—hush!"

"Oh, you do adore the fair Countess of Koe——"

"Hush, again! Would you embroil us with Scandinavia?"

"Cease to jest! for——"

"Murtheration! as Jack Johnstone says! Then the count was on the scent! You did not have that coxcomb Newell here—it was——"

"Lady Elena came, to meet your highness here!"

"What a slight! As if I had not trysting-places a-many! Edmund, this woman is dangerous, all over Europe! I was warned against her!"

"She was to have brought Miss Danby with her, for Miss Danby is sadly in want of support!"

"Edmund, my jewel of a friend, since your confidence

has been full, so I make no half-promises! You shall
wed Miss Danby, if I can help to bring that about! As
for the intriguing countess——"

He frowned darkly for a *débonnaire* gallant.

"My prince, if you have any regard for your name,
your title, your yearning to have the nation acquit your
debts, and place you foremost in its regard, do not let
this inveigler entangle you! Drive away all chance of
a scandal, which will convulse Europe! cause you to be
refused—think of that! by all the marriageable princesses,
who now long for your hand! Do not let the count even
be brought to your box! and do not let her receive even
your equerry, as though you had a secret understanding!"

The stage manager's bell tinkled. Kean started, like
a soldier at the trumpet call of "Look to yourself, sentinel!"

George simply held out his hand, and gave the other's
a hearty pressure.

Moses, who came in, saw them in this affectionate embrace, and his heart leaped with pride that he had brought
his pupil up to be the associate of the highest. But he
was full of a piece of irritating news, to tell which he
could hardly wait till the royal guest had retired, to enter
his box.

"Mr. Kean! Lady Koefeld's maid had hardly passed
through into the house, than she returned and worried
every one till she had seen Mr. Kean's man! Then, to
me, she said that her mistress, in her passage through
here, must have dropped her fan off the cord! The cord
caught in some nail——"

He began to search around.

"The devil!" muttered Kean. "Was it that the count
was fingering, over there?"

"Heavens!" cried Moses, "here is a silken thread,
frayed, snapped—her girdle did catch—the fan was torn
off, when she hastily went out!"

"Thunder! It is the count who snatched it up! I
thought his manner, though none too amicable at his coming, turned sour! He has the fan! He must believe that
his wife was here!"

A noise like thunder was heard in the upper air, toward the hall.

"The gods!" said Moses. "We are all behindhand! The audience is waxing wroth!"

"Cursed trade!" grumbled Kean. "The prince will be in trouble, after all! Unless I try to bear the brunt of it! and then, Miss Danby—oh, to be more master of one's feelings, grief, joy, calm—to play the jocund with a shivering heart and the deploring with a merry one. To wear the mask as if it were welded on the face, like that royal prisoner, over in Paris! The audience cry for me to amuse them, and I am under the millstone! And to lose Alba for a flirt, like that black-eyed 'Rosaline!' I will not be their slave! I shall not play this night!"

"Master," said the other, his voice almost soft as a woman's, "if you do not play, the money must be returned, and the poor strollers, our companions, will fall back into want!"

"Give them the prince's note!"

"But, then, the jeweler will still be able to put you in jail."

"I should have one to visit me, there!"

"Yes, master; I should not fail!"

"You! I had forgot you, when, Lord forgive me! I was thinking only of Alba!"

"Think of another!" hissed Moses, determining to appeal to the savage in his friend. "This night, you are to chastise Lord Newell, Miss Danby's greatest enemy! before all eyes! Edmund Kean, whip Tybalt like the dog he is, this time!"

Kean started out of his resolution. His eyes kindled and his whole frame quivered like a martyr's at the stake, when the burning torch is applied.

"My sword-belt! my cap!—there! there! Ring up! I am going on! Now I am with my harness on my back, set me in the field! I will trace another furrow for the glory of Shakespeare!"

They heard the orchestra playing "God Save!" indicating that the Prince of Wales had taken his place in the royal box, and Kean, as Romeo, stepped into the garden to say that prolonged farewell to Juliet.

CHAPTER XXXII.

Kean, as Romeo, in the "balcony scene," was uniformly delightful. As he leaned on the flower urn, contemplating the fair Veronese above his enraptured eyes, artists were impressed by his striking, yet graceful, pose. They said that Barry's Romeo was after Poussin; Garrick's after a Louis XIV. court-painter; but this exponent's by a Sassoferrato. On this exceptional evening, his fancy was on the play, and his deep intention on the stern prospect beyond. While lightened by having the susceptible George against the arch-diplomatist, and charmed by his Sylvia watching how he should bear himself as a lover, and afterwards as her avenger, he broadened all views, instead of confining them to the scenic bounds.

In every feeling line there was such variety, though the tone is of love-making pure and torrentuous, that monotony was absent.

This time the people were with him; he was succoring poor brothers of his profession; he had been mean and beggarly as they, but had risen through all difficulties to be the most prominent. In the low-priced parts of the house was repeated the tale that he had as a child been led on in the processions—at the head of which he was now exultantly borne. He was the paragon, and it was doubtful if he would leave a "legitimate" successor.

Old Richardson tramped at the back of the pit, accompanied by his forlorn troupe, and old cronies of the shows and circuses, reiterating:

"This here Rumbelow is too intrepid for me, but it fastenates the high-and-mighty ladies, bless 'em! Look at their eyes sticking out behind their fans, going flicketty-flicker! That shows he touches them in the heart. But you have to see him in 'Dicky the Three-Strokes' to gauge his compacity! Give me leave to tell 'ee, I were sure that he would end up the fust theayter, because once, when we differed on how to play the Blackey in 'The Padlock,' he threatened to punch my nose! Yes, he offered to square up to me, and he not kneehigh to the back of them boxes! That's the pluck as wins Waterloos! and I knowed that he would carry all afore him at the Lane!"

The curtain had noiselessly descended on the Lovers' Lullaby: "Sleep on thine eyes—peace in thy breast!" to rise on Verona's public square, where the quarrelers were stirring on the hot day.

It was a clever pendant with the delicious garden-scene, these daggers bristling after the roses.

Unlike Garrick, Kean was not "a great fidget." Even now, he who could brook no competition in love, felt not a twitter at the expectation of conflicting with Lord Newell, on his own territory, sword in hand. It was a critical hour. Never had he incurred the popular displeasure, for, adoring his profession, he was leal to it, and, thanks to Moses, who redeemed and palliated everything, his divergences toward late suppers, coaching trips out of town to make him late to the theatre, etc., were made at least amusing, and were laughed away. But, since it was possible that the new actor would carry his part literally to the sword-point, or over the line, haply, to risk all in the endeavor to disable his rival—if not to kill him! to prevent that stroke by a counter one might compel his flight from the stage—ay, from the country.

An accident to a playfellow on the stage with the always perilous foils, would be pardonable, but when the temporary actor is discovered to be a peer and the affianced of a woman for whose love the two were rivals, one whose recent adventure had welded her name with Kean's, all would look black to a jury of unromantic citizens abhorring players and kotowing to the nobility and wealth.

In his studied vagary, Newell had not made friends behind the footlights, where he briefly ventured. Absorbed in his revengeful thirst, feeling that all was a passing diversion, scorning the actors, who, in turn, repaid him with lofty derision, since he was not going to be long of their number, he learned his lesson dutifully, spoke and acted with unsuspected intelligence, but it was all because this served and masked his end.

He gave full time to the fencing-master in vogue, but begrudged an hour to the stage. Its gloomy, deterrent aspect by day damped his ardor for theatrical honors, while deepening his unhallowed intention.

He was fool enough, in his ferocity, to ascribe to fear Kean's wary avoidance of contact with him, by sending Moses to go over the lines and action with his Tybalt, and the fencing-master to repeat the set battle with rapiers, in its set progress.

Newell retained Gideon as his "groom of the chambers," and dresser here, because he needed an accomplice more than a valet. He bade him, at the last favorable moment, to nick his foil-button with a file so that it could be snapped off at will. He even wished in his virulence that he could have the falsified weapon poisoned, as in "Hamlet."

Though careful of his person, like all cowardly at bottom, and dreading to die soon, like all young in evil-doing, when they perceive the sweet but ashen fruit only, he believed that vice protects her votaries—or, at least, the choicest ones; he would, somehow, escape the penalty. At the worst, if only he disabled his adversary, he would flee to the Continent; his friends were agreed to see him to the stage door, where a fleet conveyance would be waiting. There was the *Rose,* of Rotherithe, ready to slip her cable.

If he inflicted a mortal hurt, this flight would keep him an exile abroad, but, with his brother's experience, he believed that, to a man of means, this would not be onerous. Paris or Brussels was the asylum of broken gamesters and murderer-duellists.

Kean, dying in the greenroom, would not cast any sorrow on him sailing across the Straits.

As for his being harmed, he pooh-poohed the idea. Angelo had felicitated him on his prowess with the small-sword. He could not believe that his contestant, with his burlesque practice, could compete with him, inured to the long-sword since his 'teens. On departing from the plan laid down, he trusted to dazzle and confuse the actor with his non-simulated attacks. Kean was forewarned, since he could not believe that the new actor would submit to stage regulations; but this only made the combat fair. He hoped to have his unwritten act set down to "stage fever"—the elation of being pitted before the multitude with a celebrity like Edmund Kean. In the panic, anything was explicable, if not excusable, that an amateur was guilty of.

To be sure, his escape would forbid his hoping to see Alba a second time, but if only his rival were dead, or lost to the stage through crippling, or disfiguring wound, that was filling his cup with delight; he would, in his loneliness, picture Alba in anguish, and be consoled.

So Newell, who looked "the Prince of Cats, the duellist-gentleman of the first house," came on, strutting like the veritable Champion of the Capulets; the applause of more than his *clique* told him that he was not risible or unseemly. Long debarred from participating in swordplay by the laws, the mob always rejoice in stage combats. They echoed the greeting. Flushed with his accelerated blood-flow, superheated by seeing that Alba was on the watch, he bore himself with supreme conceit, justified by the excellent carriage he had in the preliminary encounter with Mercutio. Him he finished off with a gusto, arising from his feeling it was the prelude to his more dangerous attack.

His conquering swagger was better founded, and his hope invigorated him from its deep seat, that he might with one push cancel the scorn and humiliate the actor who had heaped so much on him.

He had seen Edmund act more than once. But he was not nerved for his transformation from the lover's sugary lines to his fiery passion on seeing Mercutio slain and his slayer doubly jubilant.

"The pit is now going to have it hot," remarked Kean to Moses, who strove to cause him to be lenient and governed; "as the people craved ginger in the olden days, and want mustard with everything now, they shall have it! This new hand went from Mercutio without a scratch, but —never mind! look!"

"The next in order of the Newells should give me the order for his 'inky cloak,' " observed the tailor-prompter, quietly.

" 'This shall determine that!' " had said Romeo, as he
bounded on like a panther, afraid that a prey long eluding
him might again flee afar.

Never before had an audience learned how comprehensive is stage diction.

"They fight; Tybalt is slain!" is a short phrase. But
as the two interpreted it, there was much in it. As Garrick made his cane act so the thin laths of steel revealed
the vindictiveness electrifying them.

In a twinkling, the least experienced in the drama saw
that strict order was wantonly departed form. It was
full of the wicked tricks—this combat—of the rope-
dancer, who, to show his perfect command. pretends to
make a deadly slip! The actors in the wings, crowded
on these exceptional nights, lost track of the passes. The
stage had become an arena for gladiators. It would be to
the death, as at Rome, unless there was a king-at-arms in
the prince, to throw down the truncheon, putting an end
to a fray.

For, at the second turn, Tybalt's foil, like its master,
"lost its head," said Moses, alarmed, though anticipating
treachery.

"Refrain! Desist! Pluck them asunder!" rose the
cries above, below, and around. Women smothered their
shrieks, and some swooned. Alba leaned out of the box,
with set eyes and quivering lip; Lady Elena looked on
with a Gorgon's stare, as much as to impress on her
lord that never could the actor's dire predicament in-
flame a throb of her heart.

No more in the fixed positions, the two enemies occupied the stage as if revolved in a cyclone. The steel
emitted sparks as if applied to the cutler's wheel, and
the wild and remote tracings of the points forbade an
unarmed intermediator to rush between the vehement
pair.

But from the nick when Tybalt did not draw back and
lower the dangerously unbuttoned foil, who could doubt
that he had lost self-control or sober sight, or he was bent,
for reasons not generally known, on a public manifesta-
tion of private hostility?

There would have been a shout for the protection of
Kean, the favorite—a rush in a body of the stage

hands, who idolized a "great man without nonsense about him," but Kean stood the frenzied lunges so coolly now, and the smile, becoming sinister, determined, blood-thirsty too, King Richard the Third's, without his desperation, it reassured all, even to Alba.

She could, at last, understand how her sisters of three or four centuries before could calmly witness their knights ply the battle-ax on sheathed heads and charge on their ponderous horses with the long lance poised to perforate a mailed breast.

Throughout the house, Koefeld was amazed to see the English spirit of fair play take the upper hand.

"Let the best man win!" seemed to be on every lip, almost steady.

Moses, in the wing, held up his brown hand, as if, he staying his fond heart, none other should feel anxiety.

"Let be! let be!" said he, softly, but forcibly still. "That's the wand of justice!" he added, like a prophet. "Kean's skean!" and he laughed low and grisly at his own pun.

The third curt onset ended soon. This time, in beating off the rapid thrusts, Kean deigned to retaliate. He advanced as Newell receded for a respite in order to renew when breathed, and twice slashed him with the studded foil-end, so that, on his cheeks, right and left, a red spot appeared as if inflicted by the knot in a "cat." Then he began to let out the long steel lash, so to liken it to what it most resembled, in fact. Newell quaked; he began to pray—he who had forgot how to pray!—that the sea of faces on either side would break the barrier of stage etiquette and separate the two.

He despaired of any success now—any moderation in this signal defeat, which he had sedately brought about. He believed that he would no more be spared than he had resolved. He brought his sword round with a hand beginning to feel slow and benumbed, to ward off this fatal point. Kean, with a dextrous and strong engagement of his supple half of the blade, twisted it with the opposing; with a similar trick of the school-of-arms, he detached it entirely from his grasp, and sent it whirling up in the air. It stuck in the woodwork of a scene-frame, and, holding by the jagged end, vibrated to the handle, dancing up and down, like a reptile deferring quiet to the last.

Disarmed, feeling that he deserved his death—no less! Newell suffered those pangs of foiled rage, enmity, and revenge through which Brian de Bois-Gilbert perished in his shame. But the victor, while a thousand beholders suspended their breathing, as quickly reversed his own arm; he caught the blade in the middle, and, using the hilt as a club, smote his antagonist across the forehead. The blow must have broken off the blade or felled the man; the latter ensued. Newell gave a howl of shame more than pain. He reeled, caught at nothing, and fell at the actor's foot.

"Come off, Romeo!" called the acting-manager in the wing, showing a little of his body and head in his excitement.

There was an outcry of mixed pain, horror, and delight.

It was the stage combat to be remembered in Drury's records.

Kean stood over the body, and, with his eyes rolling in an indescribable expression, cried, in a hoarse voice, scarcely human—unearthly, indeed:

" 'Romeo!' Wherefore am I Romeo? I am your Prince Hal! See you not Jack Falstaff, rolling at my knee—overcome with the sack—choken with the penn'-'orth of bread! and, there, laughing at him, are Peto, Pistol, and my convivial crew! Is not that Poins? Oh, let Ned in! Drawer!" he shouted till the chandelier swung, "Dame Quickly, taverner of my bosom, bring in —pour out—pour up! a brimmer to the health of your coming king and his speedy crowning!"

There ran a shudder through the house; only a madman could hurl out this unloyal and personally offensive allusion to the occupant of the royal box.

Kean imitated the lifting of a cup to his mouth, saying, as wildly:

"To your prince! the liveliest, deadliest, bonniest of the Ring of Red Noses!"

"Order! order! He must be mad!"

Some out of the pit climbed over the spiked orchestral

"He reeled, caught at nothing, and fell at the actor's feet."

(See page 244)

box upon the stage; gentlemen on the stage ran under the royal box, as if to defend it.

The stage assistants rushed out with other performers to seize the tragedian while gentlemen lifted up Newell. All in the house had pushed as far forward as possible. The clamor was deafening and indefinable. Without orders, the curtain and the drop fell abruptly.

Belliston rushed before it; he had the gift of oiling the waters, and he could pacify even the Drury gallery and pit, but this time he was barely listened to by the boxes.

"Ladies and gentlemen," he faltered, waving a handkerchief before his eyes, and speaking with pathos. "There can be no further performance this ill-fated evening! The star of the Lane is eclipsed! On account of the lunacy of that brainless fool, the contagion has infected and prostrated our beloved and inimitable!"

As few heard clearly this specimen of Bellistonese language, it passed unchecked.

In the meantime, Sir John had failed to rouse his friend.

"A doctor! a doctor!" cried he.

"Our house physician is beside Mr. Kean," said an employee, loftily.

"Any doctor, then! Brandy—water! A dash of cold water, if you will so please!" appealed Whipstaffe, cowed by finding a nobleman so far below an actor, behind the scenes.

The old stage carpenter had returned from transporting Kean to his rooms. He looked, not ill-pleased, on the prostrate man.

"Water, is it?" said he, with affectation of interest. "Should we hang back from the new actor joined the Co.?" To his minions, he said this with his tongue in his cheek like a quid of tobacco. "Here, mateys, water! Water for the chicken who nearly got the best of our high-flyer by foul play!"

"This way for water!" said the chief fireman.

Indeed, at three steps, in a dark spot, unfindable by the unversed in the mysteries of the stage, there was ranged, on a stout oaken shelf, eight or ten leather buckets, kept full, according to the ordinance of the lord chamberlain, countersigned by the common council.

"No stint! Load up, lads!" continued Mr. Chips, delighted at being the Good Samaritan to the interloper,
above his *rôle*.

Each took up a bucket, and he carried a pair. This new
Aquarius and his nymphs strode back to where Newell
was going to be bled by the hair-dresser's second hand,
who, as one trained in barber-surgery, flourished a pen-
knife.

"Hold! Water is come!"

"Sprinkle his face! said Whipstaffe, relieved.

"Stand from under! Sprinkle is the cue!" said Chips,
setting down one bucket and taking the other between
both hands. His action was closely imitated by his followers, an imposing file. " 'Chuck!' is the word, one at
a turn!"

Before the gentlemen could temper this excess of zeal,
the long row of water-carriers discharged in regularity,
admirable under other circumstances, as upon a fire, each
his bucketful of icy liquid, all to drench "the fiery Tybalt." At the first shock, the victim opened his eyes, but
the second mass closed them and knocked him down.
His friends leaped away not to be swamped. Again,
Newell tried to assume a semi-upright posture, and to
expostulate. But as a sheep fallen is felled by the next
of his flock pursuing the straight line, and rises only to
be laid flat, so the noble lord kept rising and falling under
the douches like·a sawyer in and out of his pit. This went
on till the supply was exhausted.

"There is," observed the fireman, professionally, "more
at the main pipe!"

"Stay! stay! dash you!" roared Whipstaffe, who had
received some splashes.

And, with his friends, he extricated his suffering leader
from the sea. They bore him, dripping so that his track
was plain, to the street, finding their way by a miracle.

"That," remarked the stage carpenter to his rude, in-
sensate helpers, who actually broadly grinned where they
were not loudly laughing, "that will, another time, l'arn
Mr. Parkiness to be as liberal with his small coin behind
the scenes as we have been with the water! Footing
money, my boys, if an intersloper hopes to keep his stand-

ing good where there are greasy slides and no end of splintered flooring!"

"But, Mr. Kean," said the fireman, "how is Mr. Kean? Did they not say that this flimflamming ruffler had druv him mad?"

"Mad be fired! If Mr. Kean went off his head, it was with intention! Who knows but that limp-rag will go show his scarred cheek to 'the beak' at Bow street, and swear out a warrant ag'in him? They will believe white eye is black, if a lord vows to it! Mad? Him mad? Mad as he is in 'King Leary' and 'Homlet,' which they both knows their way about! Look ye, a man what brings us in ten thousand poun's a year, a-hacting only three nights a week, don't lose his balance in the head, or at his banker's for a shindy with a flippant fop like that! You are going to hear St. James' bells and the Royal Fiddles strike up Mr. Kean's wedding march, with some huge catch out of Mayfair, afore you hear St. Paul's boom his funeral knell."

"Why, Chips, you are out there! They puts such genuses us him in the Abbey, don't they?"

"Along of Mr. Garrick? Well, I don't know about that! I were a-talking with that Mr. Richardson, for whom we got up this marred benefit—a showman, and who has brought us plenty of grist! And he says, says he, Garrick and them chaps had not the eddication for the stage! He never were with me, as Edmund Kean and all the regulars has been! No, Kean, when his time comes—and may he outlive old Drury itself, ought to have a mouseholeum of his own separate from the ruck, in Paul's!"

"Amen!" said the chorus.

CHAPTER XXXIII.

A MAN IN LOVE.

Kean had returned to his lodgings, thanks to the embargo being raised through the prince's generosity. The rumor that an actor could "raise" a thousand pounds for his needy friends by his "sporting" in portions of two pieces, without regard to his fit of madness, real or simulated, to boot, made the tradesmen of London look at him with credit-giving eyes.

Under counsel, until the outcome was settled about Lord Newell, invalid or pretending so, it was judged advisable for the tragedian to keep *perdu*.

So the silence of the sick-chamber reigned in Southampton street. There were callers to sign the call-book, from the cabinet ministers to the least professional, and the minutest writer upon the stage and for it.

Kean chafed at this inaction, and his heart beat so that he had no need to affect insanity. Any mad-doctor would have declared, on his pulse, that he was out of his wits—but a wise one would have added it may be with more love for something or some person than hate for the noble baron who spoiled the Richardsonian benefit night.

Kean, in a dressing-gown, came into the sitting-room. Moses had established himself as sentinel at the door.

"Has the doctor been?" inquired Kean. "Is this trickery never to cease? I might as well have these rooms converted into an asylum."

"Dr. Cheeseden was here; he did not care to disturb you, but he wrote out a prescription all the same. He said, went on the faithful one, "that any other course would only imperil the patient's safety!"

Kean turned the paper over and over, and stared; it was blank on both sides. Then, appreciating the humor of the great trick in which all his friends were conjoined, he dropped the sheet, and laughed.

"Who has called?" said he, sinking into a seat.

"Everybody! Some several times, as the Count of

Koefeld. He was furiously desirous of knowing when
you would be on your feet again!"

"Oh! he was?" and he began to muse.

"Old Richardson has been here many a time, too. He
has, with the cash, set up a new show from the canvas
paintings to the clown's toupee and voluminous breeches.
He is so glad, and will appear in London at Smithfield!
He has never missed the Fair since ever so long back!"

Kean looked at him fixedly, and very inquiringly.

"Mr. Danby has called."

"Oh! we are getting warmer!"

"He is getting colder. His daughter will not leave
Lady Gorsewold's—those two are thick as weavers! Lord
Newell——"

"Go on!"

"He had the impudence to go there! What do you
think the amiable countess did to him? Rang for her
man, and ordered him to fetch in a constable! She was
going to have Lord Newell put under bail not to annoy
any more!"

"Not to annoy her or her guest?"

"Oh, she declared that her maids complained of the
lunatic, and that, for their sake, she would have him kept
from pestering!"

"And Miss Danby——"

Moses hesitated, seeing the color come to his master's
cheek.

"She is one of the few who believe that you really
were driven frantic by Newell's attack! She called at
once, saying to me that she was bound to come, as she
knew that you were a foundling—with no parents and
no relatives! Ah, she has a good, loyal and devoted
heart! Belliston, who happened to be here, was surprised at a great change in her! He has said all along
that she would be an acquisition to the stage!"

"He had better mind his own business!" savagely com-
mented the actor.

"It is his business, as recruiting sergeant for Drury
Lane, is it not?"

"Don't be provoking! When does she renew her call,
know you?"

"She may be afraid of being summoned as witness that you insulted the prince regent in your outburst!"

"I care as little as the prince for such speeches!"

"You might be punished!"

"I said that this is my Bedlam, so it will be merely a change of place, not of name, into a prison! I am ready to go!"

"Bah! I am not, and I cannot dispense with you!"

"Oh! if that is all!"

"It is far from all! How about Miss Danby, if your next address is Newgate?"

"If I am going to be imprisoned, it will be more just to incarcerate me for the blow to Lord Newell than the clumsy jest at the prince!"

"Why did you make it?"

"Because it was the strongest point to have it believed that I was crazed. Nobody but the crazed would thus poke fun at his august patron! If Lord Newell dies of the blow on his head—his weakest spot, eh?—it would be a good plea for Mr. Erskine to clear me!"

"I don't believe Lord Newell is dying—the direst punishment for such 'things' is to give them a long life to pass away amid accumulated contumely and reminders of the opportunities they lost."

Kean paused, and then, as if recollecting of a sudden, inquired:

"That Dane—the fan! Have you heard anything about the Koefeld family?"

"How can there ooze news of a private nature out of an establishment like that? Lady Koefeld's confidential maid might tell tales, but how can a poor man bribe such a well-paid hand? All is serene. And yet a rumor reaches Belliston that the state council has debated upon your unlicensed speech at the theatre. The prince and his colleagues tried to hush all up, but Koefeld asserts that he is only too ready to testify to the exact words of the outbreak."

"That's the voice of an enemy. What else can he be? Moses," speaking with an effort, "that confounded fan!"

"Hark!"

"Would it be the officers of the high court already on the march to seize me?" said the actor. "Shame and eternal shame, nothing but shame, if I am punished for insulting my best friend and the highest!"

Without a knock at the door, it was opened. A servant presented himself, and whispered, as if under searching and terrible eyes:

"Miss Danby!"

"I knew she would not be long a-calling!" triumphantly said the prompter.

"I will see the lady!" said Kean to the other, taking up a playbook and sitting to read it, so as to be interrupted, as it were, at work.

The servant and Moses withdrew by different doors at the same time.

The tragedian kept his eyes on his book, though he heard steps, very hurried and not like Miss Danby's, even to read, but he would not budge.

But, as there was silence, he looked up. He hurled the book from him, bounded to his feet, and stared like one perceiving a spirit.

It was Lady Koefeld, within a yard of him. She was in gray, as if beginning mourning by half-measure instead of fully.

"Lady Koefeld!" he uttered, scarcely audibly.

"Mr. Kean, I shall be pursued, I know! My destination will be divined if not tracked. That fan! my fan! Have you found it?"

"I am more interested, madam, in knowing why you adopt the name of Miss Danby as your fan!"

"Oh! I was to serve as her screen, was I not? To serve your whim—well, I use her to be my shield when I am in peril!"

"Well," returned Kean, coldly, "the fan has been rigorously searched for, but it has not been found!"

Galled by his pretended coolness, she said, angrily:

"You are wrong—it has been found!"

"Not here, then!"

"Indeed, it was found here, and that makes the affair worse!"

"Here? Who finds things here, and does not tell me, the master?" he proudly demanded.

"My master!"

"The count——"

"Found the fan here!"

"Heaven save—you! What did he say?"

"To me? Nothing—yet!"

"What does he think?"

"It is not what he thinks! It is what I think! You must leave the country!"

"Everybody is saying that! But if I would not leave because it might be said that I was afraid of Lord Newell, though it seems to me that I bore the brunt of his treacherous attack—well, I should not have it said that I was afraid of a Koefeld!"

"You must flee, because only with you would I have ample protection!"

"With you? Come, come; you don't understand Englishmen, players or prince! The prince would be the first to exclaim against any one bearing a revenge for him! At least, let him choose his champion! Any but myself, who, it seems, have grossly and publicly decried him, my good friend, if he no longer is yours!"

"Sir, you will bring about a war between two great powers! Perhaps embroil others!"

"Fie! You diplomatists think too much of yourselves! Once, perhaps, prime ministers could declare war, but it is no longer so—not in England! The commons hold the purse, and devilish tightly, too! There will be no war because you wished to set our Hercules to spin at your feet, fair Omphale of Italia!"

"I sacrificed my pride to come into your rooms!"

"Your pride? That is sensible, for you could not ascribe your action about our court to love, could you? Ah, one could fight for his prince to keep his hand around his scepter, but a fan! Our future king will never forgive you, madam! He will be ridiculed, and all for a fan!"

She set her eyes on him fixedly.

What was this hero of an hour—of a night to resist her? to be adamant when men of the utmost note had melted like quicksilver and been scattered at her will?

"If," he continued, "the prince chooses me to meet the Count of Koefeld—which I do not think in the least likely under the circumstances in which I faced him last! I called him Fat Jack, I think! in which case never will he forgive me—well, I should embark for a lone isle in the South Seas, or the North one, to combat with your husband, with weapons mortal far more than those Lord Newell uses! but—in the meanwhile, permit me to kiss your ladyship's hand in farewell!"

He was bent to take her hand, but it was abruptly drawn from possible contact.

CHAPTER XXXIV.

"TARRY, SWEET SOUL."

The incident little availed, for there were heard hurried steps at the inner door, and that sound of one man seizing and staying another against his will, which is unmistakable.

The lady did not turn pale; she did not wince a hair's breadth; but she had the rigidity of a petrified creature, by a horror unfathomable.

So far she had preserved herself on the pinnacle from more than tottering—never had she fallen—never lost her balance. No court could contest her credentials since they were without stain.

This time she feared ostracism; to be barred out from the pale of the European courts, since she had entered them all for her prey, was torment to render life the weightiest of burdens.

Born in society and reared in it, to live for an hour outside, without even a peep in at the gates, was agony.

"I say, fellow, that I am to enter!"

"I say, my lord, that enter you do not!"

The first of the voices was Koefeld's; both recognized that, though rarely had the woman heard it in that authoritative tone. The second voice Kean knew, and yet hardly knew; the English Jew, liberally dealt with since Cromwell's time in England, does not employ the submissive tone of the foreign Jews; on this occasion, Moses spoke with all the firmness of a man on his own ground, no longer a servant; a man of the theatre in the theatre.

"The count! It is the count!" just breathed Elena, seeing that a confrontation would lead to the death of a man, and the social death of the woman.

"Well?" asked Kean, as if he politely desired her answer, but it was not on that depended his next step.

"He will challenge you——"

"I suppose so. I am determined not to fight again except as before, in defense of my honor and the safety of those dear to me."

His slight was supreme.

"Still, if you stay, I think, I shall throw him out of the window! that window! It is a fall of sixteen feet—and, unless he has my acrobatic experience—but I believe it is only on the tight-rope that diplomats are practiced!—he will—oh, I see you remember how you eluded him before!"

Indeed, she had crossed the room; but she could not issue by the door where Moses offered himself as well to the infuriated man.

"Not there! Here!" and he opened another.

"If Miss Danby had come," said he, reproachfully, "this would not have been so difficult to conjure away!"

Turning, he lifted up his voice.

"Moses, if that be you, why should you not let the Count of Koefeld in?"

The count flew in, but, reining himself up, he over-ruled his rudeness, seeing that he could not expect to find his prize.

"But you said, sir!" stammered Moses, having the sagacity not to look around.

"That I was not receiving; but I had no idea that I should have the honor of my lord's visit!"

If the count had required a convincing proof that the speaker was the most excellent of actors, here was it.

Moses was reassured by the admirable smoothness and tranquillity; he bowed to the count to excuse his roughness, and went out.

"Sir, I should have thought, quite to the contrary, that your doors were closed to me, because you expected my visit!"

"What would occasion such an assumption?"

"It was recently that I said, before you, that, unlike the English, becoming squeamish, that we Norsemen fought with any one. I am offended, and I come to claim a meeting. The cause should not be trumpeted forth. You are said to be convalescent of an illness. What more natural than that you should complete your cure by taking the sea air at Ostend? If a passing treatment, with steel, happens there, no one will be surprised. Besides, we can put forth that I, a scandalized plenipotentiary, seeing that no Englishman resents your public branding of your ruler, took up the sword on his behalf."

"I alone should be able to say, *'Sic vos non vobis!'* I shrink from putting that in our plain English, as, 'Wait till you are asked!' but if you like to fence for another, it is more than I do! For that dog won't fight! I fight only where I have wronged, and as I have not wronged any one——"

"I understand your delicacy; but it is next to a fresh insult! Do you shelter yourself by being still out of your senses?"

"Not at all; only, if I am insulted without grounds, I set down the blunder to madness, and I am sorry for the hasty speaker!"

"I have seen you taken unawares, yet fight very handsomely with that genteel murderer, Lord Newell; since you refuse to run the risk of being pierced by the sword, what say you if I strike you with a—a—a—fan?"

"A fan? Woman's weapon!" said Kean, unconcernedly.

"When a man fights with the injurer of women, he may choose his weapon!"

"If I were compelled to meet such a thing, I should simply have recourse to a whip. I have one somewhere for aldermen, and critics, and those who dally with serious questions on insufficient grounds!"

"A whip to a gentleman?"

"You suggested a fan to—Edmund Kean!"

"It is the countess' fan which I found——" He drew from cover, and held up high, the Indian present, stirring up a pretty kettle of fish.

The count was startled to see the great and deep impression this sight made upon the tragedian; at least, he stopped short, his color fled, and he stared as if a murderer to whom the still wet dagger of his crime was shaken.

But the count was more surprised at feeling a hand, soft enough, but firm, too, so as to snatch the article from him, and, turning, he and the actor uttered the same sound of recognition:

"Miss Danby!"

Miss Danby had beauty; London and elsewhere acknowledged it; she had winning personality, and adjust-
ment to the situation, which all go toward making a successful actress; but, now, she had tact, which shows the
exceptional creature.

With infinite store of this valuable, she stroked the fluff
edge like a woman with no idea as much above the toilet,
and in a singularly sweet, though empty voice, remarked,
with a smile:

"My sincere thanks, dear count! for restoring it!"

"My wife's? Restoring it, for truth!"

"Oh, I stick to 'restore!' for the countess, through our
dear Lady Gorsewold, allowed me to have it to show to
Lord Gorsewold, maniac on these Eastern curios! I
think," said she, turning to Kean, as though that branch
of the explanation was incontestably settled, "I think I
must have left it at the theatre in your rooms, Mr. Kean,
when intrusion of strangers broke off our business interview!"

Rarely was the count's diplomacy put to such a test.
But he had the sense to conclude that Miss Danby would
not have thrust herself between the hammer and the
anvil, instead of Elena, unless her reason was potent.
Now, to do this and compromise herself inextricably with
the actor, was such an act as he ought to contribute toward, not cross.

He assumed a smile almost honeyed as hers, bowed in
the extreme taste, and said:

"Mr. Kean, I hear something of your violent language
toward the royal box, causing a meeting of the council,
which may have emanated, by this hour, in a warrant to
seize your person. I beg you to recall that the residence
of an ambassador is his own ground, and that the doors
of Scandinavia House are open to you—which I did not
find yours were!"

"My dear lord," returned the player, glad that he had
at least repulsed this charge with success, "may your
courtesy and your wit never be offered to less grateful
objects."

He bowed him to the door with one of those bows
which marked the prince and his select companions, and,
not to be outdone, Miss Danby added courtesy so low

and prolonged that Koefeld was in his carriage before she had resumed the upright attitude.

"God bless my heart and yours!" cried Kean, in fullness of joy; "what a woman! You have saved that diplomatic Circe!"

"Do you, then, forgive me for having intruded?" asked she, with slyness.

"Why, it is not I alone you have saved from an awkward situation, but the prince! I wish I had your father's money—oh, with no proviso!—and I would make terms with one of those kings who have a marriageable daughter, for England! Till that rake is tied hand-and-heart, there is no peace! He embroils his friends! To die for your king on the battlefield, well and good! but to die for him on an oyster shell heap at Ostend, through a Dane's foil, hang it! I prefer to be hissed by an American audience!"

"So you overlook my anxiety about you? Attained by madness?"

"Oh, let Newell plead that, to cover his treachery and cowardly attack! A madman knows nothing—no one—he is happy to all seeming! He sings, jests, laughs! I——"

"Well, since the count scared away somebody annoying——"

"Plaguing—oh, I do not mince words!"

"And I have repelled the count, I shall in my turn go, and you will be tranquil!"

"Oh, you have not taken your lessons yet, dear pupil!"

"No, but I have, I trust, profited by your advice!"

"Profited! You are an actress already—I watched you with astonishment! It tasked me to keep my voice and face before that aggravated husband, and I ought to be hardened under the mask—but you! I do think you ought to take that course of instruction, or, rather, finishing after having heard the argument!"

"I believe you are right, without flattery! Words may deceive, but, says my father, a written contract is proof! Well, to make it short, I—I——" she hesitated. "I am going out of the country—as far as North America."

Her hearer stared at her, unable to believe.

"Another one off to America!" said he, trying to make merry, and alluding to his rivals, Booth and Cooke.

"I have signed a theatrical engagement with the agent here for the Boston Theatre."

"Boston! What do you know about Boston?"

"Oh, I asked·Lord Gorsewold, who had something to do with the envoy to the United States and has lived in Washington. He gave me his opinion, somewhat gastronomical. He said he liked everything, and the table was immortally fine! Their bill of fare is the very poetry of eating and drinking! Only—for there is a fly in the wine every time—he wondered how we ever made peace with a people who did not use oil with their salads!"

She was trying to be joyous, too.

"I like Gorsewold criticizing the Yankees! He, whom I have seen cut a *fricandeau* with a knife——"

"Is not that right?" queried she, guilelessly.

"A *fricandeau*," replied Kean, becoming a *bon vivant,* since he offered Prettiman donkey for deer, "A *fricandeau* demands a spoon!"

"I see, then, that it is a lesson or two in dining, as well as the Americans that I should have; but, unfortunately, I cannot stay."

"Did not the picture I drew of the theatrical career restrain you?"

"Oh, it damped the poor girl's ardor, but my father, uneasy about the future, has settled a goodish sum on me, so as to have a resource, he so says, in his old age!"

"Rich!" muttered Kean, disconsolately.

"Do·you not think that the span of my success will be expanded if I can spend twenty thousand pounds on my dresses for the stage?"

"Poor child!" He thought that the love for finery, inseparable from the unmarried woman, had seized her.

"The Atlantic is a stream of Lethe for many voyagers; will Mr. Kean, in the thick of his triumphs, gayeties and recreations, have one thought for the exile who quits her country to enrich her dower with talent?"

She was grave, indeed.

"I suppose you will allow me to send you a newspaper, when the comment on me is not too bitter, and—true! I should like also to burden you with my progress, my work, even my failures! Even at that distance, you might cheer me, advise me, buoy me up!"

"I can—thank Heaven! do better than that! I may be a rush-light, but my rays have traversed the ocean! I have friends in Boston, New York and Charleston. All that a man can do for his dearest friend—all that an actor can do for a sister in his profession, I will do! Is there anything else?"

She looked pained and embarrassed.

"Mr. Kean, I have a weight on my mind. My father's settlement on me was not so much a gift as a hoarding. I never knew his business, but it seems to me that lately he has been led into unfertile schemes."

"Oh, what he lent the prince will be repaid him!"

"I am not alluding to that! It ought to be an honor to hold a king under obligations, like that. But he dabbles still in the gold operations—is there not a law against it?"

"The necessity of money-spinners knows no law!"

"I should go hence with a lighter heart, if I knew that you, who have all the news penetrate to you, should help him, if he is caught in the gilded web! He has his faults, as who has not? But he loves me dearly!"

Kean hid a doubtful grimace; he did not place faith in the paternal love of a worshiper of Mammon; one cannot serve two such contrary masters.

He bowed assent, but merely said:

"When do you go?"

"I have my room already in the *Yorktown* packet, lying off Greenwich."

"So soon?" sighed he.

Two little words, but they were the "open sesame" to her heart. She wavered, turned away, turned back, and, suddenly, came toward him.

"I see!" cried he, and then, with a burst of the poetry to which he recurred as if he were the author, he added, holding out his arms: "'Tarry, sweet soul! for mine— then, let us fly abreast!'"

CHAPTER XXXV.

THE PRINCE FINDS A WAY.

The happy pair were interrupted, almost as Kean had been by the Count of Koefeld; a man burst through the opposition of Moses, and entered.

"Prettiman!" cried Kean, angrily. "Is this Moses of mine letting all the world in?"

"A thousand pardons, Mr. Kean!" said the constable, "but I am forced! Your friend might have resisted the crowned staff, though I never knew that, but, this time, I carry the Black Wand! Yes, the Black Wand! I am empowered with serving the warrants under the serjeant of Parliament, when it comes to making arrests of commoners!"

"Arrest?" said the lady and her host at the same time. Moses wrung his hands at the door, as if the house had fallen in on him.

"Yes, I had a couple to make, but I left to my deputy the one I had not appetite for." He approached Kean, and said, in an undertone: "I let my deputy go to Mr. Danby's! He has got himself in a mess over the importation of gold and the exportation thereof!"

"My father arrested!" cried the lady.

"You dullard! to blurt that out before the daughter!"

Prettiman looked a dullard, indeed; he eyed the woman as if he expected her to rush out of the room; but she bore the blow with the fortitude of a millionaire's daughter, who little dreams that any offense her father can commit does not admit of bail—and subsequent throttling of the prosecution. We may recall that Danby was noted for having had a special act to rescind a law under which he might have sorely suffered.

Since she did not stir, he sighed woefully, and, looking at Moses, to convey the hope that he had done his utmost to execute his office delicately, proceeded to say:

"In the king's name, and by warrant of Parliament, I

arrest Edmund Kean!" He pulled out a short ebony truncheon and touched the actor on the shoulder with it.

"It's a pretty stick!" said Kean, coolly, "and I shall take a hint when next I 'do' Richard! But, after being touched with that king's evil, what the deuce and all do you expect me to do?"

"I suppose you must follow me! I have a staff in the passage! I expect there is accommodation at Westminster. There's a clerk out there called the *chafferer,* who *chauffés* the wax to seal up your desk and rooms——"

"Oh, I don't suppose you are going to seal up, with Moses herein, and Miss Danby?"

"Oh, only papers and such!"

"If the lady can go, it will be the more kind, as she is due aboard the American packet."

"There!" said the promoted constable, "what a mistake! If only you had booked yourself on board and started an hour ago!"

"If we could alter the name of the passenger!" whispered Miss Danby, blushing at her own audacity.

"Oh, you can alter yours, but I would not. I must refuse, for I am sure I should be timid at sea—to sail so far, alone!"

"Then I stay, doubly bound, for my father and——"

"You forget your contract! My dear child, a theatrical engagement is sacred, because the manager of the first part is nothing save a representative of the public, to whom we owe all duty and obligation!"

Prettiman hemmed.

"If I might for the second time take the lady under my charge," ventured he, "I would conduct her to her father, and reach him in whatever close custody he is."

"Thank you," said Miss Danby, placidly.

"Meanwhile, Mr. Kean, honoring artistes as I do, I will beg Mr. Chaffwax to have the greatest consideration for you. By reason of your high and influential associations, I doubt not that you will soon be free to embark——"

He went to the door, but Moses anticipated him, for he had gone out there, and, as was his duty, announced in a voice not rueful:

"His worship the Chaffwax of the two houses of Parliament!"

And as this important dignitary entered pompously, to which pomposity he might aspire as being a kind of keeper-of-the-seals, or, at least, the sealing-wax, Moses gave Prettiman a push and neatly obtruded him to the outer side of the door. Miss Danby, who felt no interest in this official, save so far as custodian of her lover, was giving him but a cursory glance when she stopped short. Her surprise was only equalled by Kean's.

Mr. Chaffwax, finding that they were alone, since Moses showed a pleased face, quickly removed a reverend beard and a gray wig, dusted with powder, and disclosed the countenance of George, Prince of Wales.

"His royal highness!" said the actor, while Miss Danby, suddenly relieved since the arrival's smile was so broad, courtesied to the floor.

"I have not come to set the seal upon our friendship," explained the pretender to parliamentary honors, "but to save you as I have saved Mr. Danby."

The young lady repeated her salutation and ventured to take and kiss the royal hand.

"Oh, I deserve to be whipped," said Kean. "I thought —on my soul, I must out with it!—I thought you were too frivolous to bother about one who cast ignomy on you in his pretended frenzy, and I shall go to prison with pleasure!"

"I prefer you should go aboard the ship—which, as a new dictionary interprets it, is a prison with the prospect of being drowned!"

"Ship?"

"Why, surely, since we must let the little tempest in the royal box blow over! By the time you reach Boston, it will be an old tale, and by the time you return after your honeymoon trip no one will refer to it without being supposed to be one of the Seven Sleepers."

"Honeymoon?"

"Why, Kean, dear child, I know everything! What I was ignorant of, this worthy valet of yours dilated upon!"

"I suppose," said Kean, with his former lively spirit, "that, as, for the time, I pass as having offended my dearest friend and patron, your highness will not provide a man-of-war for my voyage, as was done for theatricals such as Catalani!"

"Well, no; but you can take any vessel you like!"

"With preference for the *Yorktown!*" said Kean, glancing inquiringly at Miss Danby.

"All its rooms are taken, sir!"

"I'll appoint you special royal messenger to convey a message of mine to our ambassador at Washington," interpolated the prince, never fond of obstacles, "and the ship captain must make room for you!"

"Hum!" said Kean, as if he had deeply reflected. "Your highness' suggestion of it being a honeymoon trip gives me an idea. We will send Moses to have the registration altered to 'Edmund Kean and his wife.' With a special dispensation from my well-wisher, the Bishop of London, we can go aboard man and wife!"

"Splendid!" said George; "I am afraid you will yield to temptation, to be like all great actors!"

"What temptation? Marrying my leading lady?"

"No, to write a play! And yet it is so easy, to me, anyway, not to write a five-act tragedy!"

Then all laughed and Moses was not reprimanded, because he joined in with his low, musical peal.

"I will write that letter of recommendation for you offhand!" said the prince.

"Include my wife professionally! She is engaged to play principal ladies at the Boston Theatre!"

"Oh, if you go away hoaxing me——" and he frowned a little.

"Not at all, highness! I ought to be a judge! This *débutante* has, by her excellent acting, deceived that arch-diplomatist, the Count of Koefeld."

The regent frowned again at this name.

"Sending him away home, happy to think that his wife is as commendable as she is admirable!"

"Fireation! as that rogue Johnstone says! It is not you that I have saved, but you—that is, your wife to be, that saves me!"

There was no time to lose. Miss Danby did not hasten to welcome her liberated father, who gave her away in the private chapel of the Savoy, where the marriage was celebrated privately. This shut out the prince from the act which he had offered to perform.

But he meant to be kept in remembrance.

The packet dropped down the river, but at Tilbury a shot was fired from the fort. The *Yorktown* hove to, and waited. A boat came off with a naval crew; in the stern sat Mr. Bonnell, carrying on his knees a box carefully wrapped up.

"With the prince's compliments to Mrs. Kean!" said he. Then to the actor, he added, "By the way, I have allowed to accompany me, in the *Spitfire's* cutter, as you see, a man who insisted on being brought aboard, as he loved his master."

It was Moses.

"I thought I left you provided for?"

"As you did your lion! Yes, but I want something more than meat and drink! I am a dog, not a lion! You are not going to give up your art because you go to America?"

"Well, no; the people among whom I go do not like men who stroll about looking on, but doing nothing. I and my wife are going to act!"

"That harmonizes with my notion, too! When a man is in love, he stands very badly in need of a prompter!"

"But I am more than in love—I am married to my beloved!"

"Then you will be so absent to all other things that you will need a prompter more than ever."

Scarcely was the ship out of the sight of the last light than impatience induced Mrs. Kean to open the box sent by the prince.

Besides the usual packing of a court jeweler's, there was a newspaper wrapped around it to keep off the sea-water by the careful Mr. Bonnell. A marked paragraph excited Kean's attention while his wife undid the tissue paper and disclosed a casket.

"Scandinavia House, seat of the Danish embassy, is being refitted for its new tenant. The Count Koefeld has been promoted to the Court of St. Petersburg, and leaves town at once. The countess, to whom the Russian winter offers unbearable rigors, will retire for the season to Torquay, where she will dwell in seclusion."

"Well?" asked Mrs. Kean, absently, for her eyes were on the contents of the box.

"Oh, that Koefeld couple have parted—the czar has

sent for the count to Siberia on thereabouts! Well—on your side?"

"Look!"

"The casket was roomy, but full of an admirable set of jewelry f r a lady. A little strip of parchment was inscribed: "Will Mrs. Edmund Kean please accept this token of respect and gratitude. George, Regent."

"By Jove," said Kean, "that is indeed an acceptable royal box!"

THE END.

Printed in the United Kingdom
by Lightning Source UK Ltd.
106734UKS00001B/8